Carrying the Light

A Collection of Short Stories
by Graduates of the
University of Hull's MA in Creative Writing

For all the graduates

(past present and future)

of the

University of Hull's MA in Creative Writing

Table of Contents by Story Title

Table of Contents by Author

Foreword

Writing well is hard work.

I have never quite understood the debate about whether 'creative writing can be taught' or whether creative writing courses are worth the investment. It's not something we say about any other art such as painting or music. Yet just as artists and musicians have to learn certain skills to create a beautiful painting, or write a symphony, writers have to understand certain techniques and elements of the craft in order to make their words shine in a tough, competitive publishing environment.

Hull University's Creative Writing MA course is not for the faint-hearted. Students are asked to write to deadlines, to write through those days (or weeks) when they feel 'blocked', to write to specific requirements or prompts, to accept regular feedback from tutors and peers, and to critique the work of others like an editor. Everyone featured in this anthology survived the process and came out a better, more skilled writer.

There is a myth that creative writing courses encourage a kind of homogenisation. You only have to read this anthology to see what little basis this has. Students come to the course with their own ideas – we can't put them there – and all the course does is help make the work the best it can be. We don't offer 'rules' exactly – more guidance and tools and solutions, so that the more confident writer can become more experimental when they have those fundamental skills in place.

Not all aspiring writers want to admit that their craft needs work, and not all aspiring writers dedicate time and effort to it. The writers in this anthology have accepted that writing is a discipline, albeit one with creativity and imagination at its heart.

The way all the students here have supported each other and formed lasting writing critiquing groups and friendships is one of the best things to come out of a course like ours. The anthology is a wonderful testament to it.

I'm very proud to have worked with all the graduates here and to see this evidence of their hard work and continued dedication to writing. I wish all of them well, and hope to see their names on further publications in the future.

Dr Barbara Henderson PhD
(Hull Creative Writing MA Online Tutor)

Barbara Henderson is a former newspaper and BBC journalist. She has a Creative Writing PhD from Newcastle University where she studied under the supervision of award-winning writer Jackie Kay and renowned literature expert Professor Kim Reynolds. Her debut novel, a crime/suspense novel titled *In Too Deep*, and a second in the genre, *This Little Piggy*, were published by Legend Press. She also writes for younger readers. *The Serpent House* is a historical time fantasy and was shortlisted for a Times/Chicken House award. Her latest novel is *The Misper*, aimed at a teen readership. She writes under the name Bea Davenport.

A Note for Readers

Although they all studied at the University of Hull, the following stories, essays and poems have been produced by writers from all over the world. It contains some stories written in US English and some in UK English. Some writers have used double quotation marks for speech and some have used single. Some have used indented paragraphs and a simple line gap for time breaks, some used a *** 'dinkus' and non-indented paragraphs to mark the same. We decided to leave all these as the author had written them and so we shall ask for your flexibility in conventions as you read through this anthology. What is consistent is the high standard of the writing.

I trust that you will be immersed into this world of words, be impressed with the writing skills on display and perhaps be inspired to write (or continue to write) your own stories. I also hope that through these pages you can discover a new, favourite author.

Ian Hooper
Editor and Compiler

A Certain Someone

The home phone rang. Another call about that bloody accident I wasn't involved in. I pounced on the receiver, ready to snarl. There was a hesitant pause.

'Ruth. Hello… don't know if you remember me… It's been thirty years… from school… I tracked you down through Facebook. Your surname's different, but I found you through your brother, Marc.'

I remembered, but a soft Irish drawl had replaced the familiar accent.

'My dad's died… I have to fly over from Kilkenny to arrange… he's ninety-six… was. I've lost contact with the old crowd and I'm in a really bad place… . Can we meet?'

What could I say? 'Of course. Just tell me when and where.'

Over the next week, we chatted by text. Found many parallels — both of us had shaped a career in a high-street bank, married, raised two sons and lost our mothers, too soon, to cancer. I sent a few links for half-decent hotels.

On the day, I sat facing the door of the little café in the university quarter, balancing calm and chaos like a juggler. A few enduring childhood friendships are dear to me, but on the rare occasion I happen upon someone from school, it's never when I'm in a fancy frock with a full face of makeup. Oh no, it'll be a tap, tap on the shoulder, 'fancy meeting you here' shock whilst

I'm queuing in Tesco to pay for a tube of Voltarol. In a pair of gardening Crocs. With a forsythia twig in the back of my hair — invisible on setting off, but waving at me in the hallway mirror when I walk back through the front door.

I steer a wide berth from the one-upmanship gameplay of Facebook school reunions. Usually. But today I'd fussed with the belt of my blue midi-dress. Dithered over pearls or a pendant. Today I'd triple-checked my reflection before stepping out. New shoes were a poor choice. They'd rubbed by the time I turned the street corner. Today was different.

I waited. There was time to straighten up the sugar sachets in the bowl, check my hair again (in selfie setting) and flick my phone to silent. I could have said no. Made excuses. Too late now. And there she was — the same, yet completely different to how I had imagined. Striking. Slim. Straight dark hair in a short bob, leather-look leggings and a biker jacket all accented with leopard print. She clutched the gold chain of her shoulder bag as she scanned the room. A teenage girl glanced up as she passed, held the gaze a little too long, then went back to her phone. We hugged.

The tension in her shoulders subsided a little. With my cheek to her neck, and a heartbeat pulsing between my ears, I closed my eyes and inhaled. She was wearing a scent I had almost forgotten — the lemon and jasmine of my teenage perfume. What was it called? Charlie. Where on earth can you still find that? As I exhaled, the years peeled back, to lay bare the raw emotion of High School. Essence of gym bag. School choir and end-of-term disco. Sherbert dip from the Tuck Shop. Linked arms all the way to the bus stop.

We ordered coffee. Sitting opposite gave me the chance to scrutinize her face. Up close, the heavy but flawlessly applied make-up didn't quite disguise the age lines. Those beautiful brown eyes were the same, but they had a sorrow behind them so intense it made my heart ache. She rubbed at a lipstick mark on her cup, squeezed her right earlobe, yanked off a clip-on earring and dropped it in her saucer, flexing a long, pink, false thumbnail with her forefinger until I feared it would snap.

'Relax Louise,' I smiled. 'You look amazing!'

She closed her eyes. 'I'm dreading the funeral,' she whispered.

We sat in silence until she was composed enough to speak. She bit the corner of her bottom lip. Exhaled audibly. 'Sure, it wasn't a surprise. When you get to your nineties, you're on borrowed time. He was in a care home… their house is gone to fund it. I used to be so close to my Mam and Dad, you know. They only had me. Devoted themselves to securing me a good Catholic upbringing. I found a job, married and gave them the grandchildren they expected. But after the divorce, I couldn't face their disappointment… so I put an ocean between us. As time sailed by, I couldn't find a way to cross it.'

I shook my head. 'I'm sure they loved you.' I reached in deep to pull up a memory. 'I came to your sixteenth birthday party. Your mother sat us all around that polished dining table of hers and served up cheese souffle and a black forest gateau. They were both so proud. Your dad gave me a lift home.'

She slapped a hand to her forehead. 'Oh God, I'll never forget that night. Everyone else's parents turned a blind eye while their kids sneaked off to the Bali Hai disco for a boogie and an underage bevvy on their birthday. My parents threw me a dinner party. Although… as I recall, I wasn't the only one with a crazy mother. Your mam gave us a Christmas party that June after our 'O' Levels, did she not? Put up decorations and baked mince pies all laced with sherry. And the games! The boys had to roll up their trousers and stand behind a sheet hung on the lounge door, with their knobbly knees on show. The girls had to guess whose knees they were… You wore a white boiler suit.'

She was right. I'd all but forgotten. How could she remember that detail? Boiler suits were all the rage in the seventies, and I was slim and brazen enough to carry it off, in those days.

'The last time I saw you,' she continued, 'was Alan's eighteenth. Bali Hai of course, but a private party. Official like. You'd got rid of your glasses and stole the show in Olivia Newton-John painted-on black satin trousers and a boob tube. Nobody could take their eyes off you. You were with some tall guy with long blond hair. Not from our school'

Still am. Never left Hull.

Her shoulders dropped. 'Oh, Ruth. You haven't changed a bit. I knew you were the one to share my secret with… but how the hell am I going to get through the funeral? Not to mention the wake. None of the family over here knows… None of my old schoolmates. I'm going to cause so much pain when this comes out.'

I dropped a sugar lump into my cup, fragmenting the wings of the barista butterfly floating there. In the foam, an image appeared of a younger me, wiping away stinging tears after the postman delivered the other half of the sixpence I'd had cut up and hung on chains for us. Without so much as a note attached. I stirred my coffee. My childish bitterness melted away. Never have I so deeply appreciated the unpretentious deck that life has cut and shuffled for me. Full of love and family. The biggest secret that I have to keep, is the true price of a pair of new shoes.

'You can trust me,' I said. 'We'll always have a special bond. How could I forget the first boy I ever kissed?' I took her hand. 'Look, I can help you work out the funeral arrangements. We'll do a list. Make some calls. But later. First, come on, start at the beginning. When did you first know?'

Louise hesitated, 'I suppose I've always known. But I really knew when I saw you in that white boiler suit. My mind was clear. I knew who I was supposed to be. The only problem was… it took me another twenty-five years to say it out loud.'

Corrine Aveyard

Corinne is proud to call Kingston upon Hull her home. After the premature death of her mother she took early retirement and became the legal guardian of her brother who lives with Down Syndrome. This change in the family dynamic enabled her to complete a Masters in Creative Writing and she plans to give her brother a voice and write his memoir.

Aleesha

That summer, I spent the muggy nights walking the streets of Oxford. The ferocity of the neighbours' fighting shook the wall behind my bed, making it impossible to sleep.

I took photographs on my phone, streaky, wobbly pictures as I walked. Sometimes, the camera lens pointed at people's windows, sometimes inside cars, sometimes at foxes or cats or homeless people slumped in doorways. Maybe I thought I'd make a book of the photographs, black and white and moody, a coffee table edition with clever words to make people think. I'm not sure now.

The sun rose high over the honey-coloured stone, throwing golden light over the buildings, ruining the mood. Birds started their morning chorus. I wandered home.

The neighbours were asleep, exhausted from the effort of hating each other. Silence but for the creaking of pipes. Flicking the kettle on, I scrolled through the pictures, deleting the ones I didn't like. Sometimes I'd captured something interesting, a woman staring back at me from between pulled curtains, eyes puffy with sleep, a child gazing at the stars. Once, I saw a man sleeping in his car, arms folded across his chest, head hidden in the shadows. Once, a fox pulling the carcass of an unknown animal into a hedge. The pictures asked more questions than they answered.

It was a scorching summer. People complained about the heat, left their windows open wide at night. Babies cried in sweaty tempers. The blue light of televisions flickered behind curtains. Pyjamas were discarded and fans blew the only breeze in stuffy rooms. Only the homeless wrapped themselves up, hiding from a world afraid of them and what they meant.

In those stale early hours, life ebbed and flowed in the city. Ravers staggered on towering heels, chucked out of clubs which had made their money and needed to wipe cocaine off toilet cisterns. Men and women with dreams, mopped floors to earn enough to pay the rent. The night watchman patrolled.

Then the quiet space between three and five. The time the city was mine. When night still stretched her silent cloak over the roof tops. Before the early commuters stumbled from their doors, before the birds sang their chorus. Once, I took off my shoes and carried them in my hand, feeling the cool tarmac beneath my feet, stray stones poking soft soles.

Once, I got home and a woman was sitting on the step to the front door. She was crying, hair tied up with a dressing gown chord, curls escaping which she pushed behind her ears as she wept. I couldn't get past her so I hovered for a minute, waiting for her to move. She didn't seem to notice me so I turned towards the street and watched commuters head for the station. They wore sandals and shorts and several were wiping sweat from their necks, the sun already hot as it hit my forehead.

'I'm sorry.'

I spun round and the woman looked up at me.

'I'm sorry,' she said again. 'I'm the reason you go out at night. I'm the one that causes the rows.'

I sat down on the step next to her, nudging her slightly to make some space. She wasn't a woman really, a girl, barely out of her teens. Mascara ran down her cheeks. She had a nose piercing. I didn't know what to say so I didn't say anything, just sat next to her. I hoped it was enough.

'He's left,' she said.

She held a damp tissue between her fingers. I felt small, inadequate somehow, searching for profound words. A bee buzzed close by her hands.

'Maybe that's a good thing,' I said.

'I don't know what I'll do without him,' she said.

I remembered a time when I felt that way too, a time long ago when 'he' left me and I didn't know what to do or how to do it.

'You'll be ok,' I said. 'You'll get through it in your own way.'

'Can I come to yours for a bit? Have you got to go to work?'

'I work from home,' I said. 'You can come and have a coffee or something.' I didn't want her in my flat, didn't want to bring her into my life but nor could I say no. That's how people get you, just blurting something out, needing something, and then you're stuck with them. I stood up. 'Come on then, one coffee and then I'll have to get on.'

She followed me up the stairs and into my flat, looking around before sitting on a stool by the breakfast bar. 'This is nice,' she said.

I flicked the kettle switch and took two mugs from the cupboard. 'Coffee?'

'Milk, two sugars.'

No please, no thank you, no this is nice of you. Just milk, two sugars. I poured the coffee and put the mug in front of her.

'I'm Aleesha,' she said, 'With two Es.'

'Penny.' With two Ns, I thought, but didn't say. Instead, I asked, 'Do you think he'll come back?' The thought of him hammering on my door sent a shiver down my back.

'I don't know. He's never left before.' She slurped coffee, wiping a drip from her chin. 'He took our stash. You don't have any weed, do you? I could do with a spliff.'

'No.'

She finished her coffee. Her eyes darted around my flat, up across walls, down across the rug. Over the mantelpiece and the family candlesticks. I wondered if she was casing the joint for later. Then she got up and walked towards the door.

'I'd better start sorting my life out,' she said. No please. No thank you. And then she closed the door behind her.

That night I waited for the shouting to start but silence filled every corner of the bedroom. It weighed on my chest as I lay under a sheet, no air drifting through the window.

I got out of the sweat-stained sheets, pulled on shorts and a T-shirt, slipped on slides and picked up my phone.

A fox crossed the street, stared at me for a second and carried on. I walked towards the canal bridge, hungry for the coolness rising from the water. The ducks were still asleep. But Aleesha was there, leaning over the railings, her toes just touching the pavement.

Rocking.

I stopped, was going to say something but didn't.

The camera lens caught her fall, click, click, click, click.

The weather broke that morning, fat raindrops bouncing off the pavement. Tiny, dancing fairies. The police cordoned off the bridge. A group of people stood under umbrellas, shaking their heads. My camera recorded them all, those laying flowers. Rubber-neckers. Ambulance chasers. Her partner supported by a police officer who was as young as him.

That afternoon, the rain pelted my window as I looked at the photographs.

Like a black and white film, her legs flying as she back flipped into the water.

I moved them into the cloud folder and went back to work.

Sarah Wilson

Sarah was born in London but moved to rural Oxfordshire twenty years ago and the magical city often inspires her stories. She can mainly be found writing at her kitchen table with a greyhound draped elegantly across her feet. Her first novel, *Out There*, was published in 2017.

Always Another Day

Sylvia had no idea where she was. It was too hot, too dark. An alarm sounded in the distance, incessant and terrifying. She felt a familiar hand take hers and heard a voice telling her it was alright and the panic let go in an instant. She was in their bed, in their little room under the eaves, next to Michael. Of course. She squeezed his hand, gladdened as she always was, by the warmth and solidity of him. She could number the mornings she hadn't woken with Michael by her side. First when she'd given birth to Anna, again when she'd given birth to David, and lastly when he'd been in hospital having his appendix out. Three nights apart in almost fifty years.

She snuggled closer to Michael, listening as the songbirds began their early morning chorus in the garden. He could distinguish the songs of the robins and the blackbirds, the thrushes and the wrens, but to her they blended into a delightful symphony. A private concert every morning.

She watched as the faint line around the curtains turned from pale blue, to pink, to gold. She knew that the sun had risen over the silver birch trees at the bottom of the garden, the soft golden light creeping across the lawn to the kitchen window. The grass would be sparkling with dew, the primroses and narcissus just opening in the early sun. The robins and blue tits would be flitting back and forth, squabbling round the feeders, and the swallows would be darting into their nests under the eaves. They had returned, as they did year after year, travelling thousands of miles across desert, mountains and ocean, coming back to this same spot. The heat and dust of Africa a distant memory. The fat pigeons would be fussing in the birdbath Michael had bought her for her fortieth birthday, the day they'd found out they were finally expecting a baby - Anna - after years of hope and grinding disappointment.

It had been their garden for over forty years, and she knew it all without looking.

"I'll get us some tea, love," she said, kissing Michael and getting out of bed. "And then I'm off into town. Lots to do."

She took her dressing-gown from the back of the chair and pulled it tight round her. Michael had bought it for her birthday a few years ago and she treasured it. Pure white silk, covered in blowsy pink roses. It was the most glamorous thing she had ever owned. He said she looked like a film star in it.

Down in the kitchen, waiting for the kettle to boil, she stood at the window and felt familiar joy at the sight of the garden. A lawn you could play bowls on, Michael boasted. The trees were still bare but tiny green buds promised blossom and shade. In summer, helter-skelter borders would be crammed with flowers; there would be bees and butterflies fluttering; dragonflies skimming the little pond; irises standing tall over the waterlilies. They had brought so much life to this little patch over the years, filling it with colour and delicious fragrance. And happiness too. She remembered the endless summers of Anna and David's childhoods. She could see them splashing in the paddling pool, hear their giggles and shrieks, the thud of the cricket ball and the creak of the swing. *Mummy! Mummy, watch! Can we? Mummy look! More, more, more!!*

The whistle of the kettle brought her back to the kitchen. She had to get on and daydreaming wouldn't do at all. She made two cups of tea and carried them back upstairs.

"Come back to bed, love," Michael said. "It's early."

"No, I've got lots to do today. Can't waste half the morning in bed."

"I can give you a lift later. We could grab a spot of lunch. Pick up some Egypt brochures so we can get it booked, see the pyramids at last."

She ignored him. She was going to the jewellers to pick up the watch she'd had engraved for his birthday next week. The last thing she wanted was for him to tag along.

She got dressed quickly, choosing her favourite dress, yellow to match the sunshine. She sat at her dressing table to put on the gold chain she'd bought a few years ago on a weekend away.

"We must go back to Venice," she said as she fastened it.

"Venice?"

"Yes! Do you remember that lovely little hotel we stayed at by the canal. It's where I got this."

"That was Amsterdam, love."

Sylvia laughed. "Oh, yes. Amsterdam. Of course."

She crossed to the window and pulled open the curtains. "It's going to be a beautiful day," she said. "Nothing but blue skies."

"I'm off, love," she called up the stairs as she left. "I'll get some Egypt brochures to look at later."

The postman was heading up the path towards her as she stepped out.

"Morning, Mrs Hammond. Lovely morning!"

"Morning, Richard. Isn't it gorgeous?" Sylvia replied. "Lifts the spirits."

He handed her a couple of letters and a card. She knew the card would be from Anna. She always liked to get cards in the post early. *So they definitely get there in time, Mum.* Anna had always been the organised one.

As she closed the gate she saw their neighbour across the road pushing a pram. Caroline was a couple of years older than Anna, and Sylvia could remember them playing on the swing in the garden for hours, and hopscotch on the pavement outside. It was hard to believe that almost two decades had passed and now Caroline was a mother herself. Sylvia hurried over to say hello and fuss over the baby.

"He gets more grown up every time I see him," she said. "Such a handsome lad!"

Caroline looked proud, exhausted and indulgent all at once.

"He kept me up half the night, little terror!"

"You make the most of it. He'll be married with a little one of his own before you know it."

Sylvia knew Caroline wouldn't believe it; couldn't know that one moment it was all sleepless nights and dirty nappies, and the next it was first steps, university applications and an empty nest. Sylvia said goodbye and strolled on. The entrance to the park was at the end of their road, the ornate gold gates glittering in the sunshine. She stopped at the gates, undecided for a moment whether to go through the park or follow the main road into town. There was no rush she thought, she'd go through the park. Couples ambled along enjoying morning coffee, joggers and dog walkers weaved between them. Shouts and laughter drifted over from the play area near the bandstand.

Just a few more minutes, Mum, please. Ten more minutes!

She could hear Anna and David's relentless pleas. They never wanted to leave the park. Always wanting just a few minutes more.

The sun was overhead now, the path shaded by the canopy of enormous elm trees on either side. Dancing shadows rippled in front of her. It was glorious. When Sylvia reached the lake in the middle of the park, she sat on one of the benches facing the water. There was time to stop for a while. This is where she and Michael came the first time they went out together. Almost half a century ago. Meet me at the bandstand, he said, we'll have a picnic. He was twenty and she was nineteen. He wore a suit a size too big and had shined his shoes good as new. He brought iced lemon buns and a flask of tea. He knew the way to my heart even then, she thought. It had been sunny that day too. They had sat on this bench until it was almost dark, then he had walked her home. Their first kiss had been here as they stood to leave. She could still feel his hand on her cheek, drawing her to him.

In front of Sylvia at the water's edge sat two young children — a boy and a girl — their bare feet dangling in the water. They were throwing bread for the ducks and geese, shrieking with terrified delight and splashing their legs wildly as the geese approached. Sylvia laughed out loud watching them. When all the bread had gone their mother called to them.

"Come on you two! Time to go."

"Oh mum, can't we stay a bit longer? Five more minutes. Please!"

Their mother took no notice and gathered up their picnic things and bags.

"Come on!" she urged the children. "Dad'll be waiting. Get your shoes on."

The little girl, so like Anna with her tangled blonde hair and patchwork summer dress, jumped up and did as her mother asked. The little boy stayed where he was, his whole face a frown, kicking his feet hard and sending water scattering.

"David. Now please."

Sylvia smiled. Just like her David. Stubborn, making sure everyone knew how cross he was. She caught his eye and gave him a little wave.

"There's always another day," she said.

The three of them set off, the little girl holding her mother's hand, little David kicking his feet grumpily behind them. As they passed, Sylvia caught the scent of Lily of the Valley, the perfume her mother wore. Sylvia had gone to the Yardley counter every Christmas to buy it, and it sat on her mother's dressing table amongst the other bottles and jars and pots. Sylvia would spend hours transfixed, watching her mother apply lotions, powder, make up, perfume. It was like being granted access to an unfathomable ritual. She'd hardly dared to breathe for fear of breaking the spell.

The woman and her children reached the bend in the path and the sound of their chatter faded away. Silence. Sylvia closed her eyes. Everything was still. Then, the tap, tap, tap of an unseen woodpecker, the distant cries of children in the play area, the whisper of wind through the leaves. Sylvia opened her eyes as the day surged back. She must get on.

She left the park and walked along the High Street to the travel agents.

"Hello, Sarah," she greeted the woman at the desk warmly. "Michael's sent me in for brochures. He wants to go to back to Venice. We had such a wonderful time there before."

They chatted for a few minutes, then Sylvia stepped back out into the sunshine. Just to the post office now for a passport form, then the jewellers and home. She could get out into the garden for a few hours before dinner.

As she passed the primary school the children were swarming out of the gates. How had it got so late? Shrieks and giggles and shouts rang out as they ran to mums, dads and grandparents. Sylvia smiled at the sight. It was no time at all since Anna and David had run through those same gates to hug her and chatter about their days, talking over each other in their excitement, begging for ice-creams from the van.

The post office was busy when Sylvia got there. She was irritated by everybody taking so long. The queue didn't seem to move.

"Good afternoon, Sylvia," said the postmistress when Sylvia finally got to the counter. "Sorry you've had to—"

"I do think you might have a separate waiting line for people who don't need to take forever," Sylvia snapped. "I've got better things to do than stand in here all day."

"Oh, I am sorry dear. What can I do for you today?"

Sylvia hesitated. For a moment she couldn't remember what she'd come in for.

"Sylvia?" the woman said kindly.

"I need some stamps. A book of first class, please. Six."

"Here you go, love. That's £5.70."

Sylvia reached into her bag for her purse. She frowned, finding it empty. She was sure she had change.

"Sorry. I thought— I can't—"

She rummaged through her bag. Where was it? She could hear muttering and tuts from the queue behind her. She searched again. Increasingly frantic. Nothing.

"I'm so sorry. I'll have to— I'm sorry."

She left the stamps where they sat on the counter and turned, desperate to get away.

"Would you like me to   "

Sylvia cut her off. "Just forget it. I've wasted enough time in here."

Such a waste of time, and what a rude woman. She wouldn't go there again.

She clutched the rail as she came down the post office steps, dismayed by the leaden sky and the chill in the air. She pulled her cardigan tight, but it was little use against the fierce wind. The jewellers was a little further up the street and she walked as quickly as she could manage, wanting to get there and get home. As she got close, she could hear the sign above the jewellers creaking as it swung wildly. An empty crisp packet rustled round her feet. She bent to pick it up, but it whirled away. As she straightened up, she noticed the display in the jeweller's window and frowned. Why had she come all the way up here? It was the wrong direction for home.

A can clattering into the gutter startled her. She saw the little boy she'd seen in the park earlier. David. He was hitting at the can with a stick. What on earth was he doing here on his own? He must be freezing, in shorts and a T-shirt.

"What are you doing?" she asked. "You'll catch your death. Where's Mummy?"

She heard a sudden loud beep behind her and turned in panic. So loud. A lorry reversing? But there was nothing there. She turned back to the little boy.

"Where's—"

But he had vanished. Sylvia was bewildered. Couldn't understand where he'd gone. She was exhausted. Just wanted to be home. Warm and safe.

She re-traced her steps back towards the park. Gusts of wind sent flurries of leaves swirling down the pavement towards her, and she felt the first drops of rain. Why was she out in this awful weather wearing such a flimsy dress and sandals?

Ahead of her, on the other side of the road, she saw David heading into the park. He was far too young to be out on his own. It was cold, and would be dark soon. Sylvia crossed and went through the park gates. She had to make sure he was safe.

"David! David!" Her voice was thin, whipped away by the wind. He would never hear her.

"Out the way, grandma," yelled a boy careening towards her, chased by another boy. He knocked her bag out of her hand, sending her things sprawling over the path. They carried on running, laughing as they went. "You should be in an old people's home," one of them jeered over his shoulder.

"Have you seen a little boy? David? Have you seen him?"

But they had gone.

Sylvia stooped down to pick up the scattered things. Purse, keys, pills, five-pound notes, coins, lipstick. A little further way, in a shallow puddle, lay a couple of holiday brochures. Ruined. She saw that one had a crooked tower on front, the other a man in fancy dress stood in a boat. It all looked foreign. They weren't hers; they never went anywhere other than Scarborough for a holiday. Their little caravan with the red and white curtains; the condensation running down the inside of the windows when it rained; fish and chips, straight from the paper, scalding hot and doused with vinegar.

David loved to play hide-and-seek in the woods. He'd have gone that way. She set off down the path towards the wooded area by the river. She called for David again and again. She had to get him home. It was getting dark, almost dinner time. She was worried he'd be climbing trees. It wasn't safe. He'd fallen out of the apple tree at home when he was nine and broken his arm. She could still hear the scream as he fell and the terrible silence as he lay on the grass.

She heard voices ahead. A man and a woman just out of sight in the gloom. She heard her name. Had Michael come to look for her? She tried to head in the direction of the voices, but the path had disappeared. She stumbled over branches and nettles, brambles tearing at her bare legs. The trees were so close together, tangled branches blocking her way.

She heard the voices again. Distant and indistinct.

"… not a good day…agitated."

"… managed to eat?"

"… refusing… later."

Peculiar sort of conversation for them to be having.

Finally, she reached them, a young man and a middle-aged woman in a clearing. The man looked like he was wearing pyjamas. Very odd. The woman looked familiar, but Sylvia couldn't think where she had seen her before. It was so bright suddenly, making Sylvia squint. She could hear the beep again, somewhere in the distance. She wished it would stop. Made it hard to think.

"Have you seen David?" she said. They did not answer. "Have you seen David? He's lost." Louder this time, angry at being ignored. Why weren't they listening?

"Have you seen—"

She was suddenly blank. Silence filled her head. No room in the blankness for thoughts. Nothing but that incessant beeping.

The man in pyjamas touched her arm and told her everything was fine; she didn't need to worry. Everything was fine.

She tried to pull her arm away. Nothing was fine. Why was he lurking around in the woods in pyjamas at night. She must get away. She wrenched her arm from his grip and her legs went from under her. She clutched at the man's arm, but she couldn't hold on. Her hands scrabbling, grabbing nothing. She sank down to the sodden ground, unable to hold herself up a moment longer.

Sylvia opened her eyes but struggled to see in the dim light. She had no idea where she was, couldn't breathe. Someone took her hand. Soft hands stroked hers. She caught the faint scent of

Lily of the Valley and knew her mother had found her. The familiar voice soothed her, told her everything was alright and the dread which had been crushing her finally lifted. She closed her eyes. She didn't have to worry.

It was almost midnight. Snow had been falling for hours, muffling the sounds of occasional cars on the street below. Anna had been at her mother's bedside all day. It wouldn't be long now, the doctor said and asked if there was anyone they could call for her. She shook her head.

"No, my dad died a couple of years ago. And my brother, David, he— No, it's just me."

The room was dark apart from the faint glow from the lights on the monitors. These were silent now, the alarms no longer needed. Anna held her mother's hands. Those hands which had so often held hers. They were still now, the constant fluttering and anxious twisting of the last year finally stopped. Anna caressed the misshapen fingers and let silent tears fall.

Jodie Kennedy

Jodie has worked in the travel industry for the last twenty years. Despite living in Australia, Indonesia and the United States, she has always returned to the quiet Buckinghamshire village where she was born. A husband, two teenage daughters, a dog and a goldfish, and half a life of memories, are currently providing material for her first novel.

Big Ted's Fall from Grace

"Tonight, on A2Z TV, we conclude our series "BearTorx". Saving the scoop of the season till last, we meet Big Ted, that infamous bear of the 1970s children's programme, *Play Days*, as he struggles to gain a paw hold in the industry that made… and ultimately broke him."

With the headline introduction to the programme finished, Big Ted settled down to watch what he hoped would be a way back to the big time, a gamble he was all too keen to take. "It'll show them all," he muttered to himself.

"Big Ted. That once loveable rogue bear is living in somewhat reduced circumstances, housed in a rundown static home somewhere on the South Coast. We tracked him down to let him have his say on *that* incident," the voiceover person intoned.

Big Ted cringed and shrank back into the faded and overstuffed settee. It wasn't what he had expected to hear. They promised to be fair. Yet it made him sound guilty all over again. The programme continued, Big Ted talking directly to the camera.

"What a life! Well, I can't lie, it's been hard these last few years. Can't deny that. Not my fault either, see. Was a set-up from start to finish. Used to be the toast of kiddies TV back then. Hmm, it all started when I got picked at the audition. Hundreds of us teddies back then, it was hard to get into show business. Tough days. Down to the economy and all that. Only alternative was the dole queue. Well, they only went and chose me. ME! Big Ted. Who'd have thought? Well, Play Days was brand new, see, it was me and that Jemima Ragdoll, Mr. Bryan and Jodie.

"Never saw anything coming though, did we? We didn't know what a huge smash show it was going to be. Overnight sensation it was. Mr. Bryan and Jodie, well, they told us that we were up for some TV award nonsense. None of us thought we'd stand a chance, first year and all that. Not a chance. Well, we only went and won the blimmin' thing, didn't we?

"I s'pose things were already getting out of hand. We were everywhere. Did all the top shows, Parky and Russell Harty, fancy that! Talk about the high life. We had it all. On the day of the awards, well that Jemima, she was half-cut before we'd even gone out. She was a goer alright. Heady times. Well, we wrapped the series that afternoon, we had the debrief, the ratings were going through the roof. Through. The. Roof. I don't need to tell you what that meant. The world was our oyster.

"My, what a night that was. At the Albert Hall no less! Ma Bear was so proud of me. Mr. Bryan, he carried us onto the stage, and that nice Mr Craven off *Newsround* gave us the award! Had our photos taken with him, think I've still got one somewhere 'round here. Anyway, the champagne was flowing and well, I don't remember much after that, brain not as sharp as it was. Could quote another bear but you get the drift.

"So, they told me we went to another party, and it was very late when they put us back in the toy box. I was just getting me head down when the lid flies open, and I'm blinded. Blinded I tell you. Couldn't see who was there, camera flashes going off left, right and centre. Couldn't see a thing. So, there's me like doing what any decent bear would do, trying to calm everyone down and then that Jemima starts screaming blue murder. Blue murder I tell you. Always wanted to be centre of attention that one. Anyway, she blames me, tells me it's all my fault. Didn't even know what she was going on about.

"Next day, they show me the *News of the Day*. Someone's sent the Polaroid pictures in and they're all over the front page. 'Big Ted Guilty!'

"Well, there's me with Jemima, and me paw's up her skirt. Now I tell you, she led me on that one. And you know the rest. The show dropped me like a hot brick. Jemima went to some sort of institution. Never made it to court, too ill they said. Too ill my arse, in rehab. None of the others came to defend me. No one told the truth. The evidence was incriminating, and I went down. Did two years, for an egregious misdemeanour in a toybox. I tell you; they made that one up just for me!

"So, as I say, it's been a tough few decades. No one's wanted anything to do with me. Toxic they call it nowadays. I've had to paw me way back, been left to fend for me self. Mr. Bryan and Jodie stayed well away. Last I heard, they were scrabbling about on the festival circuit trying to resurrect their careers. Least said about that then. And don't even mention *her*, she's left me with a phobia of ragdolls. Those long stripey legs. Ugh! Makes me fur stand on end.

"Look, I've clawed me way back. It's not much I admit, but as Ma Bear always said, 'no point growling over an empty honey jar'. But the biggest laugh is, I've been doing me own tribute act, no one knows it's the real Big Ted playing Big Ted! Lost some weight when I got out the Scrubs so thought it might just work, no one was going to recognise me. Well, keeps the kids happy, they don't know my past and the parents just look at me and remember Play Days.

"Been getting by on that for years! Well, the tummy's rounder and the snout's going grey, and I can't keep on doing the rough and tumble much longer. Maybe fame and fortune ain't all it's cracked up to be. I'll be alright though, been saving up for years on the side, I'm CEO of Big Bear Business Holdings, owner of A2Z TV…"

Stephanie Wilson

Stephanie is nearly considered a Meltonian after thirty plus years of residency in Melton Mowbray, Leicestershire, England. A semi-retired nurse by day, she is also a curator of every "how to" writing guide known to humanity, in a vain attempt to aid writing of her current work in progress. Mainly at night.

Bread Eaten in Secret

Even seven floors up, the sound of the front door wakes me. We still call it the front door, as if there were any others. Seven floors of shuffling feet and heavy breathing are plenty of time to prepare. I am the first to the tap, washing my face and hands in water so cold it takes my breath away. The others press behind me. I push fly-away hairs from my face and pad back to the cot in the front room. My bare feet stick to the plastic flooring that tries to look like wood. I haven't seen it since the end of the summer when there was enough light to notice such things. Sometimes, the water in the tap flowed brown, and I longed for the ignorance of dark winter mornings. Today, the apartment is dark, like the inside of an ear. I read that somewhere, back before, when there were books. There is a drawn-out squelch as the last door frame peels away from the wall. The glue finally giving way. We ignore it. The ventilation fan in the ceiling leads to the apartment above us, and sometimes, it feels as if those women are standing in our kitchen instead of their own. They haunt us. Ghostly feet avoiding disrobed door jams and poking down unpeeled corners with bare toes.

Mother Angela lights up the hallway. When I first got here and was still asleep when the beam of her lamp fell on me, I would be woken by the leather strap she carries. The new girl in the second room wakes up this way. She's getting better, and today, she climbs out of bed, shielding her face, without screaming or confusion. The rest of us wait for it to be over. I stand by my cot, fingertips on the windowsill, gentle. Painted wood on freshly washed skin. Mother Angela catches her breath and straightens her clothes. She nods, sending us down to housekeeping on the ground floor, where we queue for our uniforms. There is a patch on the wall where the postboxes once were. I miss reading their names and making up stories about the lives they lived. Wind whistles and cries beyond the door. There is no sound of traffic. The woman at the laundry yawns as she hands me a cap, shirt and trousers. There are burns on her fingers and arms where her tattoos were removed. Her earlobes hang loose and empty. I step to the side and pull on the clothes over my underwear. Today's shirt is too tight under the armpits. It is a cotton and linen mix. The irony is not lost on me.

We walk to the bakery, heads bowed—a procession of mourners. The way is short and so familiar now that I do not have to count my way to the curb. Some women hesitate, looking both ways before stepping into the road. I remember when the lampposts worked. The bakery is ablaze with light, ceilings higher than the sky outside, where I am blanketed by darkness. I squint but do not pause. The day truly begins. We wash our hands, the bakery mother checks our fingernails, and our hair is under our caps. I heft bags of flour, slashing the sacking, filling the enormous bins, weighing as I go. On the fifth bag, something spasmed in my back, and I cut the wrong place, flour spilling out onto the floor. The new girl runs over and helps me. Together, we empty the remains of the bag into the bin and clean up the mess I made. On my knees, I tell her that she doesn't need to. She doesn't say anything, looks at me and smiles. It's a disconcerting moment. She tucks strands of hair back up under her cap, and light buzzes across the welts on her forearms. Memories of you stab into me. When I wore your pyjamas, they were tight under the armpits, and I never complained. My shirt pulls me back to your bed.

I almost scramble away from the new girl. I don't trust her help. She was beaten while I stood by, and still, she smiled. A sad smile. An unbelievable smile. We don't help each other here. We don't talk. We learned that lesson long ago. Some new girls were mothers in disguise, and we were punished for the things we let slip. We complained about the current order. We reminisced about our lives before. Speaking of that time is forbidden. We are supposed to be born anew in the light. We are shaped by the work we do now, not the sins we committed before. We all pretend that we are not serving indefinite penance for those sins. It must be the same for you.

We were taken, and no one fought for us. We screamed, and no one heard. When we tried to fight, they locked the doors and left us without food or water until we'd calmed down. That thirst. The way it drags at every cell of your body. Fighting was an impossibility. So, we were returned to the flats and put back into our cots. Not knowing if the woman sleeping next to us had been taken or if she was watching us. We could not trust each other. The new girl breathes strangely in her sleep. Shallow and rapid. As if she were running or preparing to fight. I should not be noticing such things.

I walk into the fridge in search of butter. Hands pressed against the clammy walls, deep breaths in the cold air. The cloy of dairy and mould. I hate this fridge. I pull crates of milk and wedge the door open. If someone tried to shut me in, I'd hear them moving the crates first. The thought lurks here every time. The inside of this fridge has no handle, just a metal spike in its place. I doubt that anyone would notice if it shut. I worry that someone will lock me in out of malice or apathy. And I will die in this fridge, trying to turn this spike with butter-slick fingers and running out of air. I dream of that. Over and over. Wrapping my cap around my hand in a futile attempt at purchase. It would take a long time, and there might be moments of hope. I might get bored before I die. It would be a quicker death than the one I live, but I still fear it. I kick the fridge shut behind me. Not bothering to replace the milk.

I weigh the butter and cut it by hand. My fingers slip on the knife handle. Greasy, like when we sat on your sofa, eating cheesy chips and talking about poetry. I shiver, trying to shake off the feeling of your knees against mine. This bright, cold morning is nothing like that night. I am not there. I will not fall into a pit of memories. I stare at the twisting dough in the machine and throw pieces of butter into the mix. Listening for the slap. The dough grows elastic, and I clean, ignoring the pinch in my armpits as I reach and wipe. Letting the water warm my hands. The comforting smells of yeast and bleach. A mother watches me; the leather strap hangs limp at her waist. I bow my head. A good woman knows her place. All our guards are mothers. We are too dangerous. We would manipulate and seduce male guards, they say. The father visits occasionally, to proselytise. A wall of women guards him from us. Even me. In their eyes, all women who have strayed from goodliness are the same. We are all wantons and temptresses. Better to be put to work and kept away from good folk. I miss other people. I miss turning lights on and off. I miss being alone. I miss a lot of things.

I turn off the mixer. The dough can proof there. I am allowed to stop for a glass of water and a piece of fruit. Today, an apple. My saliva is thick with thirst. Somewhere, a woman like me has picked this fruit. The father says that we have become useful.

Our lives have meaning for the first time. I shut my eyes so that the mother does not see them roll. This is a good apple. Crisp and crunchy. Sometimes, the apples are mealy, and I swallow the pieces whole, trying to avoid the sensation of chewing on sand. Not greedy, not ungrateful. Eyes down. I cannot remember what fruit you liked. I cannot remember if we ever ate mango together, sticky fingers mixed with strawberries and fresh mint leaves. That might just be fantasy. There's a lot I can't remember after all these years. Nothing tangible. You only left me with a feeling of confusion. And want—almost desperation. I bite through the skin. The new girl is carefully eating her fruit with the left side of her face. Still, she winces. I wonder if one of her smiling teeth is rotting. I wonder how much pain she is in. I lost a tooth last year; I do not blame her for putting off asking for the pliers.

I pick the seeds out of my apple core and add them to the jar the mother holds. When I wash my hands, I notice how tight the skin on my hands has become. Wrinkled and red with swollen knuckles. I wonder what my face has become. I weigh the dough and shape the loaves - the satisfying part is seeing what I have made come together. Feeling it roll under my hands and knowing that I have made something tangible and good. It's better than the intangible, digital work I used to do. Now, I am making something I can see and feel and taste; I know that I have changed the world in this little way. I exist; I am real. I sound like their propaganda, but it's true. I always loved feeding people, always showed love through food. Banana bread and cakes for friends after breakups and a whole host of new recipes for a celiac diagnosis. I can only remember cooking you dinner once, but it might have been more. Fresh pasta with a soft, cheesy, garlicky sauce and wilted spinach. We watched a movie on my sofa. I put my hand on your knee, and you told me that you wanted to concentrate on the film. I pulled my hand away. You shuffled closer and twisted your fingers idly in my hair, eyes on the screen. I can't remember what we were watching. Concentrating on not gazing at your face in profile, blue light reflecting in your eyes, your jaw tense. Later, we rolled into the middle of my bed. You backed into me, and I spooned you. I put a hand on your waist, and you tensed. I pulled back. You were still tense. I felt awful. I had misunderstood. I had pushed too far. I rolled away. Replaying in my mind the difference between consent and coercion, but then your body followed mine. Without speaking, you gently stroked my thighs and the delicate skin around my hip bones. I did nothing. I could only lie there and let you touch me. Fingertips circling. We never spoke about those caresses. You fell asleep draped around me.

I leave the dough. My hands are slightly sticky, and my wrists ache. The loaves need to proof for a final time. I check the time twice before my brain takes any notice of it. The mothers cannot know what I am thinking. I tried to kiss you. Often. But you pulled away. Should I have stopped trying? Whatever we were doing, wherever we were, you would pull away. Until the goodbye, you always held my face in your hands and kissed me. In public or in private. They were long kisses with heat behind them. And then you would walk away, leaving me confused. My friends would say that maybe you didn't want to draw attention to two women kissing, and that's why you wouldn't kiss me when we hung out. But then they'd see you say goodbye to me, and they would be as confused as I was. But their lips weren't prickling with abandonment.

I fetch eggs and pour them into a bowl. I take a brush and wash the loaves. All of them the same; they come from the same dough, they weigh the same, and have been proofed for the same amount of time. The consistency — the reliability — is calming. I catch myself holding my breath. You were never consistent. There were so many times when I thought I knew what was going on between us. The time we played squash made me sure that we were just friends. And then you kissed me goodbye. Or when you called me to join you on a night out and told me you couldn't wait to see me. I arrived, nervous and excited—all fizzy at the edges. You beamed and fell about me, light rainbowing off your cheeks. Your friends gave me knowing smiles and told me how much they'd heard about me. You laughed and agreed with them, you couldn't help it, you were crazy about me. It felt simple. All of my doubts were gone. All of my questions were answered. You stroked my face. I put a hand on your hip. You smiled up at me. I leaned in to kiss you, and you turned away. I whispered something in your ear to hide my mistake. I can't remember what. Maybe I bought you a drink. I was sure, again, that we were just friends and that I had misunderstood. I laughed with you and your friends, unhurriedly finishing my glass. I thanked you for the evening and said goodbye. I turned to say goodbye to your friends, but there you were, holding your coat and telling them we were leaving. We stepped out of the bar and into the glow of the streetlight. You laughed, and it came out in a cloud. You held my hand and took me to get late-night pizza and cheesy chips. You took me home. On your sofa, we licked fat and salt from our fingers and shared poetry. I pawed through notebooks filled with your neat, blue scrawls. You told me that you'd read my story. You liked it. You wanted me to submit it to be published. You were the first person who ever told me that. Not abstractly, concretely. To this email address. Send it. My cheeks burned. I didn't kiss you.

I check the temperature. This oven doesn't hold the same dread of closing in as the fridge does. Here, it's more like a pull.

I want to step into its fiery embrace. I could stand in it and not touch the sides, but it would not be long before I slipped, stumbled, and put out a hand to stop my fall. I don't know if my skin would melt, bubble, and stick me to the black walls. It's the same feeling as when I was a child and was told not to touch the grill because it's hot. The part of me that wants to poke my fingers in - that wants to see how hot - it hasn't died. It lives, and the bread oven brings it out. That night, after eating pizza on your sofa, we went to your bedroom, and you lent me a pair of pyjamas. You turned away as I put them on. They were too tight at the armpits, but I wore them. I was scared to reject anything you gave me. I was determined not to get anything wrong and not to push. I lay in your bed and waited for any hint from you. You kissed me on the shoulder, your lips on the cotton, and rolled away. The room lightened in the dawn. You breathed deeply and slowly. Walls revealed pictures you'd taken in frames you'd made. The mess on the windowsill cast long-fingered shadows into the room.

I push the bread into the oven and shut the door. I do not shut myself in. Not today. You slept by my side, curled up, facing away. I tried to decide what we were to each other. Were we falling for each other? Your friends seemed to think so with their winks and nudges and comments. My heart seemed to think so. The way it sparked when you held my hand or played with my hair. I had no clear answer then, and I still have no idea how you felt about me. You kissed me, told me you liked me, and laughed at my jokes far more than they deserved. You flinched away from my affection and regaled me with stories about your ex-girlfriend. You called me when you were drunk and only kissed me goodbye. And how could you have liked me? I was barely myself around you. I was an awkward wreck who got lost in your eyes and forgot to reply. Once, I heard myself claiming that I believed in ghosts because you said you did. I did not like that version of myself. I cringed when she laughed her braying laugh and forgot what she was saying halfway through an anecdote. I wanted to see you, listen to you talk about poetry and opera and photography and really hear the words. Not just let it all wash over me as I bathed in the sound of your voice. I lay there in your bed and realised that I couldn't. I couldn't be around you and be myself. You were burning and bright, and I didn't want to be a moth, only dreaming of fluttering clumsily against you.

I am hit for absentmindedness—a sharp blow across the back of my thighs. I apologise to the mother and get back to work; she hasn't broken the skin. I am lucky. I don't think about you every day - or even every week. But all I have is time here, and sometimes I dwell, falling into memories. I have nothing to read except the writing on bags of flour and packets of yeast and butter kept in a fridge, which terrifies me. I tell myself stories, and I remember—or invent as if the difference matters. Once, at the start, a woman confided in me that she watches old TV shows in her head. She can't help it. She wished she could watch a good movie, a play, or even a limited series. But she is left with sitcom episodes that lived in the background of her old existence. And I have you.

I turn the bread out of its pans. All identical. Except for one, which is slightly darker than the rest. Maybe one corner of the oven is overheating. I should check that later. My hands move in a practised rhythm; they have gotten used to this new life. What are your hands doing? I wonder if your handwriting would be unchanged. If you have pen and paper squirrelled away. Where are you now? Are you picking the fruit I eat? Are you washing the uniforms I wear or the sheets I sleep in? Did you successfully convince them of your conversion? Was the tattoo on your wrist burned away? Have you been assigned to an officer as a wife? Are you a mother? Or did you escape? I cannot imagine you in a cap.

I load the bread into baskets. This close to the doors, the world outside finally feels real. I could walk out of here, if I wanted. Alarms be damned. I keep working. I am helping to feed this city. I wonder if you've ever eaten bread that I've baked. Do you even think about me? I don't know how I think about you. That's always the difficulty, isn't it? Looking back on past lovers and lacking certainty that was truly love. So much of you and us is blurred or discoloured. So much of you is my own invention. I ran my thumb over your tattoo on the bus. Delicate raised lines that crisscrossed your veins. They refuse to form a picture. Only the sensation remains. I wonder if now, surrounded by the coldness of other women, I have romanticised our strange and awkward relationship and used it to keep myself warm. I have always felt loneliest when I cannot be alone. So here, I wrap myself in the past and pretend that the last few years never happened.

The heat of the last loaf presses into my hands and a madness takes hold of me, I peel off a piece of crust and eat it. Stealing from my own creation. The new girl with welts on her arms looks up, her eyes shining. Perhaps she approves of my trivial rebellion. If she is a mother, I will be beaten later. If not, well. I will wake her up tomorrow morning before Mother Angela reaches us.

Florence Hood (For Florence's biography see page 233).

Cardigan

The tide rolled in. White foam washed against sand darkened by the intake of water. Bubbles formed after the sea had washed down, sucked into the waves again to curl back over and break in a repetitive, slow cycle. A gentle breeze rippled around her as she moved through the surf. The water was cool as it rolled over her toes. The morning had barely broken, but she was already walking along the cove. The sun had yawned wide enough that orange rays dusted the cliff tops a short distance away. Her hands delved into her cardigan pockets, digging deep within to brush over the shells she had already collected. A shell brushed against her toe as she stepped on the sand, sinking into it gradually when she came to a stop. Her hand reached down to collect the scallop shell, brushing the wet sand from the inside of it with her thumb. She stepped toward the sea. She reached down to wash the scallop shell in the water itself. Satisfied that every grain of sand had been washed away, she let it fall into her cardigan pocket. The clink of the scallop against other shells was drowned by the sound of the waves washing ashore. The satisfaction of another piece to add to her collection was evident on the smile of pure happiness spreading without a second thought.

She gathered the ends of her cardigan around her, feeling the warmth and stopping the sea spraying with little dots of wet. The sun wasn't high enough yet to warm the sand, or indeed even the sea, so the cardigan was her swaddle from the cold. Handmade, the cardigan was; the multicoloured wool knitted and stitched into the shape it was now – long sleeved and with large pockets on either side. Though a little frayed at the cuffs and with a star-shaped button missing from the bottom, it was still her most favoured item of clothing. She still remembered the day she had unwrapped the box waiting under the Christmas tree. It was one of the very last gifts she had received from her Nan, before sickness had quietly taken her eight days later. She had since clung to the cardigan as well as it clung to her — a reminder of who had made it, of who had loved her enough to create something she could keep.

She found a small collection of rocks to perch upon at the side of the cove. The rocks were carved from the cliffs, it seemed. The waves hit but didn't quite roll over them, and with a rougher tide she imagined that the rocks had been worn down over the years. The fractures in the rocks beneath her were visible, but they held strong. She drew her knees up to her chest, tucking them inside her cardigan. She fished her shells from her pocket and laid them out, one by one, on the surface of a rock in front of her. Her fingers brushed over the ridges of the shells — scallops and cowries, clams and mussels, abalones and olives. She arranged them in two lines, mixed in shapes and sizes. She smiled at the sight of the various colours, shapes and types the sea had gifted her.

A crab clambered its way across the rock, small enough to fit into the palm of her hand. She watched it go, side-walking in the way they did. It manoeuvred around the shells, avoiding them in favour of making its way to the edge. She waved as the crab disappeared into the sea and stuffed her hands up her sleeves, leaving the tips of her fingers exposed. The neon pink nail polish had cracked and flaked by now, after having it on for so long.

She pulled at a loose thread of yellow from the cuff of her cardigan, knotting it to keep from being blown by the wind. The breeze gently caressed the tail end of the thread still left unknotted.

There was something she had to let go.

She uncrossed her legs, careful to avoid the neat rows of shells, and reached inside one pocket of her paperbag waist shorts. In her hand were a folded piece of paper and a small black pouch, perfectly made to contain earrings, but earrings did not lie inside.

"I did what you asked," she murmured softly. "You're home now."

Home. That's what the cove was. Not hers, but the home of the person who had taught her to lay out shells in neat rows after collecting them. The person who had knitted her cardigan. The house further back from the shore had always stood alone, unbothered by the sea. It had belonged to her Nan, and now it was hers. But the house was a house – not home. Home was stretched out in front of her, reaching across the horizon, washing against the sand. She gently pressed a kiss to the letter in her hand and tucked it back inside her pocket to treasure the shaky handwriting upon the page. She slowly opened the small pouch as she rose to stand on the edge of the rock, stepping over her collection of shells. Seawater hit the rocks and splashed up against her toes. She rolled up the sleeves of her cardigan keeping them at the elbow. The cuffs were stretched. She emptied the contents of the pouch onto her open hand, the breeze making some of it dance and swirl. Instead of letting the grey powder be blown away by the breeze, she carefully lowered herself on one knee and placed her hand against the water. The tide brushed the ashes off her hand when it pulled back into the swell. The cardigan sleeve on her outstretched arm slipped, dipping into the water. Her expression held a watery smile as she watched the ashes be further swept away. She waited until she couldn't see traces of the ashes before moving, carefully collecting her shells one by one and slipping them back into her cardigan pocket.

Shanice Khan

Shanice is a librarian from Manchester whose love of books started at an early age. When she is not spending her time encouraging young people to read or entertaining her nieces, Shanice can be found working on her first fantasy novel in one of her many notebooks.

Day Hike

Samantha had not brought the "ten essentials," but only food, water, a compact first-aid kit, and a multitool, which all fitted loosely in her small daypack. She found the group of seven other women gathered at the trailhead, all outfitted in hardshell outer layers and serious hiking packs, some even carried trekking poles. Samantha shivered beneath her softshell jacket and took a deep breath, reminding herself that these women weren't strangers, only "friends she hadn't met." She exhaled slowly, working at the tightness in her chest.

"Welcome, everyone!" The guide, Anna, clasped her hands together next to the weathered information sign. "Thank you all for coming out on such a misty morning."

The day was cool and overcast, with tufts of fog clinging to the treetops on the mountain ahead of them. It wasn't Kilimanjaro, for sure, but as a novice rambler, Samantha marveled at the prospect of ascending so far in a single day.

Mostly she'd done easy treks on wide, flat trails. Many were family-friendly. She wouldn't say it out loud, but Samantha had become increasingly annoyed at moms on the trails who pushed their strollers past her, only to stop dead in front of her moments later, to tend to their wet-faced infants.

A pang of guilt tugged in Samantha's chest, an echo of her own mother's long-suffering disappointment. Samantha would prefer to stay home alone with Netflix and a box of wine.

However, at the insistence of her therapist and the courage fueled by Merlot, Samantha signed up for walking groups. Any other *Meetup* events at bars or restaurants typically devolved into pseudo-support groups for women to complain about their husbands. With a walking group, Samantha could just keep moving if the conversation went sideways. Even if she couldn't make any friends, at least she'd get some exercise.

Anna started the introductions.

Samantha stood nearest to Candace, who looked like the type she could have drinks with.

"We should make pretty good time," Samantha murmured to Candace, "without a bunch of kids slowing us down."

Samantha knew her sense of humor was a bit off, but Candace's reaction seemed over the top. She looked as if she'd been slapped, shifted her weight, and turned away.

Samantha's cheeks burned. Her mother's voice replayed along the well-worn groove in her head. For Christ's sake, keep your mouth shut! Better to have people think you're an idiot, than to open your mouth and prove them right.

Samantha wanted nothing more than to slink back to her car, but the confirmation email she'd received from Anna was clear. Even though it was only fifteen dollars, there would be no refunds, and signing up was itself a "firm commitment." Samantha couldn't back out; she'd promised to report her progress to her therapist on Monday. Pressing her cool fingertips against her temples, she willed her heart rate to slow down. She'd have to see this through.

Some of the women seemed to know each other, picking up conversations as they chatted. She tried not to eavesdrop, but overheard two of them say they were, "Ready to move on".

Anna held up two Kinko-printed spiral-bound booklets. "Two of you didn't pick up your copy for today's walk."

"Here," Samantha raised her hand and stepped forward, feigning confidence. She didn't know there'd be a book; that must have been what the fee was for.

Anna handed the copies to Samantha and to another woman holding a tall wooden walking stick, wearing a broad-brimmed beige hat tied beneath her chin. If this walk was a fantasy novel, this woman could be the wizard, advising a rag-tag group of reluctant heroes. Samantha smiled with renewed energy. She felt a tug of sisterhood, wondering what the adventures might be that lay ahead, and how she might find connection with these women.

Samantha flipped through the pages of the book and said aloud, "I'm just looking forward to an outing with other women that isn't a margarita-fueled support group—"

Samantha stopped short on a page in the booklet with the heading: "Grief is a Part of Life."

"That's such a shame," Anna said. "It's easy for us to fall into despair. I hope today's walk will inspire you to find other ways to process your grief."

"Oh, I don't have any grief."

The conversations stopped.

"Sorry, what walk did you sign up for," Anna asked.

"Um…the child-free, women's walk?"

"This is the 'Childless to Child-Free—Surmounting Infertility' walk."

Heat bloomed from Samantha's collar. Another of her wine-time decisions had gone wrong.

"You're welcome to join us," Anna continued, "if you're willing to support a safe space for these women."

"Of course." Samantha's eyes darted to the faces around her. She held her free hand to her heart, realizing how corny it was as she did so, but knowing it was too late to put it back down.

"My apologies, everyone," she said.

Candace nodded, tight-lipped, and looked away. The woman in the broad hat tilted her head slightly. The other women resumed their conversations, seemingly happy to ignore her. This was going to be a very long day.

Samantha never wanted children. With her first period, she burst out of the bathroom and delivered an impassioned lecture to her mother about how unfair it was she had to go through such nonsense when there was no way she would ever—EVER—have kids.

"Life might surprise you," her mother replied. "It sure surprised me."

Samantha heard everything her mother had said. Motherhood makes you fat and makes your man leave you. Motherhood means you get fired from your shitty, low-paying job when you miss a shift because your kid is sick. It means you never get to pursue your own dreams, because you're saddled with an ungrateful clone of yourself you're socially obligated to feed.

How was Samantha going to spend the next several hours with these women, bonded by their existential ache that they couldn't make babies?

Samantha opened the trail book to "*Station 1: The Bridge*." She stood with the other women at the end of a long footbridge which spanned a tumbling river.

"A bridge is a transition," Anna shouted to be heard over the rushing water. "Where we leave behind one way of being and embark on a new version of ourselves."

Anna paused, making eye contact with each of the women.

"The turbulence of the water represents the turbulence we feel as we make this transition into the unknown, but we do it together, as a community."

Anna led the way as everyone merged onto the bridge to follow. As Samantha waited for her turn to step across, she thought how much easier it would be to be swept away by the churning rapids below her.

Station 2: The Rocky Approach

The group continued beyond the bridge, up the mountain trail. As they climbed, the level, compacted tread eroded, exposing bedrock and ankle-bending divots.

Samantha leaned forward, grasping the shoulder straps of her daypack. Her heart rate quickened as she pumped her legs up the steep incline. She breathed heavily, and the cool air made her eyes and nose water. She focused on her feet, planting one step in front of the other, pushing herself up the path.

Samantha stayed at the rear of the group. Rather than make a friend today, she'd be lucky to get through this without everyone hating her. *How could she be so stupid? Fucking careless—*

"Give it a rest, will ya? Your self-flagellation is harshing my mellow."

The wizard-woman stood ahead of Samantha on the trail. She was likely in her early fifties, based on the gentle smile lines of her face, just visible beneath the shade of her hat. The woman leaned on her walking stick with a nonchalance that impressed Samantha, given the terrain.

"Go easy on yourself already."

"Sorry…" Samantha stuttered. "I guess I said that out loud."

"Yeah, ya did. You gotta let that shit go, or it'll eat you up." She extended a hand. "I'm Margaret."

Samantha and Margaret continued up the slope, concentrating on their footing. As they rounded the bend, they met the others who had gathered on a small terrace, which was no more than a widened, flat, part of the trail.

Anna addressed the group.

"At this second station of our walk, it's important for us to take a moment to consider how far we've come."

Samantha turned to acknowledge the steep incline behind her, catching her breath as she opened her water bottle.

"Each day can feel like a battle," Anna continued. "The disappointment and the continued press forward. The discomfort of IVF treatments. The heartbreak of miscarriages. What we wouldn't give for just a little success, just once."

A sense of quiet reflection settled among the women.

"Although it may not feel like 'success,' we need to stop occasionally and recognize how far we've come. There's a lot more we need to do—a lot farther we need to go—but each step we take is building on the one before it. We have made progress."

There was general agreement among the women, which morphed into some chit-chat and laughter. Samantha was on the periphery; there was no place to sit, and she was eager to keep moving. Rather than blunder another conversation, Samantha toed some of the sharp, gray-beige-colored rocks at the base of the cut slope.

Samantha put herself on 'The Pill' as soon as she could get it from the free clinic. She wouldn't have sex until later that year, but she wanted no surprises. Her mother claimed, often with a deep sigh of resignation, that she'd gotten pregnant the first time she ever had sex. Samantha took no chances.

Now that Samantha was thirty, she wondered how many pregnancies she'd avoided as she brushed her boot over the loose stones.

"We adopted," said Margaret.

Startled, Samantha took half a beat to process what she said.

She'd never considered having kids *on purpose*.

Samantha remembered how years ago, as she and her mother watched a Christmas special, a teary-eyed adoptive parent referred to the beaming child at her hip as a "gift." Samantha's mom barked at the TV, "That's no gift—just lucky sperm," and ruffled Samantha's hair. "Just like you!"

"How did that go?" Samantha asked, replacing the lid on her water bottle and slipping it into her pack.

Margaret laughed out loud. "Well, they were still alive when I last checked."

"Sorry, I—"

"You apologize a lot."

"I—"

"You're alright, kid. One of these days you'll figure that out."

They followed the others up the trail.

"What are their names?" Samantha asked, eager to change the focus from herself.

"Dylan and Cody. Two ornery little devils—thirteen and fourteen—I wouldn't have it any different and wouldn't change them for the world."

"What made you decide to adopt?"

"I never did the IVF treatments like some of the women here—the 'discomfort' Anna mentioned is one hell of an understatement—that is some hard-core shit to put yourself through. But we wanted to have a family, and it just never happened naturally. We figured there are already enough kids in this world that need loving parents, ya know?"

Samantha paused.

"Was it difficult?"

"They look into every part of your life," Margaret answered. "They make sure you're not sociopaths or pedophiles, that your house won't fall down on the kids, and that you can afford to feed them. We're not fancy, but good enough, I suppose."

"Do you miss… um… not…"

"Not squeezin' out my own pups? Nah. I've seen the birthing process, and I'm not enamored with it. This way, I get the kids without the stretch marks or the leaky bladder."

They both chuckled.

"Why did you come today?" Samantha asked.

"I understand the ache of not being able to have kids. Adoption worked for us, but it's not for everyone. Eventually, we all need to come to a point of acceptance—our life doesn't always turn out the way we hope, but that doesn't mean it can't be rewarding in other ways."

They progressed their way up the path. As Samantha placed one foot in front of the other, she allowed herself to consider her existence as more than a mere apology, that she might be worthy of a rewarding life.

The buoyancy of this realization was short-lived as a tightness crept in. *How do I know what will be rewarding? What if I get it wrong?*

Samantha shook her head to clear out the chatter and tried to latch onto the sense of lightness she'd felt when talking to Margaret, as if forcing herself to remember a dream after waking up.

Station 3: The Cave

Near the summit, a small cave awaited them, past benches of bedrock among patches of soft grass, wildflowers, and low, scraggly brush. Everyone found a place to sit and took out their books.

The clouds had burned off. Samantha was already warm from the ascent. She took off her pack and tied her jacket around her waist as Anna walked by.

"What are we doing now?" asked Samantha.

Anna held her book open above her head and kept walking, tapping the appropriate page of the book with her finger. She stopped in front of the cave to make her announcement.

"This cave represents the emptiness we feel due to our infertility. I invite you to come to the cave in turns and stand inside of it, to not be afraid to feel the emptiness, and to challenge yourself to find something you perhaps didn't know was there. We'll stay here for a while, so there's plenty of time for journaling and contemplation."

Samantha flipped to a page with an illustration of a cave, while many of the others queued up to go inside. She wasn't going to write about the pain of not having children, of course, but she still felt the urge to write something.

By default, her mother's words came first. *Selfish. Ungrateful. Mistake.* Samantha scribbled hard on her page, as if to scrub the voice out. Then she closed her eyes, shook out her hands, and started again.

Samantha made a list of the things she always thought she'd wanted. A montage of possibilities played in her mind: herself as a photojournalist; at a Moroccan market; laughing with friends over drinks; kissing a man in the sunset surf, wearing cuffed white linen pants, damp with sea water.

But these were TV commercials, not her life.

Next, the reel of her life's errors interrupted her thoughts. Her mother smirking in response to the "When I Grow Up" essay Samantha wrote in grade school. The humiliating breakups. The time she said something unkind about a friend and it had gotten back to her. That one pregnancy test she took in a panic, worried the birth control had failed.

Samantha lifted her chest and stretched to break the spell. Everyone had finished in the cave and was either seated on the ground or on a boulder, curled over their books, writing into their pages.

Samantha indulged her curiosity and took a turn in the cave. She stepped beyond the reach of the sunlight tiptoeing onto the cave floor and listened.

She wondered if Anna might be an extrovert, because Samantha didn't sense "emptiness" in the cave, but instead a solace. It was quiet, but not silent. Louder than the sound of her own breath were the soles of her boots against the grit on the floor. The cave provided a bubble away from the rest of the world; the breeze rustling in the brush outside seemed far more distant than it must have been. A slight hum of energy emanated from the cave walls, like the sound of a television with the power on and the volume muted. She couldn't explain it, but the insular nature of the space was like a portal, reintroducing her to a long-forgotten self: unknown, yet familiar.

Samantha took a deep breath, slowly inhaling the still air of the cave. She closed her eyes and exhaled with a force—her breath seemed to ricochet off the walls around her and land against her body like soap bubbles bursting in slow motion. Spots of her that had long been calloused over became tender. With each breath came the sensation of something returning to her, splashing against her, reminding her body to be curious. Reminding her that to be soft and vulnerable can make her strong. Reminding her of a well of joy within herself.

Her mother's voice was not in the cave.

Station 4: The Meadow

Samantha hadn't noticed any pain in her knees on the way up, but the descent of switchbacks down the other side made it clear how much she'd stressed them.

A younger woman bolstered herself with a pair of carbon

fiber trekking poles. She had struggled with abrupt, jerky movements on the ascent, although her gait seemed smoother on the way down. Margaret was far ahead near the front of the group, recognizable by her broad hat and her tall, wooden, walking stick. Samantha thought to stop at REI on the way home; some sort of walking support wouldn't be a bad idea.

Anna guided the group to a wide meadow and paused before her next speech. Samantha kept her eyes down while Anna spoke, not wanting to intrude upon the others any more than she already had. Once Anna had finished, everyone broke into groups for lunch.

Not wanting to press her luck, Samantha sat alone in the grass. Two women approached as she unwrapped her sandwich. One was older; the other woman, the one with the trekking poles, was quite a bit younger.

"May we sit next to you?" the older of the two women asked.

The younger woman made a sound that didn't register as words to Samantha's ears.

"Of course; welcome to *Chez Samantha*."

The older woman continued. "I'm Patsy. This is my daughter, Julia."

Julia made another sound.

Samantha pulled a container of pistachios out of her bag while the two women settled onto the grass. "Would you like some?"

"Oh yes. We would, wouldn't we? Thank you."

Julia used her voice again.

"She says we have pretzels," said Patsy, and she offered the Ziplock bag from her own pack.

"You're a mother-daughter team?" asked Samantha. "Why… um… what brought you here today?"

Julia squawked and made a murmuring sound.

"Julia has a disability, and has decided not to have children, even though she longs to be a mom."

Julia murmured in agreement.

"She says she's heartbroken." Patsy translated with gentle compassion, yet without wearing her daughter's grief as her own. "But the walk helps to process it." Patsy paused. "It helps, doesn't it? We enjoy it, don't we?"

Julia made a chirping sound and shifted her attention to the horizon.

"She's really struggled, coming to terms with this. We heard about the walk, and she insisted we come. Isn't that right?"

Julia nodded her head.

Patsy helped her daughter by opening some of the containers they'd brought, and by tucking a napkin into her collar. Julia's movements were awkward, but she ate her lunch capably.

Samantha, by contrast, managed to drip mustard on her shirt and dust herself in pretzel crumbs. She'd never witnessed such symbiosis between a mother and daughter.

Patsy anticipated every need, interpreted each slight movement and expression her daughter made. As they chatted, Samantha discovered that Patsy was more than her daughter's caregiver, but was coming to the end of a long career in education and looking forward to retirement.

"Julia has become as independent as she can; haven't you, darling?"

Julia nodded.

"Yes, you have, haven't you?" Patsy continued. "We have a team of helpers that come in on rotation, so it's not just me and her father. We went on a second honeymoon of sorts just last year, and I don't think Julia missed us at all. Julia will do well when we're gone. You'll do just fine, won't you?"

Samantha didn't know a mother could be so dialed-in to her

child's needs, without an air of martyrdom, yet independent of her daughter, with her own, separate, sense of self. The calibration between Samantha and her own mother had been only one-way: Samantha attuned to her mother, constantly adjusting to match the shifts in her moods. A look, a tone of voice, a change in her breathing—all meant Samantha would be required to react, to perform, to appease, or to disappear.

During her final days, Samantha's mother lost the ability to speak. She'd mumble only sounds, her lips kept moist by Samantha's repeated application of mouth-care gel. Her mother could not make words, but her tone, the faces she made, and the look in her eyes were clearly recognizable to Samantha. Her mother gave a wordless, critical admonition: *make it stop.*

Samantha could only watch and wait as her mother suffered, disappointing her to the end.

Station 5: The Forest

Samantha's shins balked as they adjusted to the decline of the downgrade, toward a thicket of trees flourishing at the bottom of the slope. As Samantha approached, a single path became visible through the undergrowth.

Anna paused at the head of the path as the others gathered around.

"Another word for 'descend' is to 'concede.'"

Samantha admired how well Anna projected her voice outdoors.

"The hill we've just come down represents humility. After all we've been through, we acknowledge we don't have control over the outcome. We may need to humbly accept that even if we do everything right, we might not be able to have our own children."

Several throats cleared as Samantha stood behind the others, her eyes fixed on her own boots.

"Yet through it all," Anna continued, "we find our own path. Once we identify the path that presents itself before us, and put one foot in front of the other, we'll come to accept wherever it is we find ourselves, wherever that path leads. For some, it might lead to successful childbirth."

There was a hopeful intake of breath as Anna continued.

"For others, adoption. And for most of us, acknowledging that having our own children is not going to happen. It's a lifetime journey to find meaning in our lives, while giving honor to our disappointments."

Once Anna finished, the women worked their way, two-by-two into the woods. Samantha found herself walking next to Candace.

"Hey—I'm sorry. For earlier."

"It's alright; you didn't know."

Samantha relaxed, relieved. Candace walked at an easy pace, and Samantha found herself comfortably falling into step with her.

"How has today, um…been for you?" Samantha asked.

"Good."

Samantha took the brief reply as a cue: more walking, less talking. As the clearing disappeared behind them, the others also kept their voices low, if they spoke at all. Some shifted out of step with their impromptu partners, walking their own sacred path beneath the trees.

The temperature dropped as Samantha and Candace moved deeper into the forest. The damp, pine-scented air chilled their faces. Decaying leaves and pine needles softened their path underfoot, while varieties of leggy, bushy ferns emerged from discarded branches along the edge of the trail.

"It's not what I expected," Candace whispered. "I arrived here a few hours ago feeling very sorry for myself, like no one else could possibly want this as much as I do. I mean—don't get me wrong; if you asked, I would've said there's nothing I can't stand more than a 'victim'—but I realized today I'd been wallowing there. It was eye-opening."

Samantha listened as she lifted a thin, low-hanging branch out of their way.

"And here are all these other women," Candace continued, "and I didn't feel so alone anymore."

"Well, that's something," added Samantha, unsure what else to say.

"And you know, I think I'll be able to find meaning in my life without being a mom," Candace said. "It's obvious when I say it out loud—and it's not like I won't ever be sad about it again—but I think I'll be able to have a fulfilling life. For the first time in a long time, I'm excited to see what's possible."

"Awesome—you're glad you came, then?"

Candace smiled. "Yeah. I am, actually!"

"Me too," Samantha said, beaming.

A small animal rustled in the brush

"You wanna get a couple drinks after?" Samantha asked. "Maybe a cheeseburger?"

Candace's face fell. "I'm vegan. And I don't drink."

"Oh shit! I'm sorry—"

"Kidding!" Candace chuckled. "A burger and a beer sounds awesome!"

Sarah Sharp (For Sarah's biography see page 177).

Dead in the Water

It was a warm August night when Peter wandered into the woods. He wanted time to think and that is where his idle footsteps had taken him. I could be happy if I spend my life with her, he thought. I love her, he assured himself.

Further into the woods he went, treading carefully over entwining roots. The full branches above blanketed out the indigo sky. He came upon a small stone footbridge, stopping at its centre to lean against the parapet and watch the inky water flow by. Trees parted over the stream to reveal the reflection of a single star flickering on the water's surface. He prayed upon that twinkling image for his love to be unwavering.

The wind raced through the trees, causing leaves to fall and ripple the water, and as it passed him, its icy fingers traced his exposed skin. It left a sense of unease in its wake, as the forest fell silent and still. Slow and steady, his heart's tempo rose, then behind him, soft footsteps echoed off the cobblestones. In one quick motion, he turned around to find a find a young woman stood before him. Her eyes were focussed on the ground, and she was barefoot and wearing only a blue silk gown. Her grey skin looked delicate, and limp black hair flowed over her breasts to her waist. Peter's panic changed to concern; he took in her exposed form and thought it dangerous for her to be in the woods alone.

"Is everything okay? Are you lost?" he asked.

At first, he thought she hadn't heard, but then her eyes met his, unblinking.

He tried again, "Would you like me to escort you home?" At this request, she smiled, began to walk, and motioned for him to follow. He could only stare after her; for someone so defenceless, her composure was startling. She glanced back over her shoulder, and seeing that he hadn't followed, she turned around, reached out her hand, and with a single nod of her head, asked him to follow once more. Entranced by her strange allure, he thought of nothing else he'd rather do as he placed his hand in hers.

She led him along the edge of the riverbank, through overgrown grasses and sodden soil. He didn't care that his trousers were muddy or that water seeped into his shoes, he was hypnotised by her hair as it swung like a metronome to the sway of her hips. The wind's cold caress no longer caused a chill, and the stillness of the forest felt peaceful.

"Where are we going?" he asked, as she veered off into the trees. She looked back at him, a hint of mischief in her eyes, and smiled.

They walked for some time, navigating ferns and fallen branches. The trees began to dissipate, and they came to the edge of a small lake. The still water was like black glass, reflecting the full moon and that single star. She dropped his hand and walked straight into the lake, her thin gown absorbing the water, clinging to her curves like a second skin. The sight of her caused Peter's cheeks to flush. When the water reached her waistline, she beckoned for him to come to her, and he went without hesitation.

He waded through sediment and stumbled over loose stones, cringing at the lake's frigid temperature, until he had no choice but to float and kick. He had never been a strong swimmer and wondered how she kept her shoulders above the water without making a ripple. He swore she hadn't swum far from the shore, yet getting to her felt like a never-ending struggle.

Her legs gripped his waist when he finally reached her, and the weight that threatened to drown him disappeared. She pressed a long finger to his lips, snaked her free arm around his shoulder, and pulled him beneath the water's surface. He started to panic, but then her lips were against his, and the pressure in his chest began to ease. Her lips parted his and he was compelled to inhale her gentle breath. It filled his lungs until they burned delightfully, and when she pulled away, his need for air had vanished.

They sank until their feet touched soft clay, and there she released him. Though the cold had pinched his skin, now he did not feel it. There was no urgency to breathe, and the inky water made it impossible to see. Being deprived of his senses felt heavenly. She pushed him down by his shoulders, the water acting like a guiding hand until his back was flush with the lakebed. Milfoil slithered around his limbs, holding him in place as she settled upon him. She nuzzled his neck, and though there was no external sound, he heard an ethereal voice demand, "You will love me for eternity."

The words echoed in his head, then slithered through his body. Something felt wrong. He had welcomed her touch at first, but now it made his skin crawl. She was wrong, so very wrong.

Emily, he thought, sighing as the memory of her face flooded back to him. *I do love Emily.*

He focused on his vision of Emily while the young woman moved against him. Their encounter was brief, and as soon as it was over, she detached herself and swam away, disappearing into the black abyss. When the weeds had wrapped around his limbs, he had thought himself completely stuck, but with a gentle tug, the plaited stems came undone. Above where he lay, an orb of moonlight cast hazy rays through the water. He pushed off the lakebed, intent to get back to the forest before she returned. As he neared the surface, he felt a tug in his chest: an invisible string that threatened to pull him back under. He kicked hard and grasped at the water above him, dragging himself towards the ball of light. Eventually the phantom string snapped; he shot through the surface and swam for the shallows.

As soon as he could stand, he started to run. But the water battled against his legs and pulled at his torso, hindering each step and making his escape feel impossible. Fingers clamped onto his ankle and yanked just as the waterline dropped past his knees. He collapsed onto stones in the shallows, which scratched his palms and elbows. Stiff and slow, he turned onto his back to see what had caught him, and the young woman came upon him. As she hovered above him, her long hair withered away, and her eyes turned black and beady. At the sight of this, the remaining peace he felt left his body. Her grey skin grew scaley, and her mouth split wide as she screeched into the night, revealing pointed teeth.

Helpless, he begged, "Please, the one I love waits for me."

"You were going to betray me?" The vicious grin didn't move, but the ethereal voice echoed through his skull.

He shook his head, feeling cowardly. She cocked hers, black eyes glaring into his. Her gross mouth smirked, as if she could see what he was thinking.

"If her heart is yours, then you have betrayed her."

He swore he saw lightning flash through her eyes. His muscles froze as fear pinned him to the ground. "You enchanted me!"

"If that is true, how do you run from me?" The voice became more enraged with each passing word.

His heart raced so fast it was hard to think of what to do; he failed to hold his breath as she pulled him back through the shallows. Dragging him down deep, she forced her slimy mouth to his. Despite her repulsive form, he still found himself wanting to breathe her in. But there was no air; water flooded his lungs. This time it burnt like hell. Peter's heartbeat slowed, then his squirming body began to falter. And as he sank, just before unconsciousness closed in, through the black water cold and still, he saw that lone star shining back at him.

Amy J Sayner

Amy Joan believes there's more to romance than meet-cutes and happily-ever-afters. She grew up around the castles and ancient woodlands of Wales, and her love stories take inspiration from folklore and fairy tales.

Destiny's Child

I'm here because it's all I ever wanted to do.

There was never rhyme nor reason. Or so I thought. Simply what was in my head since I was six, perhaps younger. Early primary school for certain. A desire, even then, that drove me, shaped me. I thought everyone had a clear focus on 'what they wanted to be when they grew up', yet my classmates changed their minds on a whim. A vet, an astronaut, a train driver, a footballer. A nurse, a singer, a movie star. I stayed constant; true to my belief that I was meant to do this. Never sure of why, yet now it becomes clear. Now I know. The Moirai wove me tightly, certain of my destiny. And now Atropos's abhorred shears are ready for their cut. Ha! It seems some of my schooling stuck. Ah John, how fitting that you and your poems come to me now, as I look around and see the reason I was put on this earth. Fated to be here, in this place, at this time. To save their lives.

***

'Alpha45, this is Alpha, cleared to RV14, air enroute, throw green smoke on LZ, how copy over.'

'Alpha, this is Alpha45, copy RV14, air enroute, throw green on LZ, out.'

Happy our ride home was booked, I hooked the radio handset back on to Skim's body armour and signalled across the dust track for Thomo to move out. We were split into two standard fire teams of four. Corporal Bobby Thompson and his three lads crouched down behind the corner of a fragile looking red-brick wall that was here, in the middle of sod all. Keeping nothing in or out of nowhere. A strange place to put a wall. Most things in this country looked ramshackle, yet the wall had probably been here since British troops passed by in bright red tunics. Thomo acknowledged my signal and stood up, his desert-pattern combats blending in with the surroundings better than the scarlet of our forebears. His three followers rose as one and in-synch, but distanced, they walked forward, their weapons in their shoulders, muzzles pointed down, heads in constant motion, checking for threats. I allowed Bobby to get ten yards ahead of me.

'Right Skim, lets shuffle.'

Lance Corporal Stevie Kim waited before falling-in five yards behind me. His slim-line radio pack was almost the same width as he was. Twenty-two years old and with Asian features he would proudly tell people he was from the Nam. It was true; Cheltenham, west of England.

Climbing up and out of the narrow wadi I checked over my shoulder and saw Fusiliers Danny Baines and Charlie Vaughan take up their places in our little walk through the desert. Danny was known as Ged for reasons no one understood. He carried the section Light-Support Weapon like it was made of polystyrene. His huge, yet strangely slender hands wrapped around it so it looked like a child's toy. I smiled as I thought of the first day he joined the Battalion. Turns out it was true about men with big hands and it had taken the barracks grapevine half an hour to share the news with most of the Regiment. They'd nicknamed him Donkey until he slapped a couple of people who called him it to his face. His slaps were harder than most punches, so he became, Ged. Many discussions had been had as to why. None had revealed a truth.

CV followed at the rear with bandannas of spare ammo looped over him like a sad Mexican bandit. That boy never smiled. Even when we knew he was happy he looked pissed off. Miserable little shit, but he was strong and calm and one of the best marksman in the Battalion, so I liked having him along.

The dust kicked up as I picked my way along the shambles of the long-worn track. A few steps and 'The Routine' kicked in. Scan the horizon, scan the near ground, scan the middle ground, look for anything that was out of the ordinary. The weird, the unusual. Every so often, not set or regular, a quick-step dance movement to turn around and check my rear view in the same way. A few steps backwards then around again. Start over. Scan the far ground and the horizons. The Routine. I'd patrolled the streets of Belfast, country lanes in Bosnia, burning villages in Kosovo, death alleys in Basra and it was always the same. Part of my mind searched for the person trying to kill me and the other part of my mind thought random thoughts to keep me sane. Walk and watch and be alert, because your country needs lerts. Keep your peripheral vision sharp and think random thoughts.

Sweat trickled slowly down the small of my back. Tracing its line like Morgana's gentle fingertips. Her breath teasing the touch of her lips on my neck on a lazy weekend morning. Nuzzling her head into my shoulder. Breathing tenderness onto my skin.

It was hot but not stifling. Autumn in the Afghan. A lot more bearable than my first two tours. Ah the joys that had been the summer heat of Helmand. By the time this little holiday at Her Majesty's pleasure was due to be over, I'd have spent a year and two months in this god-forsaken country. Morgana understood less and less now. Since Bethany had come along, the arguments had become worse. I couldn't really disagree with her.

'You've spent more time in fucking Afghanistan than you have with your own daughter.'

'That's not hard really, she's only nine months old.'

'You're missing her growing up.'

'There'll be time to catch up when I leave.'

I hadn't figured on being a Dad, wasn't entirely sure about the whole deal. Then my Bethany had smiled at me when she was three weeks old and I cried. I just sat there, holding her head in my hands, looking down at her smile and I cried. I've never felt closer to anyone in my life. It broke my heart to leave her. But I didn't tell Morgana. I didn't know how to. It didn't seem fair.

After a kilometre of nothing we approached the small village that lay between us and our pick-up point. A single track bisected two rows of houses. Not houses like me or the lads grew up in. These were tall boxes of sand-coloured blocks. One row above the central track, one just below. Both appeared to grow, in a gravity-defying way, straight out of the mountainside. Even Thomo had grown up in a palace compared to these ramshackle little hovels and he came from the rough end of Walthamstow in east London.

Children's voices, laughing and happily squealing came from around the corner of the sandy brick house to my front. I kept walking and soon the six little boys came into view. They were frantically running around in a circle. Kids playing catch. They stopped running when they saw us. It wasn't that they shied away, they just stopped and stared up at the soldiers and their guns. We weren't the first soldiers they'd seen, but little boys, wherever they may be, are always transfixed by the paraphernalia of soldiers. The body armour, the webbing, the boots, the weapons. I reached into my pocket for the sweets that we all carried. According to the Generals, priority one was to make the locals like us, make the kids like us, treat all well and respectfully, make friends with friends. Priority two was that when that same friend tried to pick up a Kalashnikov and blow your guts all over the street, you killed him first. We felt the Generals had their priorities wrong.

Thomo and his boys fanned out into a protective screen to the east while the kids jammed close to me to get the sweets. High-pitched voices, little brown bodies jumping up and down and reaching with their dirty hands. I laughed with them but I always thought it was the strangest thing. Kids in Belfast never came near us when we had patrolled their streets. They had stopped and stared, but they had kept their distance. Even the Protestant kids and they were meant to be on our side. I never once saw anyone, child or adult, give us the time of day over there. We were like ghosts amongst them. Crouching, covering, walking, running and they lived their lives around us. Despite us. The only people that ever paid us any attention were the snipers, bombers and rioters. We'd been told not to expect any form of interaction with the 'normal populace of Northern Ireland'. The training also said that in the beginning, back in the 60s, they'd come out and given us tea, but the welcome had dropped off rapidly when it turned out we were a permanent addition to their cityscape. Not that there had been any inkling of a long and dirty war back at the start. Don't think it bodes well for here. Ha! In hindsight Belfast had been fun; in comparison.

Yet here in this strange nation that broke empires, the women and children and men would come out to tell us how much they appreciated us being here. Kids taking sweets. Guess if history is anything to go by, we'll be here for some time. At least Belfast had bars, booze and beautiful girls. All the B's.

I'd had a theory up until 9/11. Belfast, Belgrade, Baghdad. Every country I'd fought in had a capital city that began with B. I hadn't been in the Falklands, but Buenos Aires had kept the theme intact. Even World War One and Two adhered to it, mostly. Hey, it's my theory so I can be flexible.

I daydreamed about politicians picking a fight in Bridgetown, the capital of Barbados. Would make for a nice change, somewhere idyllic. Instead, here we were… in the Afghan, spoiling my theory, like they've spoilt my family life. I suppose I could call it Bloody Kabul.

'Hey Skim, looks like your good looks are working again,' I said over the laughing of the kids.

'Well even the most demure ladies can't resist.' He laughed and knelt to greet the three little girls who had ventured shyly out of one of the houses to our left. I signalled a balled fist to Ged and CV. They set up the Light Support Weapon system, or what I'd have called a machine gun when I'd been a kid, in an overview position to cover the way we'd come in. The kids jostled for position too and we fed them sweeties and waited for the headman of the village to come out and greet us. He would tell us in nods and clapped hands how pleased he was that we were here. It was, of course, bullshit. One thing we did understand was that this place was tribal. Yet here we were trying to get them to be democratic. Might as well go to the posh neighbourhoods of London and ask them to live in hippy communes.

If they had asked me, I would have told the politicians, 'They're not going to get fucking democracy after a millennium of family ties being the only thing they've had. They're more likely to vote for their cousin's fucking dog than some tosser in

Kabul.' But no-one asked me. Perhaps I was too eloquent for them?

I looked around for the main man. The kids were still smiling and chittering as they chomped down on Liquorice Allsorts. Good old Bertie. Skim was next to the three little girls, each dressed in fine silken dresses that had seen better days. Hand me downs. Like everything here. Hand me down soldiers from hand me down wars. The little girls smiled and Skim handed them more sweets. They stood delicately, taking each sweet one at a time and eating it politely, like it was the finest of the confectioner's art. Skim grinned over at me. I winked back. Hearts and minds, one kid at a time.

The door to the house directly across from me opened, and in my periphery I registered Thomo bringing his rifle up into the aim. The man that stepped out looked about a hundred and fifty. He was probably the one that had built the wall whilst the redcoats had passed by. He did not smile. I'm not sure the sun-stretched leather face could have formed the expression. On reflection it was because he knew there was nothing to smile about.

Another door opened. This one behind me. I looked over my shoulder. The young man that came out of the house was clean shaven, a fresh complexion. Recently washed, his hair still damp. Eyes that were calm and settled; a stillness to them. His robes too big for him. He walked steadily and with purpose right towards me. I turned to face him. Skim was still kneeling down and had no clear line of sight on him. Thomo and his boys were no better placed. I couldn't swing my rifle up and take aim, there was no time. I stepped out of the circle of kids still gathered round me and ran straight at the young man. Lifted him bodily up and kept his arms away from his sides. I charged forward heading for clear ground. Behind me, Ged was shouting and I knew he was bringing the LSW around. I was going to throw this fucker off me, dive to one side and let my boys blow him to pieces. I hadn't reckoned on him head-butting me and kneeing me in the balls at the same time. I tripped, stumbled and fell right on top of him. Looking down I saw his left hand come up to his side and all of time, my time, stopped.

***

If I roll away the bomb will kill all of us. The kids, the old man, Skim, Ged and CV. Thomo and his lads might be okay but it's doubtful. I'm dead anyway. It's a fact. Plain and simple. So… I'm not going to roll. I can't anyway. My arms are trapped under this little bastard. I'm trying to pull them free but he's pressing down on them. I can't. Fucking hell, I can't. There's a weakness and a pain in my right arm. It's trapped between him and my rifle. My wrist is broken. The fall and the hard ground, this man's weight. The weight he bears. Twisting awkwardly, I see the children staring with wide eyes. No option now but to press into this strange young man as hard as I can. Still I gaze back at the nearest child. My Bethany has the most beautiful blue, wide eyes. Round and bright and shining. She'll be beautiful, she is beautiful, like Morgana. It would have broken my heart to walk her down the aisle, but I would have done it and been proud. Morgana and I would have survived. I was going to leave my Khaki mistress and become a good husband to my beautiful wife. I do truly love her. We bicker and argue but I still love her, ever since I met her, I've loved her. Growing old would have been nice, I think. Not the wrinkles or the weakness, but the contented happy times we would have shared. Bethany's kids coming to see Granda. I'll not see them now. Fuck it. I'll not see the Backs of Cambridge again. I like them. The punts. I never took one out. Always worried I'd make an arse of myself. I should have. March coldness and the Cheltenham Festival. The horses and the laughs, the mates and the fun, the lost bets and the taste of cold Guinness. I look down the length of my body and see his hand moving to his belt. Time has started again and it's true; all the clichés are true, everything is in slow motion. I'm struggling against him. I'm fighting my rising fear and panic and frustration. I don't want to be here. Skim is yelling and trying to get a sight along his rifle. He's sheltering one of the girls behind his legs. I can't hear what he's yelling. CV's standing up. His rifle steady. The cartridge casings flying acrobatically out of the breach as each bullet is fired. But even he can't bring the rounds close enough without hitting me. He's hesitating. He better smile when he realises he's alive after this. I wonder who'll win the Premiership? I hope this doesn't hurt too much. Oh God, are you there waiting for me? Or is it going to be blackness with nothing? Oh Christ, I hope not. I don't like the dark. Never have. Dear God, I believe in you now. I need to. Please don't abandon me. Dad, be waiting in the light to take my hand like you did when I was little. Mum, I love you. You always made me proud to be your son. You are the finest lady I know, my Morgana is like you. I want to smell freshly mown grass. Or bacon sandwiches, or Morgana in the morning. She smells muggy and sweet and soft. I am so sorry I won't be home sweetheart. You'll hear about your husband. They'll talk to you and give you my medals. No-one will tell you what I was thinking in these last seconds. I'm so sad my beautiful girls. I don't want to be here. I want to run away and live. I want to live my life. I want to hold you in my arms and tell you that I'll never go away. Oh sweet Christ please help me. Please. Let my arms come free. Let me stop him. Morgana tell Bethany I'm sorry. I wanted so much to be there for her. I don't want to die. I'm scared. I'm sor—

***

'Good evening. In the news tonight, another soldier has been killed on patrol in southern Afghanistan. The Ministry of Defence confirmed the serviceman, Sergeant Barry McMaster from the 2nd Battalion Royal Regiment of Fusiliers, was caught in a suicide bombing south of Nawzad in Helmand Province. He leaves a wife and baby daughter. His Commanding Officer said that Sergeant McMaster was a credit to the Armed Forces and had died whilst leading from the front, defending the people of Afghanistan.

In other news, London Underground are preparing for the chaos expected during the one-hour stoppage called by the Transport Union for tomorrow. This special report from our correspondent at Kings Cross Station...' [1]

Ian Hooper

Originally from Northern Ireland, Ian served two decades with the UK's Royal Air Force and now lives in Western Australia. Always a writer, he has dashed off daft poems and silly rhymes, speculative fiction and a series of crime novels (some under the penname of Ian Andrew). He is now the executive director of indie publisher, Leschenault Press.

---

[1] With due acknowledgment to the inspiration derived from Harvey Andrews's 1972 recording of *The Soldier*.

For My Mother Ivy, Who Believed

We met, eye to eye, on the stairs. Me in my wedding dress, you in a navy school pinafore. A life-changing moment. Time stood still.

I know you, Little Ivy, I know all about you. Since your mam swaddled you in flannelette on the scullery hearth of the two-up two-down terrace in Middleton Street, half a spoon of brandy for your blue lips. But you don't know me. I watch you and I watch your Evelyn with her Bisto stockings. She's more my age. Now she's got that job at Wrights, she's hardly home. I hear her vent if you eye her Max Factor pan-stick on the dresser. Spends too much time painting her face, Evelyn.

'You're not my sister,' she snarls.

Wants to mind who hears her say that. Makes out you're the cuckoo, not her. I've seen your face drop when she says it. Yet I remember another story. About the beating your mam got from your granny on her sixteenth birthday, when her straining coat buttons drew too much attention, and the third-trimester bulge in her belly was discovered.

'Skinned rabbit,' your mam said when she saw her firstborn. 'Put it back!'

The midwife laughed. But Georgy Crick's parents didn't. Georgy Crick's parents packed a bag and shipped their son far away from Hull. He embarked upon a trans-Atlantic crossing to a better life and didn't look back. Soon after, the shy Tommy

Jickells stepped forward and spent his savings on a gold band. He raised the bairn as his own, with never a mention of her pedigree. Evelyn reckons to have forgotten that story.

It was a spring Sunday in 1948 when my troubles began. An unfamiliar sense of excitement in the air. You perched on the faded candlewick bedspread, which once was turquoise, and Evelyn calls *eau de nil.* I saw you stretch down and pull on a new white ankle sock.

Your Holy Communion frock hung on the door. The one the nuns lent you from the box they keep for girls who… for girls like you whose mams have had a telegram. In homes like yours where the piano lid in the parlour stays closed, and no one visits because there's nothing to celebrate, and sisters work days and mothers do nights but there's still nothing nice in the pantry. Or coal in the scuttle.

'Now you've a spare pair of socks,' your mam smiled. 'You won't have to wear damp ones for school if the fire goes out.'

Evelyn pinned on your lace veil. 'Dad would be proud. Let's get to church.'

You paused a moment at the mirror on the dresser. Morning sun through cloudy panes made a halo of the strawberry blonde plaits framing your scrubbed face, and the ribbons matched your speedwell eyes. I used to fear your lonely heart might not mend, Little Ivy, but I see now that it will.

Where did it stem from, my longing to gaze in that mirror? There is no explanation. For the waiting and listening and planning. For the when and the how to break the rules and make the forbidden climb. What place had a looking glass in my world? Vanity. Oh, I'd envied your life before. Dreamed of leaning out of a window, palms upturned to catch a snowflake or kneeling by a crack in the flagstones to sniff a golden buttercup wet with morning dew. But we live in an indoor world. I respect danger. Yet…

'Our sort doesn't wear white,' my mother insisted when I rooted out the swathe of cotton she'd acquired years before and stored for "something". 'It might mean a matter of life or death.'

She was right. Better for us to blend, invisible in plain sight. Just once, though, I ached to cast aside all practicality. To stand before that dresser mirror in my wedding dress, dappled rays of summer sun dancing down, and shake my chestnut curls. I vowed that if I could stand there to take in my reflection, the memory would last a lifetime.

I begged till my mother gave in. No need for a pattern or a fitting. She's raised and schooled me, so knows my shape better than she knows her own. While she sewed, she rested from time to time to push a silver thread of hair behind her ear. I hadn't noticed those silver threads before. Tiny hand-worked stitches fashioned the seams and folds until it was made. As I slipped it on, my mother smiled. A flicker in the corner of her eye might have been a tear.

***

It is almost Summer. After school, I watch you fold your socks, ozone fresh from the washing line and slip them in a drawer. You take the string of pale blue rosary beads from their tin, stretch out on the bed, and swing them from a finger as you mouth a couple of Hail Marys. You push up on your elbows and cock your head, listening. I freeze. Could you have heard me? You swing your legs over the side of the bed, tiptoe to the dresser, slide the lid off Evelyn's pan stick and dab it on your nose. Soon it will be the holidays, Little Ivy. You will be home all day and I will have missed my chance.

'I'm ready,' I hear myself say. 'It will be tomorrow.' A new chapter of my life is about to begin. As a wife, I will have less time to watch and dream. One day, like my mother, I will tuck silver threads in my hair behind my ears and smile when a daughter of mine is ready to shape her destiny.

In my world, we are born, we marry, we die. Just like you. Yet nothing like you. I'm the ear at a grate, the eye at a crack. I sleep beneath the floor by the scullery fireplace. Hidden. You may call me a fairy, a little person, but you may never, never call me a friend. I stand at the foot of the staircase in your empty house and start upwards. Below, the porch door opens with a click, and I freeze. We meet eye to eye on the stairs - me in my wedding dress, you in a navy school pinafore.

'My name's Ivy,' you say. 'What's yours?'

Corrine Aveyard

Grandparents

Gothic House.

The name is elegantly swirled in a gothic black and silver script on the large brown front gate. Initially, it was house number 36 but became known as Gothic House when my aunt thought up the title. It was home to my large, Catholic family who had a reputation for taking in sick and injured animals. The flowerbeds are probably still full of small remains, buried, wrapped in tea towels. Half-dead pigeons with broken wings, concussed chicks freshly tumbled from their nests, stray moggies with weepy eyes, even a dead seagull, were brought to our front gate for help. All this despite no one in the family having any veterinary training beyond putting the kettle on and applying an old blanket.

In 1979, ten members of my family, across three generations, clubbed together to buy the house in the hope that it would be an affordable way to own the property. Despite the best efforts of my grandparents, an uncle, and two aunts, plus my mum and dad, the house remained in a perpetual state of disrepair. The hall ceiling collapsed one Christmas Eve. A storm blew the roof off my grandparents' bedroom in the middle of the night. Life revolved around an endless list of jobs to keep the rain out (the flat roof always leaked) or the walls up (built on clay soil, cracks in the plaster gaped wide in the summer and closed in the winter, showering the floor with specks of plaster and brick dust). Despite this, the tumbledown house was a home for us all, along with the many creatures that spent time under its roof or in the backyard.

***

Dressed in itchy orange pyjamas that were once curtains, I am sitting on a settee arm chewing my grandad's thumb. There is a taste of soil and varnish, probably from a recent attempt to tame the unruly garden or preserve a decaying window frame. There is a sweet smell, with a slightly acrid taste, from his yellowing thumbnail. My grandad, Albert Pile, is laughing while my grandma is ordering me – and him – to behave. My toes brush the pink carpet as I remain firmly attached to my grandad's thumb. It is not clear why I am biting it, except that both of us are red-cheeked with laughter.

Their dog is lying still next to the electric fire; a blind, silver-flecked griffon named Rory. Quite how he got the name has been lost in time, but it always seemed a rather unfitting name for a dog who was as mute as a pious nun (except for the odd mid-dream snort or *yip*.) Rory is unperturbed by the childish assault on his master's thumb and has passed out on a small green rug.

Grandma Pile has had enough, cautiously getting to her feet. The settee is too deep and low for her, but pride prevents her from asking for help (and the other family members have no appetite for that conversation). Daily dog walks and feeding the birds in the garden are part of her daily routine - anything less would be letting the animals down. As she would earnestly tell me in more serious moments, God forbid the animals go hungry or thirsty. She walks to the kitchen, and I hear the hollow clang of ancient pipes as the kettle is filled, followed by the *kktsch* of a Ship Safety Match to light the hob.

The arrival of tea is a sign to my grandad that the biting game is over. He looks down at me with tender resignation, reaching for his pipe with his unfettered hand. I unlock my milk teeth from their task and slide onto his lap to play with the large brown buttons on his favourite cardigan. Whether in his workshop, painting skirting boards, out in the garden or sitting at the dinner table, this item of clothing is a constant. Except at mass.

Grandma never let him go to church in that cardigan. The quarter-past-six Sunday service at Our Lady of the Sacred Heart church is the one event of the week where he wore a shirt and tie. By five past six every Sunday evening the whole family is sitting in church on the back row, to the left of the aisle. We smile politely at the try-hards, posing like doomed mantises in the front pews. Rosaries held out like medals of honour and eyes squeezed shut, they silently whisper a Hail Mary or two in pious penance.

The tea arrives, on a plastic tray, in two cups with saucers, along with a weak orange squash and a plate with four biscuits. Despite a daily walk, Rory is fat. Probably due to his diet of biscuits and sausages. The result was a terrier shaped like a Baltic seal, often carried outside for his daily ablutions. This made me giggle every time he was inelegantly hoicked up by his front legs, exposing his wrinkly pink keel. I wonder if my dad might carry me out into the garden when I needed a wee, though that never happened. But then I never asked.

Many years later I found out that, beneath his cardigan, my Grandad had three scars across his tummy. He was shot by a Messerschmidt 109 while sailing a boat full of soldiers back from Dunkirk. Very nearly bled to death laid out on the deck.

He never mentioned his involvement in that historic event, despite my childhood love of anything World War II-related. He was a genius at sorting out tricky Airfix models or knocking up a wooden castle but skilfully avoided any war stories. So, my abiding memory of him is the cardigan. And his thumb.

Ian Harris

Ian Harris is a schoolteacher and aspiring writer. After completing a Theology degree, he has been a teacher for over twenty-four years and since completing the MA at Hull is planning a new career in writing and publishing. He lives with his wife, six-year-old daughter, and cat in Dorset in a converted pub full of books, music and toys.

Here I Am

The Times Obituaries, 3rd July 2020.
Professor Mary Hartford.

Mary Hartford, who has died aged 75, was one of Britain's leading Egyptologists and a collector of Egyptian tomb antiquities.

Mary was born in Chester in March 1950, the daughter of Henry Hartford, an under clerk, and his wife, Lily (nee Hodge), a nanny. After attaining a scholarship, she attended the Bluecoats Grammar School. She studied Egyptology at Oxford University from 1968 to 1971, where she was inspired by her first-year tutor Professor Harry Smith. After graduating, in 1973 she was appointed Lecturer in Egyptian Antiquities at the University of Liverpool, a post she held until her retirement in 2015. Her undergraduate courses on the rise of the ceremonial mid-period funeral rites were always particularly well attended.

Mary authored books including her two-volume *Tombs of the Pharaohs* (2014), *Dictionary of Egyptian Funeral Rites* (1982), and The Egyptian Afterlife (1990). She served on the Council of the Egyptian Exploration Society from 1975 and 2002, and also contributed to its quarterly magazine, *Archaeology of the Delta*. After she retired from the University of Liverpool she adopted a four-year-old boy, a role which gave her renewed purpose right up to her unexpected death due to brain cancer.

Mary was a kind person with an impish sense of humour and a love of wine. She combined thorough academic study with humorous and engrossing stories.

Mary never married but is survived by her son, Oliver. Much of her extensive collection of Egyptian artefacts has been kindly donated to the Ashmolean Museum, Oxford.

***

The journey to Blackpool is uneventful. After an hour and twenty minutes on the motorway, neither the young woman driving nor the boy in the passenger seat says a word. On arrival, they drive along the promenade with its illuminations hanging lifeless, waiting for darkness to spark them back into life. The social worker checks her mileage, ready for the claim form, as the small boy gazes out the window to look for the tower. Eventually, the promenade turns into Fleetwood Avenue, where the illuminations and gift shops end, replaced by cramped rows of terraced houses and the occasional vaping shop.

Ollie squirms in the passenger seat. His view of the beach is blocked by tired iron railings, blue paint flaking off like ancient skin onto the pavement. Small cyclones of sand scuttle across the pavement, blown by unpredictable gusts off the Irish Sea. Further out, mobs of gulls loiter near mounds of rotting seaweed, as they wait for bins to overflow. He closes his eyes.

Mum's desk was big and wide with three drawers underneath. On the left were two piles of neatly stacked books, with a tray of letters on the other side. His favourite things on the desk were the statues around the edge: cats, soldiers, men with heads like dogs or birds. Just before she went into hospital she said he could choose a statue to keep safe.

'Pick anyone you want. But be careful, some of them have special powers,' Mum said, smiling.

He usually played with Anubis' spear and his funny dog's head, but looked down the line and finally chose a shiny little blue man.

79

'Interesting choice Ollie. This is a *shabti*, an answerer. The Egyptians used to put these in tombs so to help their masters in the afterlife.' She passed the statue to him, and he turned it round in his hands. On the bottom were some little drawings.

'Those are hieroglyphics. This says, '*Here I am, you shall say when.*' The Egyptians believed this figure could be called upon and would obey their owner's commands after they had passed into the afterlife. Take good care of him, he's incredibly old and very precious.'

Ollie turns around, checking for his rucksack and new coat on the back seat.

'You'll like it here Oliver. Once you settle down and make a few friends you'll be right at home,' says the social worker, nodding to herself.

He doesn't reply, knowing that nodding indicates an adult is saying something that usually isn't true. He thinks back to the last time he saw his Mum, as she held his hand at the hospital. She never lied to him, even when he asked if she was dying.

'Right then, this is the one.'

They sit and look out at a small terrace of red brick houses, identical except for the faded colour of the window frames. The doors that aren't boarded look new, with shiny locks and peepholes. As Ollie gets out, he grabs the coat and checks the little blue man Mum gave him is still in the pocket. The social worker zips her coat against the biting wind and heads up the path. Ollie follows.

Mallory walks into the living room, checking that any unpaid bills or prescriptions are hidden away. Anything an eagle-eyed social worker might spot. The agency paperwork is all signed and ready. The photo on the front sheet shows a small boy with a ragged fringe almost covering his eyes.

The clatter of an ageing diesel alerts her to visitors. She squints through the bay window, coiling long, brittle hair away from her face, and watches as the new arrival gets out. The boy's hand pats at his coat pocket, as if checking something. The social worker joins him on the pavement and they walk up the path but don't get the chance to knock; the door has already been opened.

'Do come in, quick, before the sand blows in. Have a seat. And you, young man, there's a stool under all that. Sorry about the mess – laundry day.' Mallory says and rolls her eyes. She lifts a pile of clothes off the stool, being careful not to crease them.

'This is Oliver. You've completed the sign-off form we sent you?' The social worker remains standing, coat still on, cleaning her jam jar glasses on a tissue. Oliver hovers by the front door, trying not to attract attention.

'Yes, all done. Here you go. I'll take good care of him. Cup of tea before you go?' Mallory raises her eyebrows but makes no attempt to put the laundry down.

'Erm, no thanks, must dash. Right, Oliver, we all hope you're happy here, I'll pop by in a few weeks to see how you're settling in. See you soon.'

The social worker gives a quick wave towards Ollie and retreats, pulling hard on the door to shut it against the wind. The door clicks shut; the boy has been successfully rehoused.

'Right then, Oliver. I'm Mallory, call me Malls. You must be hungry after your journey? Let me get you something.' Mallory returns from the kitchen with a glass of weak orange squash and a saucer with two digestives. 'Here you go. I need to finish some jobs upstairs. You eat up and I'll take you through a few things in a bit, okay?'

Left alone in the living room, Ollie looks around at his new home. A well-used sofa propped up against the far wall, opposite a large TV. A plastic chair in the corner with another pile of clothes on top, next to a large dark wood unit that takes up most of the wall space. Just as he is swallowing the last biscuit, Mallory comes downstairs with a pen and notepad.

'Right Oliver, first thing we do here is make an inventory. Things are always going missing in this place. Empty your rucksack and I'll write a list of everything you've got.'

Ollie shuffles over and tips the bag onto the table. Out comes the usual two sets of clothes, most with tags.

'Lovely job, now your pockets.' The boy shakes his head and shuffles backwards. She tilts her head, her eyes locking on to his.

'Now then Oliver, let's not get off on the wrong foot. Empty your pockets pet.'

He takes another step back. She springs forward, spinning him round and bending him over the settee, one hand pinning his arm painfully up his back as the other hand searches his pockets.

'This. Is for your own good. Now, let's empty those pockets.' She tuts as the first pocket yields an empty key ring and a tatty toy soldier. But the second one is a better harvest; a small blue statue. Ollie tries to wriggle out of her hold, but she is expecting it and leans forward to push his face further into the settee.

'I'll keep this safe pet. You wouldn't want it to go missing while you're here. I'm going to let you go, and you'll go to your room to calm down. Down there, through the kitchen then second door past the loo.' She places the statue on the mantelpiece, beyond his reach.

Ollie circles around Mallory towards the kitchen, hot tears dripping off his quivering chin. Mallory looks down at him and mutters under her breath, following him towards the bedroom. After locking the door behind him she pulls out her phone to begin listing the new items on Ebay.

Ollie wakes up the following day. It takes a few seconds to recall where he is. The white ceiling is blistered and peeling, peeling paint held in check by thick cobwebs running wall to wall. He watches them rise and fall, moved by some unseen draught blowing through one of the cracks around the window frame. The door has been unlocked and left ajar, allowing noises from the kitchen to seep in. As he tip-toes in, Mallory shuffles a hot frying pan on the hob, filling the room with smells of over-used oil and soot.

'Take a seat, it'll be ready in a minute.'

She doesn't look at him, as he sits down on the plastic chair. He looks down at the Formica table, with its chipped edges and deep scratches. FUC U is etched through the plastic edging, down to the chipboard beneath. Mallory appears, putting cutlery and a loaded plate down in front of him.

'As it's your first day, I thought I'd treat you. Don't expect this all the time though.'

Sat on the plate are two charred sausages, congealing into a pool of beans and fried bread.

'Go on, eat up.'

'I'm not hungry.'

Mallory cocks her head. 'Well, you either eat it, or you don't eat. I haven't got the time or money to waste good food.' She waits for a second before snatching the plate away.

Ollie pulls something out of his pocket and starts turning it over in his hand, half-hidden under the table. Mallory wolfs down the sausage and beans, before rising to leave the greasy plate in the sink.

'Your loss. What you got there? Wait… you little… that's mine.' Mallory grabs his hand and pulls the small blue statue out of his fingers. 'How the hell did you get this? Hmm? I put this away for your own good. You get away to your room.'

Ollie backs out the door, keeping his eyes on this new guardian all the way back to his bedroom.

The room smelt like the frogspawn he used to collect in jars with his mum. Like a bend in a river where water has remained for too long in the sun. Sprays of mould pattern the wall by the bed below the window. Oliver stands on the bed. The window is still too high to reach. All he can see is the tight curls of paint around the window frame like angry coils of hard parchment, where paint has split to reveal the ancient powdery wood beneath. Beyond the frame is a grey featureless sky. He can hear seagulls, but none fly above the house. When his Mum took him to the seaside he used to be scared if seagulls came too close to him. She'd shoo them away with her cross voice, and they'd always scatter. He sits back down on the bed and wipes his eyes with his sleeve.

'Come out and get your lunch.'

Ollie doesn't move, and remains at the foot of the bed, kicking his feet against the wardrobe.

'I said come and get your lunch.'

Mallory's tone carries a warning. He heaves himself up and shuffles through to the kitchen.

'It's all you're getting so don't waste it this time.'

He sits at the table, looking down at the neat edge of processed cheese poking out between slices of white bread. She brushes past him to check his bedroom.

'What the fuck is…?'

Ollie hears the coming rage before he sees it, like an approaching storm.

Mallory is back in the kitchen, shoving the small blue statue in his face.

'When did you nick this off of me again? You little shit.' As she spits out the final 't', Mallory pulls Ollie back by the hair. He tries to pull away, but she is too strong. 'No one ever nicks off of me, especially not some shitty little kid. You need a bloody lesson in how to behave. You're not in Liverpool anymore.' She jostles him to the bedroom and shoves him in.

Ollie falls, hitting the side of the bed on his way down. Off balance, his head swings out of control, stopping only when it hits the back wall. Seeing him slumped quietly onto the stained carpet, Mallory locks the door and heads out into the yard for a cigarette.

Half-lying up against the corner of the bedroom, Ollie's sobs decrease to the occasional involuntary chest heave. He gently touches the back of his head where it hit the wall, and finds his hair sticky to the touch. Sniffing, he wipes the drips from his nose with the back of his hand. He screws up his eyes, hugs his legs and rests his head on his knees. He whispers, 'Make her go away,' until he falls into an endless sleep.

Here I am, you shall say when.

The fat from the pan has leaked to form a viscous layer in the sink. Inedible remnants of breakfast are scattered across the scarred table. Trails of sand snake their way across the kitchen floor, pushed by some unseen draught from the back window. Mallory shivers. She puts her hand on the cooker to steady herself as the coughing intensifies. Her throat feels raspy and tight. She falls to her knees, her fingers wide apart, attempting to steady herself. Mallory's eyes shut with the effort, as she frantically tries to breathe. She dry gulps one last time, leans to one side and looks up. Above her on the table is the blue statue.

HM Coroner Blackpool and Fylde,
PO Box 966, Blackpool FY9 9GB
Telephone 01632 477222

Inquest into the death of Mallory Elkington
Hearing date: 14 December 2020

Date of findings: 29 September 2020

Location: HM Coroner, Blackpool
File number: 2015/282722

I find that Mallory Elkington died on 25 September 2020 at 27 Chaunce Street, Blackpool, Lancashire FY9 9NJ. Cause of death was asphyxiation, shown by visceral congestion via dilation of the venous blood vessels and blood stasis.

Additionally, PM confirmed advanced cirrhosis, as well as significant vascular disease.

PM also found unexplained traces of $SiO2$ (silica dioxide, i.e., sand) in the airway and mouth. This would not have caused the asphyxiation, but swelling around the throat suggests that bronchial tissue was irritated along the length of the airway, which may have contributed to the restriction of normal airflow.

George Peake
Coroner

Ian Harris

Heritage

Try as she might, Grandma couldn't get me to knit. "Grandma, it's for sissies," I remember shouting as I dashed through the front door, always on the go. She would smile and wag her finger, never shouting or getting mad at me, God knows, she's had enough reason to over the years. Grandma raised me when Mum walked out. Mum had me at 16 – maybe she couldn't cope. Grandma and I didn't speak about it much as I grew up. I'd wake to hear her crying late into the night. I'd creep into her room, getting into bed beside her under the heavy, scratchy blankets. We'd wrap our arms around each other, waiting for the dawn, light seeping through the chink in the too-cheerful, flowery curtains. I don't remember Mum, save for some old, dog-eared photos where she's frozen in Polaroid black and white. While I lost my mum, Grandma lost her daughter too.

***

Now Grandma's dying so I've come home to the only place I've got left. Maybe I am too like Mum. I've run from things all my life, my education, my relationships. I have nothing to show, but best to be on the run than garner another black eye from some lousy boyfriend. The cancer had spread and there was no further treatment the doctors could offer, other than palliative care. I could only give her my time; so little in return for what she had done for me.

"I want you to try and learn to knit again Abby," Grandma said. "For me."

She only had to look at me and know exactly what I was thinking. I looked away because I didn't want her to see my reaction. I've always been fascinated by the way her arthritic hands masterfully coerced the wool around the needles to produce some beautiful, cobweb-like creation. She looked at me again, waiting for my answer. The power of her gaze a magnet pulling my attention back towards her.

"Alright Grandma, I'll try." I already knew any effort on my part would end up in tears of frustration and failure, just like everything else. I faked a smile, but she was ahead of that already.

"Abby, don't be so hard on yourself." Grandma reached out with her fragile, white hand. It was cold, marbled with blue veins and lichened age spots. She guided me gently as she always had. The needles felt like telegraph poles in my hands and the wool might as well have been marine rope for all the progress I made. I dropped stitches, made holes and my tension was all over the place. My fingers felt as if they'd been plaited. I tried to quell the rising impatience and anger because I could not master it. Failed, again. Yet Grandma patiently and quietly cajoled, "You can do this Abby. Have faith in yourself."

***

On my next visit, Grandma had found a charity seeking knitted squares to make blankets. The smartphone I had bought her was to blame. I rolled my eyes, but she was undeterred.

"Let's knit a few Abby, they're so quick and easy." She'd also managed to order an industrial amount of the most lurid coloured wool I had ever seen, spilling out of the packaging like a riotous rainbow. "What a bargain!" she said. "And next-day delivery!" Her beautiful, pain-riven face lit up. "I know, let's have a knitathon Abby!" Her wheezy laugh made me catch my breath.

Should I do it to humour her? I wondered. But that wasn't fair. I had made a promise after all. So, once again, she helped me cast on, wrap the wool around the needle and bring the stitch from right to left.

"Stitch by stitch Abby, stitch by stitch. If you go wrong, you can always undo it and start over. That's how you learn, a bit like life you know."

***

Grandma died a few months back. I went to pick up her meagre belongings from the home.

Margaret the matron took me aside, "You know Abby, I see so much of your grandma in you. She was very proud of you. I know it hasn't been easy but if there is anything you think I can do, let me know."

I put the plain brown box on the table and stared at it. Carefully placed on the top were the hideous bright red cable mittens Grandma had knitted for me one Christmas. I hated them so much, yet Grandma had kept them all these years. The black elastic that once went up and down my coat sleeves was now stretched out and useless. As I turned them over and over in my hands, I felt the stitching, imbued with all the love Grandma had for me. A deluge of grief, rage and loneliness poured out, for myself and everything I'd lost.

***

I stayed home following Grandma's funeral. I figured it was time I stopped running. A few weeks after I'd spoken to Margaret, she phoned me.

"Abby, I don't know if you'd be interested but I've got a few hours work. I thought it might suit you in the short term, till you decide what you want to do." Not knowing what to do, I took a walk up to Grandma's graveside. The walk cleared my head, and I heard Grandma's reassuring voice, "It'll work out just fine Abby".

It wasn't much to begin with. I started in the kitchen, preparing vegetables and doing some cleaning. I loved spending time with the residents, hearing their stories and listening to their wise words. Two residents, Edie and Ron, were getting married. Edie had taken me under her wing in the early days when I told her how much I missed Grandma.

"Abby love, you need to find yourself a young man, like me!" Ron was her toyboy at eighty-two.

Margaret asked if I wanted to think about doing some training and getting a qualification. She thought I'd make a great carer and the home could sponsor me. For the first time in my life, I felt proud as I accepted.

I wasn't planning to meet anyone. Sam, the gardener and handyman who worked at the home saw me carrying a bouquet I'd picked up from the garage shop and asked where I was off to.

"I go up to my grandma's grave. She loved bright colours, so I take her flowers." I tried to explain that I went there to talk to her, suddenly feeling as shy and embarrassed as a teenager. Sam fell into step beside me and took my hand. It's early days but I feel strangely optimistic.

✶✶✶

On a rare day off, with nothing to do, I heard Grandma's voice in the still quiet. "Just have a go Abby, you'll never know if you don't try!"

91

Tears blur my vision. "I'm trying my hardest Grandma, I really am," I tell her. The wool feels thick, the needles clumsy in my unyielding and inarticulate hands but I am keeping my promise. I'm knitting that square, stitch by stitch.

Stephanie Wilson

Home Is but a Dream

"Green Vista Hills," Madeleine instructed the driver.

The car, a sleek Lexus in midnight blue, pulled up just as she came out of the hotel lobby. The plush caramel interior and smell of premium leather gave an impression that the hotel treated their accommodation services with serious consideration. Madeleine had never given as much thought about the make of a car as she did about its colour. When she was little, her mother said that red cars brought their family bad luck. Years later, those words came back to mind as she stood in the middle of their family home's emptied garage watching her mother close the tall metal gate whose rusty hinges wailed. Madeleine never owned a red car.

She took the seat directly behind the driver for the least chances of eye contact or interaction. Small talk, especially in an enclosed space, made her uncomfortable much more than silence. She hid behind the seat and her sunglasses. The driver asked if the air-con was cold enough, and if he could turn the radio on. "Of course," she replied. He scrolled through his phone to select a tune. Madeleine also listened to music when she drove the 15 minutes it took to the train station back in Oxfordshire. If she had enough time, she sat in her car to finish listening to a song rather than wait on the platform. Music played in the shower, while she cooked, when she tidied up after her husband and two teenagers, before she started her workday at home, and after the bedside lamp had been turned off. Sometimes her thoughts lost their way around and between the lyrics, which served her some respite from overthinking.

A shrill guitar riff blared from the car speaker.

"Sorry, sorry," said the driver, as he fumbled with the volume control. The tune switched to a Tagalog ballad. The lyrics, melody and the voice lamented a familiar despair. She thought she had outgrown listening to thematic Tagalog songs about leaving, losing, mourning, desperately holding on, searching, refusing to let go, and summoning to return. Emotions implored deliverance from guilt, regret and the past. The music became an invisible shutter between Madeleine and the driver. She adjusted her watch to the local time, and hoped, as the car rolled out of the hotel driveway, that they wouldn't be caught in Metro Manila's infamous traffic gridlock.

***

The driver set the air-con at 18 degrees Celsius which he deemed comfortable for his passengers when it was a sweltering 36 outside. No one had ever requested him to adjust it, but he always asked about the temperature as a matter of politeness more than routine. He had music on at all times when he drove, at a modulated volume, that so far had not challenged the tolerance of his passengers. He had never sought permission to play music from anyone he'd driven for, except from this morning's passenger. He had met most of them in his years on the road: the deviant, the distracted, the emotional, the lonely, the rushed, the ones who talk too much, the unsure, the drunk. He had learned to read his passenger's moods, the day's moral and emotional inclinations, and their destinations even without being told. The woman behind him had a determination that seemed far from being interrupted. She came out of the lobby just as he pulled up in the driveway, wearing a staunch face only softened by her airy and bright, yellow floral, knee-length summer dress. Her movements were precise: she glanced at her phone, briefly stood back, moved towards the boot to check the plate, then opened the car door herself before he or the hotel door attendant could get to it. Only the humidity could possibly faze her.

He slowly manoeuvred the car out of the hotel driveway. "Ma'am, are you okay with the music?" he asked, a few minutes on the road, not so much concerned with the volume as with the selection. The playlist was a collection of songs he turned to for background music when mindlessly going about his chores or while on video calls with his wife. The stiff atmosphere nudged an awareness in him of the awkward incongruity of his choice. "Let me know if there's something else you want to listen to. I can also put on the news."

"Oh, don't bother. You're the one driving, so it's best if you're listening to something that you like," she replied. He thought he hadn't listened to it in a while; he typed the name on the search box and put on Eraserheads' *Circus*.

***

Madeleine scanned the streets they slowly drove past between traffic lights and deadlocks. Stuck before a red signal, a group of boys and girls, all seemingly not more than 10 years old, took turns cupping their faces with their small hands and pressing their noses on the tinted windows of the car. They laughed as they attempted to view what or who was inside. The driver shooed them with a hard knock on the windows. The car barely moved when the light turned green, but it prompted the children to dart back to the shanties that lined the service road.

Either the food was better in one *carinderia*, or cheaper, as there were more punters than the other one a couple of doors away. A barber's, a couple of *sari-sari* stores and a billiard corner sat side by side. The mixed commercial and residential spaces stood jagged like crooked teeth. Some had broken away from the stigma of squatting by demolishing their four walls of plywood, replacing with concrete to build permanence and set roots. But the walls were stained by stagnancy. The white, dusky rose, mustard yellow and burnt orange paints were overcast by soot. Exhaust fumes clung like an almost indelible fate.

From the service road, the car nosed towards a bridge. Across, they converged with other vehicles at the foot, shaded from the vicious sun by shiny, tall office buildings and condominiums. The glossy transformation was a concrete tale of acquired privilege. On the other side were those who had yet to cross the bridge. Most would likely not have the chance.

"I just realised I only told you the name of the subdivision. You do know we're off to 16 Morley Street?" she asked.

"Yes, ma'am, I've been briefed," the driver confirmed.

Her old route had become a friend from more than two decades ago that she would no longer recognise in the crowd until they were reintroduced. Flyovers crisscrossed the sky like tangled cable wires, modern mammoth shopping malls imposingly sat on the once vast wastelands, and vehicles were like several sets of jacks tossed in the air and scattered to clog the roads. *"Walang hiya!"* the driver muttered under his breath as he swerved to avoid a car that was impatiently squeezing its way into their lane.

"Sorry about that, ma'am," he said, as he looked at her through the rear-view mirror.

Madeleine looked up from her phone. "Don't worry about that," she reassured him. "So much has changed around here, but I guess the way Filipinos drive has not at all."

"Hah! There are some rude habits we can't break," he laughed.

"Have you been driving for long?" asked Madeleine, easing on her characteristic silence around anyone she just met.

"On and off for about 10 years, ma'am, and only for special trips and occasional driving for events and hotels. I had a job in IT, which I now do freelance while I wait for my wife's petition papers for the US," he said, as he looked to his right to inch his way in for a U-turn. "She's a nurse."

"I see. My mother was a nurse, too, in the Middle East, back in the '80s. I think there's always at least one nurse in every Filipino family," Madeleine smiled as she put her phone on her lap.

"That's true, ma'am, and everyone leaves."

"You must be excited to join her. It's not easy to be away from each other."

"I'm really looking forward to it. We have lots of plans. We'll buy a house, maybe have children if we still can by the time I get my papers, maybe work in IT — a fresh start," he said, while rhythmically tapping his fingers on the steering wheel in sync with the drumbeats of the music streaming from his phone.

A fresh start.

Madeleine thought of her family's. It was a forced start. Years of their physical memories were crammed in a single removal lorry, but all the other memories attached to those objects could not be contained in one tight space. Pieces were left behind. There were parts of that life they were constrained to relinquish. Loss had a cruel regard in presenting itself.

The driver slowed down to the gated entrance of Green Vista Hills. It was less green, less spacious and less intimidating than she could remember. Time and the seasons had weathered the wooden signage; the letters R, E, V, I and S needed regilding. In place of the once lush manicured and landscaped frontage in the shape of a roundabout were yellow leaves and bald stems that begged to be tended. When Green Vista Hills opened to its first homeowners in the early 1980s, the entrance to the gated subdivision glowed with golden lights that illuminated the darkness of the suburban highway. In the beginning, and for many years, driving into Green Vista Hills was akin to arriving in an exclusive resort for a holiday. But holidays weren't permanent; even the extended ones had to end.

After the security guard had given them the clearance, the driver proceeded to a tree-lined stretch of road. A well-maintained American suburban-style house with a white picket fence reminiscent of a *Southern Living* magazine cover prominently looked out to oncoming motorists. It was like a familiar face from the past who was happy to show Madeleine around her childhood haunts. The car cruised the streets which bore names she recognised: Earl, Irvine, Ravendale, Kent. The buzzing in her head intensified as they turned into Morley Street. Her hands were clammy as the driver gently pulled up in front of number 16. Her feet were just as heavy as her heart.

"I won't be long," she told the driver.

"Take your time, ma'am," he nodded.

Modern vibrant hues of deep grey, beige-grey and teal stripped the house of its former sombre deep brown and sepia exterior. Its minimalist black, wrought iron gate was lower, flat on top, and had horizontal rather than vertical bars. The house was welcoming and would not be a recluse's dream. She was expected, as the housekeeper was waiting to let her in.

She walked into an unfamiliar layout, but memories led her to an intimate territory. Her father spent countless mornings listening to music — turned up to festival volume — with his head leaned back on the reclining chair and his eyes closed. In the same spot, a bright yellow occasional chair now sat — empty — save for the multicoloured batik-print scarf slung around the backrest. A baby grand piano was poised next to double French doors that opened to an entertainment and recreational space. In the silence, the noise from past celebrations rushed back: the birthdays, graduations, reunions, wedding after-parties, births, sleepovers of relatives and friends, late-night chats and midnight snacks. Those who visited and came to stay lingered for as long as the aroma of her mother's cooking wafted in the air.

Her mother's meals brought everyone together, from the morning, until all the dishes had been cleared at night. She deboned fish and dressed chicken as easy as opening a tin can. Madeleine had seen her mother sway and hum only once — in her kitchen — to some Connie Francis songs, when the kitchen hood light was her spotlight and the steam from the pots and pans her fog machine. The kitchen was her stage and the dishes her sold-out performances.

But the one Madeleine now stepped into was not her mother's kitchen. The varnished mahogany cupboards and panels had been refreshed to a matte palette of blue-greys and ecru — a redemption from years of darkness, neglect and uncertainty. At the centre was a granite-topped kitchen island with a decorative overhead rack for pots and pans. A light breeze blew a pan to clink against a pot and another, breaking the silence like a wind chime. Black and white framed photos of pestle and mortar, rolling pin and diverse types of bread lined the walls. The wall to the right of the dining room now extended to a lanai ideal for hosting on balmy evenings. To one side were the French doors that kept the piano from view. Foliage and flowers softened the un-plastered concrete. The lapping sound of a miniature waterfall in the corner soothed her wistful sentiments. She remembered those home interior magazines her parents collected. Her mother would have wanted these kitchen and outdoor spaces. But the money had dried up, and the dreams that came with it. Not a fatty whiff of Minola cooking oil trapped on the walls, but rather a sweetness that was slowly warming up the room, wrapping her senses. She had visions of her mother standing by the oven, wiping her hands on her apron. She turned to Madeleine and her two siblings, Roanna and Oliver. "Start setting the table; we'll be eating soon." She told Roanna, Madeleine's youngest sister, to go and get their father.

"Do we put the saucers on the daisy, too?" asked Roanna.

"Who's Daisy?" Madeleine teased her.

"Mama's friend," replied Oliver, while mustering up not to giggle.

Madeleine and Roanna rolled their eyes at Oliver, then Roanna turned to Madeleine, "That round thing on the table!"

"It's lazy! Lazy Susan, you idiot!" Madeleine shouted.

They all burst out laughing.

Their mother took the chiffon cake out of the oven.

"Do we have to have icing on the cake, Mama?" Madeleine asked.

"We've always had it with icing; you all love it with icing," her mother replied while she prepared the platter on which to transfer the cake when it had cooled down.

Madeleine was always in awe of the toasty brown sloping smoothness of the cake fresh out of the mould, as if seeing one for the first time. The tip of her nose almost touched it as she breathed in its buttery sweetness, redolent of a comfortable and warm home on a wet and rainy day. But then the rain came with monsoon gales which on the darkest days turned into furious storms. Their home succumbed to vulnerability, its warmth obliterated by dampness, and the air weighed of a suffocating desperation.

"Are you alright?" A soft voice echoed behind her.

Madeleine turned around. "Oh hello, I'm sorry, I was lost in my thoughts."

She could be in her late 60s or early 70s, but her professionally dyed, yet un-styled short hair, coral clam-diggers, Sabrina-cut Tiffany-blue tent blouse and light make-up did not give away any number. Her contentment and happiness shone through her uncontrived appearance and disarming presence.

"You must be Mrs. Rivera," Madeline continued. "Thank you for letting me have this time here."

"I am. Sorry, I had to wrap up a call. Just call me Irene, by the way. It's nice to meet you, Madeleine. I can show you around or I'll leave you to it." She excused herself and made her way to the oven. "I nearly forgot about my sponge cake. Trying out this new recipe. Have some later with me and let me know if you prefer coffee or tea — you probably prefer tea, *ano*?" Mrs. Rivera glanced at Madeleine while she reached out in the cupboard, searching between canisters and jars on a shelf. She took out a carton still wrapped in plastic, and an ornate caddy. "I have Twinings and some very *sosyal* Fortnum and Mason from a friend," she said, showing both to Madeleine. *"Pero* if you want coffee, I have ground from Rustan's, *barako* from Batangas — you probably don't have it in England — and even instant," she ended, half-smiling with her mouth closed, now awkwardly aware that she prattled before her guest whose stone-cold face didn't look impressed. Mrs. Rivera placed the carton and caddy on the granite worktop, and wiped her hands on her immaculate apron.

Distracted by her trepidation, Madeleine couldn't bring herself to interrupt Mrs. Rivera's gregariousness. She managed a faint smile, looked down and back at Mrs. Rivera. "I'd love to, Irene. Thank you."

The sweetness of vanilla slowly released a bitter aftertaste. "May I?" Madeleine asked as she turned towards the solid wood staircase.

Irene smiled. "Of course. This was your home."

The floor-to-ceiling window was still the focal feature on the staircase's landing. Madeline never understood the purpose of the design as the sun did not rise or set from that side of the house, and when a new house was built next door, the uninspiring view of the empty lot was replaced by the neighbour's firewall. A contemporary chandelier took over her parents' antique piece which they proudly told guests was imported from some country she couldn't remember. But she could remember being scared at night when she had to come down to get some snacks; she might startle a lurking intruder when she turned on the lights. Large artwork pieces accentuated both walls. She had seen images of similar paintings from the website of nearby Pinto Art Museum. She must visit before flying back to England. As she reached the top of the stairs, the brightness towards her right, which used to be the family library, spurred her curiosity. Family portraits furnished the sideboard in the hallway. Wall-to-wall bookshelves occupied the space where her family used to keep *Encyclopedia Americana* and *Collier's*. Tall artificial and live foliage decorated the corners, with the more imposing ones flanking each side of the French door that opened to a balcony. She used to imagine a similar outdoor space in the same room, especially during the hottest summer days. Madeleine stepped onto the balcony overlooking the swimming pool, sat down on a lounge chair, closed her eyes, took a deep breath, and imagined getting together with her siblings, mother and father.

Her phone vibrated several times.

She stood up to view the old rooms. Her room. She fondly recalled the day they moved in, on her 12th birthday, when she and her younger sister scrambled up the stairs to pick their bedrooms. Madeleine claimed the one with the windows that greeted the sunrise every day. It was where she blockaded herself during episodes of tantrums, where she tempered the angst that came with turbulent hormones, consoled her tears, tucked away her secrets, and sobered up from intoxicating young love. When she moved abroad and found herself having to move out of house and flat shares, move on from relationship breakdowns or recover from job meltdowns, she was envious of friends who had family homes to hibernate to. She pined for the familiarity of her room where she could lock herself away from the turmoil of adulthood. She wanted to go home. But that home had become mere images in her memory. All the photographs had been misplaced in the chaos.

She pressed down the door handle. A Juliet balcony now stood where the East-facing window used to. The early morning sunshine used to wake her up before her alarm clock did. Gone were the old rose curtains she drew to keep away the brightness when sunny, and the lightning during thunderstorms. She would have known that a teenage girl had taken up her childhood bedroom even if Mrs. Rivera did not tell her that her grandchild did. The room was spotless; the parquet floor was as glossy as she had left it. She must have been told to tidy up as a guest will come up. A quirky rug was placed by the foot of the bed, which reminded her of the one she made for Home Economics class in high school, with the image of a cheerleading girl confidently perched on top of a big letter M. *The Book Thief, Aristotle and Dante Discover the Secrets of the Universe, Love from A to Z, The Perks of Being a Wallflower,* a few of the titles on her headboard that doubled as a bookshelf. Madeleine admired teenagers who read in the age of distractions. Several strings of fairy lights hung on the wall and at the balcony. Some trinkets laid on the dresser, mixed with cables for gadgets. On the nightstand was a note.

Hi,
Mommy found this when they moved. I wasn't even born then. She gave it to me to keep. I think this is yours. I won't lie, I tried unlocking it. Sorry.
Mitch

On the cushioned PVC cover of the locked diary was an image of a teenage girl in a floral yellow skirt and frilly white blouse sitting in a field of grass surrounded by daffodils. She was pensive while looking out into the fields, her right hand holding a pen and resting on a notebook. In cursive, on the cloudless blue skies, were the words, *'Life is but a dream'.* Madeleine bought it with her birthday money when she turned 13. It was the last piece at her local National Bookstore. One day, she brought her journal to school to write down her thoughts during breaks. She decided to freshen up before the next class started, tucking her pen between the pages and closing her journal before leaving it on her desk. When she returned, some girls with whom she rarely hung out, were unusually affable and attentive. A few who were huddled in a corner — giggling — dispersed as soon as she walked in. Madeleine thought of how strange it was until she reached her desk. Her journal was gone. "We'll tell Vince you have a crush on him," mocked one of the girls. Laughter erupted from the others. Madeleine turned around to find Ayesha, the ringleader, dangling her journal between her fingers. A scuffle ensued after Madeleine's unsuccessful attempt to snatch her journal off Ayesha's hand. With the intervention of their homeroom teacher, Madeleine got her journal back, but not her trust of the people around her. She had not forgotten to lock her journal since.

She sat on the edge of Mitch's bed and clutched her diary close to her chest. The keys were no longer just charms in her necklace. Madeleine pushed one into the padlock. It clicked. She opened a world she once knew, flicked through the pages, smiled upon seeing her teenage handwriting and reading her innocent words. She stared at her reflection in the teenage girl's full-length mirror, looked around Mitch's room, and thought of all the other rooms in the house. They had been coated with fresh layers of paint and decorated with charming wallpaper but some of the original features were retained. She returned to a house that was not the same one that she left, but bore touches of what her family would have wanted had they been able to afford them at the time. But the financial misfortunes happened one after another. The house collapsed with the death of her father. Life was no longer a dream; it turned into a nightmare. Her silence was broken by her flashing phone.

"Hello?" Madeleine reluctantly picked up the call. She stared at the parquet floor as her sister spoke. Her tears were held back, but her face could not escape the grief. She hung up and looked for a piece of paper.

Dear Mitch,
Thank you for keeping my diary safe. I see you've been taking care of my old room, too. Keep it up. Take care.
Madeleine

The housekeeper had invited the driver in while he waited for Madeleine, but he decided to wait in the car. He took his eyes off the newspaper he was reading when he heard voices in the garage. He checked his watch: one and a half hours had passed. Madeleine shook the hands of a woman who seemed to be the owner of the house. They embraced, and Madeleine headed back to the car. He glanced to his right just as Madeleine slid into the backseat. Her face was veiled in tenderness and her eyes had a watery blankness.

"I'm sorry, I didn't even ask for your name."

"It's Marlon, ma'am."

"Marlon, to the nearest Saint Joseph church, please."

MZ Akil

MZ Akil packed her life into two suitcases and moved to the UK in 2006. Her career has since deviated from publishing to fashion, but she always finds her way back to writing. She uses her hour-long journey to and from work in London to weave tales about cultural identity, belongingness and women's aspirations. The goal is to write more stories rather than work emails.

Jane's Quarantine Adventure

Aseptic morning sunlight pricked through the window shutters; white blades elongating across the hardwood floor, over an orange carpet and onto a disheveled bed.

"Uggh." Jane pulled the comforter over her head.

The flapping sound of minutes turning over came from the chunky aqua-green alarm clock on the bedside table. It was supposed to be, 'the perfect second-hand statement piece for the eco-conscious bedroom' but, in those days of quarantine, felt more like a torture instrument.

Jane pushed herself up. "Happy birthday to me." Her feet sank into the fuzzy carpet as she stood. She wriggled her toes and a smile wrinkled the corners of her mouth. The tickling orange bedside rug had been a great purchase and became the only good reason to step out of bed. Jane stretched and yawned. "Good morning, old lady." Jane stepped toward her reflection silhouetted by the flickering sunlight on the Victorian full-figure silver mirror leaning against the nearest corner of the room. "Thirty years old, eh?" She tied her hair up in a bun with the thin black scrunchy that lived on her right wrist when it wasn't in her hair. Scrunchies are one of the most misplaced items ever mass-produced, lost at the bottom of purses and drawers, dropped on pavements and cars' floors, and as biodegradable as the nearest plastic bottle.

Jane's eyes studied her reflection in search of any detail

betraying the loss of her youth. She palmed her heavy breasts, which had never been perky, and let them drop back down against her ribcage. Stretchmarks that had appeared back in her teens corrugated the skin. Her hands measured the fat covering her bones. She could feel the gaps between each pair of ribs, and could begin to feel her hip bones but they were still hidden from sight. Her fingers couldn't quite close around her wrists. "Stop," the word was an imperceptible gasp. She was checking her bones. This was not a good habit to start. Maybe pairing the umpteenth weight loss attempt with complete isolation hadn't been her best idea. Jane deserted the mirror. She grabbed a pair of clean panties, pulled them up her prickly legs, and slipped into an oversized t-shirt. Her pandemic uniform.

The world had become a quiet place once all humans had been caged in their dwellings, for their own good. At first, Jane had enjoyed having an excuse not to venture into society every day and having the flat all to herself; her roommate Mary having escaped to her girlfriend's place the night the Prime Minister announced the country-wide lockdown. But soon enough this well-deserved rest from mankind had turned into sour hermitage.

Jane strode to the kitchen to look for something to eat. Opening the pantry's cabinets, she was met by a disheartening sight. A couple of sprouted potatoes, one egg, a meager portion of dry pasta, half a bag of dried mushrooms left behind by Mary, and a couple of spoonful's of chocolate-hazelnut cream at the bottom of a glass jar. The fridge was empty. One sausage was the great treasure held by the freezer. She could probably put something together to get through the day, and luckily the next day was her turn to access the grocery store. It didn't make sense that they had even state-regulated access to essential stores by surname alphabetical order. Did they fear that people would have raided the grocery stores if they hadn't? Jane chuckled shaking her head. With this stupid assigned grocery day routine, she was always short on food. Her income had stayed constant, her job was already mostly on the computer so transitioning to working from home had been effortless. Money wasn't the issue, but having to account for a fortnight's worth of meals, when previously she used to go grocery shopping twice a week, was the real struggle for her.

After a long time spent staring at the ingredients at her disposal, Jane decided to keep the chocolate spread as a mid-day snack, and prepare two meals with the rest: sausage frittata with boiled potatoes as a side (if any part of the spuds was still salvageable), and pasta with mushrooms. The mushroom pasta will have to go first; eggs didn't agree with her stomach in the morning.

The mushrooms were in a Ziplock bag; good thinking on Mary's side, otherwise after four months sitting in an open bag in the pantry they would have turned mushy and stale. Jane unzipped the bag and dumped the contents in a bowl along with lukewarm water; dry mushrooms need to soak. A rich, earthy smell filled the air. While the mushrooms were in their beauty bath, turning from wrinkly old scabs to gracious fleshy caps and stems, Jane put on the water for the pasta to boil. She stir-fried the mushrooms and sautéed the cooked pasta with them, to add some crunchiness to the dish. "One fuming pasta, right up!" She served herself the meal in front of the TV, whilst *Alice in Wonderland,* the animated movie, played. The pasta didn't taste bad, even though the damp dirt and moss taste of mushrooms was way stronger than she would have expected. Jane fished her smartphone out from the trench between the couch's cushions, and shot a message to Mary, "Hope you won't be mad. I was short on food so I ate your mushrooms. I'll buy you a new bag when you're back! But what's their name? I never had any so forest-tasting."

With her belly full and her schedule empty for the day, Jane sat back, stretched her legs on the coffee table and kept watching the movie. The Cheshire Cat's fur glowed purple and pink, Alice's dress was electric blue, and all the reds had a glossy look.

"Did they remaster it?" Jane could swear the colors she remembered weren't so vibrant.

As the end credits rolled the green background began to bleed out of the screen.

"What the fuck?" Jane rushed to the TV. Her fingers trembled as she reached for the slimy green stuff oozing from the edge of the glassy surface. It tickled. Before she could retract her hand, a fuchsia beak snatched it, pulling Jane through the icy screen and into the TV. The green light blinded and engulfed her. She screwed her eyes shut. Green polka dots danced against the red and veiny inside of her eyelids. Something wet and muscular wrapped around her. Pulsating contractions propelled her forward. Jane tried to stretch her arms and legs far away from her body, to gain some level of control over her situation. The damp mucosa wound itself tighter around her. After a few more squeezes, Jane finally felt her head plop out of the luminescent organ. Fresh air wiped her face and she opened her eyes. A fluffy-looking surface spread a few feet beneath her. One last contraction expelled her body from the green muscular mass. She was free… and free-falling through cold misty clouds. Wind roared past her ears. The air attempted to strip her naked. Her hair was ripped free of its scrunchy. The clouds cleared revealing the Macedonian phalanx of New York's skyscrapers rising their menacing antennas against her. At the sight, a helpless scream escaped Jane's mouth. The shiny spikes were getting closer and closer every second. She was going to die. No way to avoid the maze of steel and cement beneath her. Jane closed her eyes, hoping for an instantaneous death. She didn't want to imagine the pain she would experience if the impact didn't cause her immediate demise.

Warm stickiness enveloped her, gradually slowing her fall. Jane opened her eyes once more. She was sinking through one of the skyscrapers, through ceilings and floors, desks and toilets, staircases and people, but all seemed to be made of thin, soft fibers. Little chunks of chairs and door handles stuck to her shirt. Jane plucked one off. The material had a familiar consistency.

"Could it be?" Jane gave a tentative lick to the doorknob's piece. It was sweet. She took a bite. "Cotton candy!" Jane broke into laughter. Tears filled her eyes. She couldn't stop laughing.

After what felt like hours, Jane's feet finally met a surface they couldn't break through.

"Ground floor, I guess," exhaustion tainted the chuckled words.

Somewhere along her descent Jane had elected to believe that she must have dozed off in front of the TV. She was dreaming, therefore anything was fair game. She dived face-first into her sweet surroundings and ate a way to the solid surface at her feet. From there, she proceeded forward, devouring a straight tunnel in hope of coming to open air sooner or later. Jane ate and ate. Maybe she was wrong, extremely wrong. She stopped. Her elbows and knees were sore. Throbbing. The firm ground under her was coarse; in the dim light of the tunnel, it seemed a continuous spread of reddish-brown debris fused from the bottom. It looked a lot like a giant strip of sandpaper. Jane sat back on her heels and unfolded her stiff arms. Bolts of pain erupted from her elbows as the metallic smell of blood melded with the sweet fragrance of the cotton candy. Wincing, she examined her forearms and elbows. Angry red abrasions flourished where her skin had repeatedly brushed against the ground. Transparent gooey liquid exuded from the smaller lacerations; blood surfaced from the deeper scratches. The sight amplified the pulsating ache. Pain doesn't belong in dreams. Tears filled her eyes once more, rose over the rim, tumbled over her lashes and rolled down her cheeks.

"What's happening to me?" Sobs broke Jane's voice. Her shoulders shook and she collapsed into a bawling ball.

The ground opened, causing her to drop, and turn into a bowling ball. She rolled and crashed.

"Strike!" Roared a male, artificial-sounding, modulated voice.

A cacophony of cheers and shrills followed.

Jane heard her back pop. Her muscles relaxed, and her body unraveled. She was lying on her back, surrounded by capsized plastic bottles. A shadow came over her. Jane squinted as a big mauve octopus came into focus. It was gliding toward her on its muscular tentacles; its bulbous head was spotted with little bumps and harbored two round cartoonish black eyes.

"C'mon, roll back up bowling ball!" One of the octopus's tentacles probed her shoulder, the little white suckers pulling the sleeve of her t-shirt.

"I'm no ball!" Jane protested, rising to her feet.

"And my garden is no dumpster, but I don't see you humans caring."

"I care." Her voice cracked. "I'm trying, okay?! It's not that easy to purchase from sustainable brands, figure out the type of plastic from which each piece of garbage is made, and how to dispose of it!"

The octopus had collected the plastic bottles and was positioning them back up as bowling pins. "And why should I pity your affliction?"

"I… I…" Jane sighed, "I'm talking with an octopus." She shook her head. "I've gone crazy."

"Aren't you all?" Noticing Jane's questioning look, the octopus elaborated forward, "You humans, aren't you all crazy? I mean, you must be! Nobody in their right mind would purposely trash, destroy and render inhospitable to themselves their own, and only, habitat."

Jane couldn't deny it, the octopus had a point.

"Okay, out of the way!" The octopus shoved her away from the pins and toward a giant chunk of truck tire used as bleachers by a school of silver and yellow butterfly fishes. Then it turned to face a tiny leafy sea dragon. "The lane is all yours, Eustace." The octopus gestured to the bowling lane it and Jane had just cleared.

Eustace grinned. With the agility of a contortionist, it hooked the tip of its tail behind its equine head and folded its leafy appendages around its body, curling into a perfect emerald bowling ball. It rocked forward and began spinning toward the unusual pins. The four plastic bottles on the right toppled over.

Trepidation muted all those present, as Eustace prepared himself for the second throw of his last frame. He hurtled himself down the lane and… completely missed the remaining pins.

Murmurs of disappointment rose from the school of butterfly fishes that were becoming more and more restless with every passing moment.

The leafy sea dragon swam back to its initial station. "It seems to be a draw. Do you want to have one more throw as a tie-break?"

"Of course! A winner must be declared," the octopus boasted.

"You are determined to see me win today, Galileo. Aren't you?" Eustace teased.

"You'd like that!" The octopus wrapped a tentacle around Jane's waist and pulled her closer. "Time to bowl, human!"

Trying to wriggle free from the suckers' hold, Jane cried, "No, no, I said I'm not a ball."

Galileo ignored her complaints and, using its multiple limbs shaped her into a bowling ball once more.

Jane gasped as the muscular tentacles found their way into her three holes. She stifled a moan as she was propelled forward, tentacles sliding out, suckers releasing her with wet pops. With dashing speed, Jane struck the front pin causing a chain effect.

"Strike!" the artificial voice declared again.

Laying sprawled between the bottles, Jane noticed an old TV tube hanging from tangled fishing nets. Was that there earlier?

Galileo appeared at her side. "Up, up, and away!" He ordered her out from the bowling lane and rushed to reposition the pins.

Recoiling from the octopus's imposing presence, Jane stumbled to her feet and hurtled herself to the edge of the playing grounds and further. The viscosity of her surroundings increased, and what had earlier seemed like nothing more than air had turned into salty molasses. She was floating. Up and down, indistinguishable twins. She could no longer breathe. Swimming in the thick syrup was burning her oxygen reserves at a fast pace. If she didn't break the surface soon, she'd drown. Her lungs screamed and burned, her diaphragm cramped and convulsed in the strenuous attempt to draw in even just one breath, her heart hammered an irregular rhythm. Jane was dying and there was nothing she could do about it, thus why keep swimming? She surrendered. Her body jolted and shuddered in the grip of her failing organs. Slowly, the salted liquid pushed Jane's body upwards and through a clingy black film. A shaky breath inhaled life back into her body together with the pungent smell of chemicals. Exhausted, terrified and covered in poisonous crude oil, Jane floated adrift on the dark ocean for hours. She hurt everywhere.

Eventually, she washed up ashore where steady waves shattered against a colorful beach. Instead of sand, there was a lush garden. Scents of rosemary and violets filled the air. Fresh and ambrosial perfumes teased Jane's nose. Her eyes fluttered open. Tall sunflowers grew in fields of forget-me-not, bright stars in a clear sky. Pristine white daisies thrived in a checkered tapestry of fiery poppies. Vibrantly orange marigolds rose between pink pansies. All these colors were mesmerizing after all that darkness.

Tender grass blades tickled Jane, they grew to entwine with her fingers and welcome her in a soft cocoon. Tar and oil melted away. A tingly sensation spread all through Jane's body, tension flooded out of her muscles. She could feel the weight of every suffering, trauma and self-imposition crushing her soul. A deep breath in, hold, a long breath out. They were gone. Her molecules unbound into a primordial broth. Jane was pure potential. Her bones calcified anew, muscle fibers and nerves wrapped around them, skin spread as a protective blanket, hair sprouted luxurious. The green cocoon cracked open, and the remolded Jane emerged. She was perfect.

The dawn song of far-away swallows animated the otherwise emptying surroundings. Jane was basking in pure white light. "Is this paradise?"

"No," a chirp echoed from the edge of existence. Fuchsia feathers waltzed down in front of Jane. Each feather stopped midair at a different height: here they coagulated in an oval shape, there in a long cylindrical one. "This is the being," peeped a now completely formed flamingo.

Jane approached the big bird with a spring in her steps. "The being?"

"Everything that is, it's part of the being," the big bird elaborated, "and everything that is, is interconnected. Animals, humans, machines, and ecosystems are all connected. You and I. The being is an ecumenical organism."

"I do see how everything can flow and connect into the other. However, some of the existing entities are overtaking and annihilating others, this must be punished and stopped."

The flamingo shook its head. "Not punished." He began to prance around. "An equilibrium is to be found without relapsing to suppression. Everything contains beauty and intrinsic value, therefore everything shall be preserved and nurtured to allow it to express all its infinite potential."

Jane nodded, entranced by the bird's wisdom. The flamingo and she searched each other's eyes, peered deep into their being to find the other and improve themselves through the acknowledgment and enhancement of the other.

After so much exertion, the flamingo enquired, "Peckish? I have snacks."

Having not eaten anything since the beginning of her adventures into the TV, Jane felt famished and accepted the offer.

The bright bird began to bob its head producing harsh guttural sounds and, after a few seconds, regurgitated a cup of grey slimy mushrooms with electric-blue rimmed caps.

At this sight, Jane's stomach turned in disgust, her head spun and everything turned black.

***

Searing white morning sunlight reached Jane on her disheveled bed. She was tangled in her comforter and when she went to pull it over her eyes, as she did every morning, she ended up tugging herself out of bed. The abrupt encounter with the floor jolted her wide awake. Her startled eyes searched her surroundings. "Where's the flamingo?" Jane staggered to her feet, a dull soreness aching through her body. "How did I get here?"

She ran to the living room to check the TV. It was off. She retrieved the remote from the coffee table and turned the TV on. No oozing green light, nor any other anomaly.

"Perhaps it was all just a dream," Jane reassured herself, "Maybe, after all, the mushrooms had gone bad sitting in the cupboard for that long." She went back to her bedroom to put some clothes on. As always, her reflection in the mirror attracted her attention. Something looked different, but it wasn't extra lines on her forehead, nor new stretchmarks, not more or less fat on her bones. Something was missing.

Her hair draped over her shoulders, and still her right wrist was naked. Her scrunchy was gone. Jane turned to go look if it was somewhere in the bed, but the corner of her eye caught something dark and iridescent in her hair. She ran her fingers through her hair and one lock at the base of the neck was covered in a slimy substance. Bringing the incriminated lock to her nose, she sniffed it. "Crude oil… Could it be?" She went back to the mirror and examined her forearms and elbows. They were not bleeding nor raw, however they looked a little pinkish and felt tender at the touch. Jane kept probing the skin of her elbows trying to understand if its redness was due to being freshly regrown or to her recent fall from the bed.

Jane's smartphone dinged. She searched for the device between the folds of her comforter. The notification displayed Mary's name.

"She must have answered my message." Jane proceeded to open the messaging application.

"Happy belated birthday! Anyway, about the mushrooms, I never had any. I'm allergic to them," read Mary's text.

Genea Piervittori-Vaughn

Genea finds talking about herself in 3rd person difficult and quite concerning. Nevertheless, since the occasion calls for it, she is thrilled to let you know she was born and grew up in Marche, Italy and now resides with her wonderful husband in the US. She has always recounted stories to whomever was so kind as to lend her an ear (or an eye) and is now trying to reach as many people as possible with her otherworldly adventures.

Jockie's Brogues

The shiny chestnut brogues she'd surprised him with that morning creak as he climbs the steps out of Leicester Square station. He emerges, blinking, onto a bustling street of tourists and traffic. Which way to go? She'd know. She loved the city. Envied his trip but hadn't wanted to come.

"Who'd want to listen to you men talking nonsense all night?"

He hadn't argued. She didn't need to hear about the day he and Lochlann had skipped school to go fishing. The priceless expression on their mother's face as Lochlann entered the kitchen, fresh trout held triumphant above his head, Jockie dripping puddles on the flagstones after ending up in the drink.

He peers through the rain, gazing over an assortment of hats and umbrellas before entering the flow of people, heading west. A queue at the Ambassadors Theatre blocks the pavement, forcing him into the road, and more puddles. The floodlit billboard reminds him of the time she volunteered him as lighting technician in the local production of "Romeo and Juliet". He'd had fun until she arrived as the director, giving him his instructions. They'd made a tragedy together. He grins. Perhaps he'll take her to the opening of 'Mousetrap' next month, as a treat. She'd enjoy that.

He turns onto Glasshouse Street. A squeak from the left shoe, and a nip at his heel from the right recall the final admonishment as she'd kissed him goodbye on the platform.

"Those shoes cost more than the rest of your wardrobe put together. Look after them. Please."

His companionable old loafers would have been ideal for this. They'd steered him home too many times to count. But not these. Not his style either. He glares at the brogues. Shakes his head. What could he have done?

The birthday invitation crinkles in his pocket along with the fistful of banknotes she'd retrieved from the stoneware jug on the mantlepiece that morning. It had been a gift from Lochlann, serving as both ornament and treasury. He hadn't touched it since their wedding day. She looked after the money, and he'd never found a good reason to object.

"Whatever you do, don't spend it all in one place!"

Stepping into a doorway, he kneels and slips off the right shoe. Lamenting his chafed heel, he places a few notes inside for safe keeping. Perhaps they will soften his hike.

Jockie breathes in the reek as he enters The Clachan, trying to relish the once familiar atmosphere. Sticky carpet of indeterminate colour cushions his limp to the bar. He is glad she can't witness his sudden unease at the ambience. She's changed him.

The tall, red-haired man entertains with a droll story about a carpenter, a cow, and some lost spectacles. Jockie is the unfortunate hero of the tale. He listens for a few moments, then rolls his shoulders and approaches under a dirty chandelier to slap Lochlann soundly on the back before the denouement can be revealed.

The hug envelopes him as always. "Wee man! Ye made it! I was about to organize a search party for you, just like that time—"

Jockie interrupts, "Enough already! Let's take the weight off!"

He sinks into a threadbare chair, resting his feet. A twinge of relief and a pang of yearning for the tweed sofa he shares with her in the evenings as she tells him about the latest at her school. He loves that she thought to buy him shoes, but who would wear new brogues on a pub crawl? Who would even think they were a good idea? He groans to himself, seeing Lochlann attract the barman's attention with his height. He might have to stop early, might not be able to go the distance tonight.

She wouldn't have thought about that. His eyes widen as he remembers her insistence that he needed to look his best for his brother, then crinkle in mirth. "Tha' cheeky minx!" he murmurs to himself. "She did an a'!"

The last mouthful goes down easily, leaving a blurred vision of Lochlann through the bottom of the glass. Jockie sighs, and places it carefully on the bar. The remnants of beige foam slide lazily down the inside wall. A bell rings and a raucous call disrupts his reverie. "Last orders!"

Lochlann pats down his pockets several times, but Jockie can tell it's all theatre. If his brother was skint the petted lip would be larger than a soup plate.

Jockie slips off the stool and after an ostentatious bow, straightens to grip Lochlann's shoulder. With a barely noticeable wobble, or so he believes, he raises his right foot, and pulls off the brogue. A single damp bank note slumps into the palm of his hand. Jockie lifts it by a corner and brandishes it under

Lochlann's nose. "We're ok for a ditcher, big man. Nae worries."

Lochlann bellows his approval, then points a finger unsteadily at Jockie. "This reminds me of that time you borrowed our Da's bicycle without asking and ended up—"

"Never mind that, what'll it be? Islay or Speyside?" Jockie cuts in, laughing.

Lochlann lifts a conspiratorial eyebrow. "Got to finish with an Islay, don't we? It's the law."

Jockie releases his grip and turns to the bar. "It should be the law!"

The rejoinder drifts over his shoulder, "Anyway, we're not finished. I know a wee place…"

Jockie spills out onto the pavement behind his brother, barely keeping his feet. He doesn't know the name of the place. The Clachan was an age ago, back when he knew where he was. He's glad she didn't come. She wouldn't like to see him like this.

Lochlann tugs the bottom of his waistcoat down and exhales into the cold night air, his breath a billowing cloud around his head. "Better get you to the train station, wee man," he observes, "and sitting down before you fall down." He pivots left and marches in a slow weave along the pavement, the first few bars of, "Donald, where's your troosers?" in his wake.

Jockie stoops over, eyes closed, hands on his knees. He swallows once. Again. Then he straightens and focusses on Lochlann. Easy to pick him out on the street, given the height. And the hair. And the singing.

Lochlann skips across a junction, leaving Jockie to totter off the edge of the kerb. He splashes though a puddle in the road, then slows. Something is wrong with his feet. The warm glow that has accompanied him over the last few hours dissipates below his ankles. He glances down to see a damp brogue on his left foot, but only a sodden Argyle sock on his right.

Jockie whirls, searching the ground around his feet. Did it come off in the puddle? He splashes a little with the already saturated sock, forlornly hoping it might find the errant shoe hiding below the surface. But there is only one thing Jockie can do. "Lochlann!"

"Ach sure it could be anywhere, couldn't it?" Lochlann purses his lips.

Jockie remembers carrying the brogue out of the Clachan. He hadn't been able to face squeezing his foot back inside. Enough of having his feet nipped. "We'll need to retrace our path. It's the only way we'll find it." He shudders. He daren't let her down.

"No, lad. There's no point in that. Those bars shut hours ago." Lochlann rubs a thumb along his jaw, his serious expression sobering Jockie up more than a cold shower or splash in a puddle ever could. He continues, "They were brand new, so I'm thinking we try Carnaby Street. I know a shop there that's open all night." He snaps his fingers, the decision made. "They'll have what we need. We'll buy another pair. C'mon, let's grab a taxi."

Jockie can't believe his luck.

The brogues are a perfect fit and a perfect match. The same warm chestnut. She'll never know. He'll be late home, but she'll have expected that and will have been planning for him to make it up tomorrow. He stares at his feet, then their reflection, and finally makes a silly face at himself in the mirror. "They are braw! I can't believe it!" He reaches over toward the manager, a tall, thin, dour man with a mild Glaswegian accent and shakes his hand. "Thank-you, sir!"

"Aye, well, yer lucky we were open. Luckier still we have them in your size. Will you be wanting the box?"

Jockie hesitates and glances at Lochlann, who is parked in a chair in the corner of the shoe shop, head tilted back, snoring gently. He bites his lip and turns to the manager. "I don't suppose you can go down a size?"

The man purses his lips while he checks the box. "We can, yes, but this is your size. I measured your feet not five minutes ago. Why would you want a size smaller?"

Jockie stammers. "Aye, I know, I know. And don't get me wrong, this new pair fit like a glove. But these were a gift, you see. And I don't… even though I lost one, I don't…" he tails off, unable to describe how important it is that he find an identical replacement.

The manager's demeanour dissolves as he bursts out laughing. "You don't want to explain how you lost a shoe. Aye, well, we can match the size and all. And I expect you won't be wanting the box. Nor even a bag, nae doubt?"

Jockie nods, removing the larger brogues from his feet with a hint of regret. "That's it. That'll do. And a pair of Argyle socks, if you have them? Thank you again."

Lochlann leaves Jockie hobbling behind as he sprints up the steps onto the brightly lit platform at Euston station. Jockie takes his time. An elderly couple pass him, arm in arm – he with a brown flat cap, and she with a matching scarf. A whistle blows. Jockie steps gingerly onto the platform, both shoes squeaking and the spare tucked under his arm. He embraces Lochlann, grateful that his brother has proved helpful for once, rather than making him the butt of the joke. "C'mon Lochlann. C'mon home wi' me. We'll have a last dram and put your birthday to bed."

Lochlann beams. "You're determined to get yourself in trouble one way or another, aren't you lad? Well, it's been a few years since I've seen your fine lady, so I guess she deserves it, if only for an hour."

The brothers board the train as the final whistle blows and wander along the aisle, past their fellow travellers. No one makes eye contact. They find an empty carriage, not difficult at this time of night. Jockie collapses into a seat, the gentle acceleration pressing him back into slightly grubby velvet fabric. He kicks off his shoes and throws the spare down into the pile as well. He can rest easy for an hour before the short walk home.

Lochlann, sitting opposite, reaches down and grabs the shoe. "You can't walk in the front door wi' this. After all the trouble we've gone to. We'll need to get rid of it before we get off the train." He scans the carriage, and spots the bin, but there is no way a leather brogue is going to fit through a flap designed for coffee cups.

Jockie leans back and lets his eyes close. "We might as well have left it in London. I don't know why I bothered carrying it this far."

There is a sudden movement, and a gust of chill air. Jockie blinks his eyes open. The harsh white glare of the artificial overhead light silhouettes his brother. Lochlann is peering out of the small glider window above their heads. With a glint in his eyes that Jockie has long learned to dread, he dusts his hands together. "Don't worry, wee lad. It's sorted. In a few years this will just be another tall tale. One of your escapades that everyone loves hearing about."

Jockie bolts upright, staring at Lochlann, then scrabbles about with desperate fingers at the remaining pair of shoes on the floor.

"Lochlann, you idiot. You've left me wi' two left feet!"

Jeff Parke

Jeff is originally from Northern Ireland, but has lived in Aberdeenshire for over twenty years. As well as enjoying time outdoors with his wife and children, he also appreciates goods books, malt whisky and a comfortable leather armchair. He started writing flash fiction in 2020, and since completing the Creative Writing Masters at Hull has been working on a historical crime novel set in the Highland town of Nairn.

Just Enough

Last night another woman died
By the hands of a man she'd stood beside
And pledged to love till death
do part The one who said he'd hold her heart
In tender hands, that curled to fists and beat her face
until it bled, while curse's spittle rained on her
and mixed with coursing tears of red.
The kicks that splintered teeth and bone
The ribs that punctured lungs and tore
Away the breath with which she'd swore…
to love him

And he'd repeated, with words to shade
from harm and hurt, the bonds they'd made.
Him, the strength within their life,
that strength he used to kill his wife
and unborn child. In silence
he steps over Matryoshka corpses curled
                          foetal-like upon the floor
and leaves as cowards have before
to take his life in solitude.

In darkest corners as he would without the glare of justice.
Without society's pound of flesh yet we lack the ways
to weigh the costs of doing wrong,
and let our senseless leaders tweet, their senseless song,
that deaths will be reduced.
By a percentage.
By enough.

But when the penalty is a slapped wrist
in payment for a broken face,
or a decade docked for death's embrace,
the politician's soundbites do not bite
as much as the joke it is, we do not laugh
as well we might, for we know the truth is rough,
and it shouts that NOT ALL MEN ARE BAD,

just enough.

Surely – enough.[2]

Ian Hooper

---

[2] Winner of the Shorelines Writing for Performance Festival, Western Australia, 2024

Lady Anne Clifford

Born in 1590 to a wealthy family of noble lineage, Anne Clifford lived her early years in the Elizabethan court, basking in the knowledge that she was heiress to a huge fortune. But life did not work out as she had planned. She lost her place at court when Elizabeth I died and James the 1st of England and 6th of Scotland came to the throne. His taste in companions was exclusively male. The cruellest blow struck two years later, when she was fifteen. Her father died suddenly, leaving his estates not to her, as she had believed, but to her uncle. Outraged, her mother Margaret set about trying to reclaim her daughter's rights, but died unsuccessful, leaving Anne to battle on alone.

Brougham Castle, Westmoreland 22nd March 1676

"Beware the man who would cause guilty men to rise, and innocent women to fall." It was a well-known saying at court, repeated to me by my mother, meant to warn young girls like me to be wary of flatterers, philanderers and fops.

My dear mother knew a thing or two about guilty men. Father was a brave soldier, a great landowner, and Earl of Cumberland. In the end, he deceived us both. For I was brought up to believe that I was his heir. My mother told me that King Edward II himself had decreed in 1310 that Clifford lands should devolve to the eldest surviving progeny, male or female. How cruel then, that my father saw fit to bequeath his entire estate to his brother, my uncle. Ninety thousand acres. The day my father died I was bereaved not just of a dear parent, but also of the land of my heart. My home. My Westmoreland.

We fought, of course. My mother explored every legal avenue and pulled every string she could at the court of old Queen Elizabeth. When Mother died in 1616, I was only twenty-six years old, married to the Earl of Dorset, Richard Sackville of Knole House who was himself not without influence at court. James had succeeded to the throne in 1603 and enjoyed the company of well-dressed young men with pretty manners. Richard agreed that the situation was a tangle of ill fortune and said he would use his influence with the King to help resolve the matter. The day we went to Whitehall together, I was wary, but I clung to the hope that justice would be done.

Whitehall Palace, Saturday 18th January 1617

I have been here before, this labyrinth, a rat-run designed to disarm and confound. Nobody knows all its secrets, or how one door may lead to another. The palace of Whitehall is a maze of conjoined apartments, grand halls, private chambers. There was a time when, as a companion of the old Queen, I thought to make it my home.

But that was many years ago and fate had other plans for me. Today I must play another part. I am not the compliant courtier, nor even the simpering courtier's wife. I am the plaintiff, and the King has agreed to hear my cause. I am fighting, if not for my life, then for something that means the world to me, and should by rights already be mine. I am struggling to keep up with my Lord Sackville as he pounds breathlessly through room after room after the eager young page boy who has been sent to fetch us. Not once does my husband look back to see how I am managing, red-faced and out of breath in a tangle of taffeta skirts and my tight silk shoes.

Memories of this place flood back. My mother brought me to court for the first time when I was just a girl. There were hopes then that if the Queen favoured me, I might in time become part of her household. And she would have taken me too if Aunt Warwick is to be believed. Just a few years' more would have done the trick, and I would have become a lady-in-waiting, a trusted companion, even a treasured friend. I remember the rustle of the ladies' silk dresses, the whispered conversations, the smell of cloves and mint leaves, chewed to sweeten the breath. My heart was pounding, excited at the thought of entering what I perceived to be a dazzling world of luxury and pleasure. What an innocent I was then.

To my horror, the poor old Queen faltered within a year, then failed utterly. Weeping, I watched the funeral procession from a balcony, as Aunt Warwick and Mother joined the mourners; twelve veiled ladies all dressed in black, parading alongside the great coffin, topped with an effigy of the Queen in glorious robes and jewels, as in life. I had not been allowed to visit the corpse as she lay in state, and it was my dearest wish to be amongst the ladies in the funeral cortège. I begged my mother and my aunt for leave to join them, but I was judged too short, too slight, too young. So that was the end of that Great Age, the reign of Queen Elizabeth. It was 1603 and I was but thirteen years of age. I felt then that my life was over before it had begun.

A new court came in, with proud King James; a Scottish king to rule the English. Mother and I went at once to pay our respects. How bitter it was to reflect that when the old Queen was alive, we were allowed to sail in state down the Thames and moor our barge at the Privy Stairs, the private royal entrance. Now we had to enter like strangers, on foot through the Holbein

Gate. We were admitted by an unshaven guard who grunted and barked at us, then had the nerve to demand a shilling.

To my young eyes the court that day resembled a farmyard, heaving with bodies and stinking of sweat and ambition. The Gallery was packed with flouncing lords and braying courtiers, all eager to be noticed, while James sat smirking on his throne like a fat tomcat. We waited in line, curtsied when the time came, and were swiftly ushered out with the other women, into the new Queen's apartments. There we saw Anne of Denmark, enthroned with her ladies. She nodded as we entered, but then her eyes slid off us and she turned back to her companions. Mother and I were, it seemed, of little consequence.

"It is well known," whispered Mother bitterly, "that the King will have only men around him. The new Queen will have her own people, come down from Scotland with her. There is nothing here for us now. We shall have to rely upon your father for our places at court."

That was fourteen years ago, a different world, before my troubles really began.

When we got home that day from our royal visit, we found ourselves to be covered in fleas.

But back to the present; we follow the capering page boy through a door and find ourselves in a set of opulent rooms, a private apartment. My husband frowns in recognition.

"By Our Lady, is this not the chamber of Lord Buckingham? Have you brought us the right way, boy?" He turns to me. "I was in here only last week playing cards with old George Buckingham. Ha! Lost ten pounds to the knave." My husband's gambling debts do not bear scrutiny. He says it is the price of influence in the right places, that you need to know how to lose, and to whom. I prefer not to argue with him. It is his fortune he is spending.

For some reason I do not understand, the page's smooth face flushes as he bites his lip and looks at the floor. "Indeed, my Lord. Yes, these rooms are Lord Buckingham's lodgings. Please wait here. I shall return presently."

The floors are thickly carpeted, like walking on clouds, soft and silent. Fat-bellied turkey-work cushions on every chair, matching curtains in weighty tasselled folds at the casements. On one wall, an enormous silver-framed mirror flashes and gleams. My reflection startles me; decked out as I am in silk and jewels. I hardly recognise myself.

Portraits of fashionable men gaze down at us, all dressed in the richest fabrics and most exquisite lace. As I scan the gold-framed earls and dukes, one seems to wink at me.

"Good Lord, Richard. What is that doing here? I thought it was on your closet wall?"

Larkin painted my husband in all his finery just four years ago. The likeness, I must admit, is good: the high forehead, a shrewd glint in the eye, the sulky mouth. But the clothes are not to my taste, and I said so when it was first painted. The rectangular lace collar is so broad and stiff that my Lord's head resembles a ceremonial boar's, served up on a tray. The silk doublet is over-embellished with intricate embroidery, the breeches impossibly voluminous, the fur-lined cloak slung awkwardly over one shoulder. Most remarkably, he is wearing tight, embroidered silk hose to exaggerate a calf that was never that shapely in life, and garters slung with pom poms the size of melons. His Spanish leather shoes have red high heels and tassels like peony flowers. One foot is turned out like a dancer to show the shoes to best advantage. A ridiculous pose. It makes him look like a pouting whore.

"You said you didn't like it."

"True."

"Well, George said it was magnificent. The finest work, he said, a wonderful likeness. So, I lent it to him. Any objections?"

I turn away. "My feet hurt."

I told my maid I wanted to look my best today, to impress His Majesty and show that I am not a woman to be trifled with. She has duly twisted and pinned my hair into an elaborate headdress, dripping with pearls. A delicate lace ruff sits like a gossamer cloud around my face. But the stays beneath my grosgrain dress are too tight, and I am not used to wearing slippers with such pointed toes.

"Try sitting down."

I find a seat by the window and gaze out at the grey afternoon. The windows on this side look out over the Privy Garden. Even in wintertime, it manages to look beautiful, like a vast black-and-white chequerboard. The gravel paths are raked and rolled, the limes pleached and trimmed, not a leaf out of place. The square plats are empty now of flowers and herbs, but the gardeners have turned over every inch of the rich brown soil and clipped the edgings into neat lines. Flurries of sleety snow are blowing in the wind like the ghosts of apple blossom.

"Have you rehearsed your lines? I do hope you will be gracious, my dear."

"The King has kindly offered to assist me in resolving my business. I am mindful of his kindness to us, and I will not risk any disgrace, if that is what you mean. But you must know how things stand with me."

My husband snorts. "Don't be stubborn, Anne, it is a dangerous game. You know as well as I do that when your father left his lands to his brother rather than to some hare-brained girl, he was acting in everybody's best interests. His farm managers, his tenants and, yes, his family."

I speak quietly, for fear of provoking him, for fear of being overheard by someone else. The walls here have ears. "I was never hare-brained, do not say so. The law states, as you well know, that the Clifford lands of Westmoreland and Craven, together with their five castles, should pass at his death to Lord Clifford's heir, be they male or female. King Edward II himself so decreed. When Father passed away, I was his only surviving child. The lands should have passed directly to me. It was my mother's contention, as it is mine, that by bequeathing his property to his brother, my uncle, my father's last will and testament was unlawful."

"…and you have been nagging and scolding about it ever since the poor man died. Surely, you must see that such a vast and wild estate is no place for a woman. Picture it, Anne. Those impossible mountains, cliffs, crags. Steep and rocky roads which no coach can pass, where the very horses lose their footing. Miles and miles of desolate moorland fit only for wolves and wild goats. You forget, madam, I have been there myself. I have seen it."

"And you forget, My Lord, that I was born there. It is my home."

My husband frowns and shakes his head and the tone changes; not angry now, more beseeching. "But your dowry, Anne. Your uncle still holds at least fifteen thousand pounds in your name and will not release it while you are in this… mind."

Yes, my husband would surely be glad to get his hands on my fifteen thousand, as would his creditors. Perhaps that is why we are here. What has he said to the King? What is already agreed between them? Perhaps this is a waste of time, my cause already lost. I must be steadfast. I must not give up hope. I turn away again. A flock of starlings has descended on the herbal bed and is pecking around the trimmed stumps of the rosemary bushes. They squawk and chatter like courtiers.

Pounding footsteps grow nearer. The page has come back for us.

"The King will see you now."

He pushes past my husband and reaches up to the rail of a woven hanging. A languid Narcissus gazes at his reflection in the pool of water. The page tugs the tapestry to one side, revealing a door. He opens it with a flourish and stands by, waving us through.

"Lord and Lady Sackville, Your Majesty."

"Through here?" So, Lord Buckingham's rooms directly adjoin those of His Majesty, it seems. I had heard rumours the two men were close companions, but this…?

We are admitted to the Presence Chamber.

The King is alone at the far end of the chamber, on an immense throne that makes him look small, like a child whose feet barely touch the floor. He holds out a limp hand and we both kneel and kiss the air above his knuckles. Even after all these years, the farmyard smell surrounding him is familiar. I remember that first visit with Mother, the odours of unwashed bodies and unclean linen, the sour tang of spirits drunk too early in the day. The throne is worn and chipped, the carpet beneath my knees stained and worn. I worry again about fleas.

"Well sit down, Sackville. Don't stand on ceremony, what?" The King smiles at Richard, a familiar smile. Complicit. A cold chill grips my heart. *Men cause guilty men to rise.* We sit down next to King James and a footman brings a tray.

"Water of Life, Sackville. That's what my countrymen call this. Gladdens the heart."

Two glasses brimming with whisky.

The King passes one to my husband, raises his own glass and declares, "To life! And to Hell with our enemies!" My husband laughingly repeats the toast, and the two men drink deep.

"Ha! Now what would my lady like? An elderflower cordial perhaps? Syrup of mulberries?"

"My wife drinks only bitter herbs, Sire, steeped in the juice of lemons."

"What? Oh, a jest! Yes, yes. Very good, Sackville."

They slam the empty glasses down on the tray and the King wipes his mouth with the back of his hand.

He turns at last to me. "My Lady Sackville, now what is this we hear from your uncle Lord Cumberland? He tells us you would have the coat off his back. Surely you would not be so unkind?" His voice has become high, soft, lisping, as one might speak to a baby, a lap dog.

"Indeed not, Your Majesty. Rather the other way around. The new Earl of Cumberland is in possession of property which is rightfully mine." I begin to tell him about the entail begun by King Edward, the illegal will, the withheld dowry. But even as I am speaking, I have the impression that my words are turning into soap bubbles, blown away on the breeze. My voice is the faint tinkle of a spoon in a cup, heard by nobody.

"Come, Madam. Can you not allow this technicality to pass? We are sure Cumberland would be relieved to have all settled, and to hand over your dowry money as he must surely have promised poor Clifford, your father. And what, pray, would a fashionable young lady such as yourself do with a few ruined castles and acres of blasted heath?"

I take a deep breath and look the King in the eye. "Sire, you must understand that I will never give up my claim to my lands in Westmoreland. There are no circumstances, no arguments, no inducements that would persuade me. I came here—"

A crash. The sound of breaking glass.

The king has flipped the tray with his fist and sent the empty glasses flying across the room. Red-faced, he leaps to his feet and points an accusing finger at me. "You came here…" he bellows, "You came here to play upon my good nature…"

Confused, I stand too. Is the audience over already? My husband is squeaking in fear like a cornered mouse, pulling at my sleeve. "Anne, please…"

The King turns away from us and roars to the room in general, "Get her out of here before I say something we shall both regret!" A guard steps forward, drawing his sword. "Take her to the Queen. Perhaps she can make her see sense. No, Sackville, you stay here, man. We still have much to say on this matter."

The guard seizes me by the elbow and propels me out of the presence chamber, alone. The door slams and I am marched down the grand stairs and back into the cold, labyrinthine depths of the palace. As I am thus forcibly escorted through chambers and halls, the people we meet fall silent and melt away, courtiers and servants alike. No-one speaks to me, looks at me. I am invisible, passing through deserted rooms. My tight little shoes patter across bare wooden floors as the guard's boots drum like a march to the scaffold.

Up another short flight of stairs to a doorway flanked by pikemen in helmets. The guard lets go of my arm and opens the door for me. "Your Majesty, this is Lady Sackville."

A cosy little room hung in shades of rose and burgundy. Lavender and woodsmoke. To my surprise, the Queen rises to greet me. She towers over me, a tall, commanding figure.

"Ah, at last. My little namesake! Come in, Anne Clifford, and welcome." She takes my hands and kisses me on both cheeks before going back to her chair by the fire, motions for me to sit opposite. She is dressed in cloth-of-silver and frothing lace. A pearl the size of a quail's egg dangles from her ear and her hair is piled high, surmounted with gold chains and rubies. She is only forty-four years of age, a woman in her middle years. And yet, I think, she already looks old, worn out. The low-cut fashion of her gown does not flatter the heavy, pendulous breasts. The long, solemn face is careworn and pale.

"Your Majesty…" I begin, but she raises a hand to silence me.

"It is peaceful in here, is it not? That intimate feeling when one is among friends. Will you take some Rhenish?" She hands me a tiny glass on a long stem, engraved with vine leaves. The syrupy white wine, fragrant with spices, warms my heart. I sink deeper into the soft cushions.

"I gather there is some dispute about your inheritance. They tell me your father's will left Craven and Westmoreland to your uncle when it was rightfully yours."

I nod. "The king has offered to help me. That is why I am here today."

"I know." She takes a sip of wine. "But what you don't understand, Anne, is that my husband is not to be trusted in this. He has no intention to help an upstart woman – yes, he called you that – but to do everything in his power to assist both your husband and your uncle to get, and to keep, the fortune to which you are entitled. He will come to an agreement whereby your uncle will hand over your dowry into Sackville's hands. Wives do not own property in this country, not in their own right. Men help men, and they help themselves." She smiles and leans towards me. "I wanted to tell you a story, Anne, which I hope you will find instructive. You see, I was married to the King when I was only a girl of fifteen. A match arranged by my parents, patently. James was kind, gracious, undemanding. I had no complaints. When I gave birth to our first child, and it was a boy, an heir to the Scottish throne, James and I were both delighted. I remember sitting in bed, cradling this beautiful baby in my arms, thinking that I was the happiest woman in the world. We christened him Henry. His baptism was in Stirling Castle, accompanied by great pomp and ceremony. There was music, dancing, a wondrous masque in celebration of the new prince.

But then everything changed. James had the baby taken from me, and given to his old nurse to look after. They kept my baby at Stirling, locked away from me, while James and I had to return to Holyrood. Reasons of security, they said. Tradition. The heir to the throne must be kept safe and separate from the king, while of course, the queen's place is by the king's side."

The poor woman has tears in her eyes. "You have children, Anne. You can imagine the agony of separation I endured. I pleaded, I wept, I denounced the king as a heartless villain. But it made no difference. I was to stay at Holyrood, while my poor sweet baby was locked away in Stirling being raised by strangers. I fought with James for months, publicly and in private. But it was all wasted effort."

"So, what did you do?"

"I came to my senses. All my hot words, my tears, my storming rage, it was all for nothing. In the end, I knew there was only one way. I had to bite my tongue, bide my time and wait for the tide to turn. Every night I prayed that my son might be restored to me."

"You never gave up?"

The queen shakes her head. "No, I never gave up. If a woman is to gain her heart's desire in the face of opposition, she must learn to play the long game.

At last, the good Lord took pity on me. When poor old Queen Elizabeth died, my husband legally became King of England. He needed to secure the throne as quickly as he could. While he and the court raced down to London. I seized my opportunity and hastened to Stirling. After nine years of bitter separation, I was reunited with dear Henry, and never again did I allow us to be apart. He is here with us now, in the palace. I remained firm to my purpose, Anne. And in the end, I triumphed." She refills my glass and raises hers. "Shall we drink a toast?"

"To what shall we drink, Your Majesty?"

"Why, to stubborn women, Anne. May they dig in their heels, dismiss their opponents, persevere, endure, persist."

"Ha. Yes, I see." I raise my glass. "To stubborn women."

Brougham Castle, Westmoreland 22nd March 1676

And that is how I eventually triumphed. Much to the disdain of the King and the increasing desperation of my spendthrift husband, I refused to back down.

Time became my friend.

In 1643, when I was an old woman of fifty-three, I finally inherited the lands and properties that had been mine all along. My uncle Cumberland had died, and his heir died soon after, leaving the field clear for me to claim my inheritance. Brough, Brougham, Skipton, Pendragon, Appleby. Five noble castles with their farms and estates. I have spent the last thirty-three years in stately royal progress from one to the other. The roads, like my life, were treacherous and steep. Sometimes we crossed heights where no carriage had ever gone before. But my companions were loyal and fearless, and I was determined. The properties had been woefully neglected, but once I was in command, I dedicated my life and my fortune to building up walls that were broken down, restoring, repairing, renewing.

Yes, I am eighty-six years old now, I have outlived them all. I have done my duty to man and God; rebuilt the churches on my estates, established alms houses for poor widows. I hope I shall be remembered fondly, for the good work I have done. But most of all, I hope those of you reading this will learn from my experience. We should all heed the advice of good Queen Anne; persevere, endure, persist.

Here's to stubborn women.

Sue Nicholson

Sue has a passion for Art and History. She has published articles and book reviews about Samuel Pepys and translated the diary of French artist Julia Burnand for the book *A Mother's Gifts*. Sue lives in the Yorkshire Dales, and her book of ten Dales tales, *Miracles at Hay Time* will be published in 2025.

Reading

D.J.H. Clifford: "The Diaries of Lady Anne Clifford" Sutton Publishing, Stroud, 1990.
G.C. Williamson: "Lady Anne Clifford" Titus Wilson, Kendal, 1922.
Vita Sackville-West: "Knole and the Sackvilles" Heinemann, London, 1922.

Online

https://www.skiptoncastle.co.uk/access.asp
https://www.english-heritage.org.uk/learn/histories/women-in-history/anne-clifford/
https://historicengland.org.uk/research/inclusive-heritage/womens-history/anne-clifford/

Love Is More Than I Know

He yanks my pigtail. Drips a smile and calls me Shortcake. I don't know this one's name, just know that half-moons of dirt nestle in his fingernails and he drops by on Tuesdays, after Uncle Pete has pedalled off to work. The hallway is dim and airless. He squats on the bottom step and loosens the laces on tired work boots, raining grit on the carpet as he tugs them on. It's threadbare but clean because Aunty dashed the carpet sweeper around first thing while I ate Cornflakes cross-legged in a squish on the sofa. She keeps a clean house. He stands, tucks his T-shirt in his shabby Levi's and shouts, "See ya" up to silence. The front door slams and through the etched petals, I watch his outline loom down the path until it's gone. There's a splatter and gush from upstairs when she cranks the shower to life. She'll go around with the sweeper again before Uncle Pete gets home.

Mama trampled on a tulip the day she walked away. A ragtag bunch in yellow and red had sprung up from the scrub of lawn out front and flopped onto the pathway. I remember the clack of the little wheels of her suitcase as she clunked it over the doorstep. The small, spinning sound as she dragged it over the pavers. A tiny piece of tulip petal got caught in the turn, came loose and fluttered off when the cab driver hoicked her suitcase into the boot and drove away.

Aunty drifts down the stairs, doll-pink lips pouting icy gloss. It is August, sickening heat. The coloured kaftan curtaining her body flaps a glow of scarlet bikini.

"You need sun on your skin," she says, her thumb and forefinger plucking my chin.

In the kitchen, dust-light tumbles through the window when she jerks the blind open and rinses out the mug he had his grubby hands around. I snap on the radio. Agnetha and Frida's glittery vocals sparkle out of the speaker.

"It's your song!" she says.

But she's wrong. It's Mama's song. It's old now but Mama loves it because it was number one when I was born. She had the record, and on good days, she'd slide it from its tatty sleeve and play it over and over and we'd sing along. When it was the two of us. Before we came here. Before everything.

Aunty sings along as she squeezes out the last drop of Hawaiian Tropic and buffs it into her arm like she's chivvying out a stain. She smells all seashells and coconuts, dotting my nose with her oily finger and don't-tell smile. But her voice is scratchy. Not like Mama's. Mama can hit the high notes like Agnetha and she's just as beautiful. Butter-coloured hair hanging at the corners of her face. Around her eyes.

The bottle, dented empty, dings in the metal drainer as it falls. Aunty is on her hands and knees, rooting around for baby oil in the cupboard under the sink where she keeps the dishcloths and the dustpan. She curses when she elbows over her secret money tin. The one she's saving for a rainy day. Agnetha and Frida are still singing about goodbyes and what means forever while Aunty crawls and reaches and scoops up the coins shimmying across the lino.

At first, I counted days. A bead a day dropped in a jar to make a rainbow reaching out to Mama. May as well count moonbeams, Aunty says, because Uncle Pete will never say no to his big sister. No point crying. And she's right. At night, I bite back tears. Picture myself in Mama's eyes, feeling her hands warm on my cheeks and her face bright; bright, but rainbow-far away. I love you more than you know, she used to say.

The beaded curtain strung across the kitchen door sounds like rain. Aunty says it stops the flies. In the backyard, sudden heat stings my feet and eyes. She clicks to the shed in studded mules. I hold the door open while she drags out a lounger laced with cobwebs. Its rusty springs creak open to a patterned bed of flat-face sunflowers and oxeye daisies. She beats the fabric, drumming fickle clouds of dust into the air.

"You need some sun," she says, letting the kaftan fall from her shoulders to a silky pool on a jagged slab. She eases onto the lounger and stretches her shiny legs out straight. Sighs. Lifts her face to the sun. "Why don't you go play?"

There's nothing to play. When we first came, I'd take a tennis ball to the wall around the maisonettes and play sevensies. But the ball got raggy, lost its bounce and I can't ask for a new one. And playing like that made me miss Heidi even more. We played everything, Heidi and me. Heidi Hart, my best friend. A true artist, preferring colouring pencils to those fruit-smelling felt tips that the girls whose mothers stand in the playground chatting at pick-up all have. Heidi has her own pencil set that she keeps in a smooth, oblong tin, each one sharpened to a careful, tender point. She always let me share them when it rained and the playground was too full of puddles to go outside. She taught me to draw and plait my pigtails myself. I miss sitting up close beside her, in our old classroom with the rain coming down. The soft scoring sound her light strokes made on the page.

When all the tulips withered and there was no word from Mama, Uncle Pete said I had missed enough school. Aunty filed her nails faster and wondered what he was thinking. Hardly worth it for the last few weeks of the year. But Uncle Pete said I'm going places. Not like him. And not like Mama.

Miss Sweeney likes indoor voices. She has a wintry face but underneath the shapeless dresses, her body looks soft. Her sleeves stop at the dimples on her elbows. She sat me next to Tansy Cotes from the flats. Tansy is tall with skinny fingers. Her dad is too. I've seen him staggering around the estate. He disappears for days then comes back, dishevelled, like peonies after a blast of spring rain. All the kids say not to play with Tansy. She hangs around the alleys behind the terraced houses and for ten pence, she shows the boys from St. Bernard's her knickers. I've watched those boys ride around on Raleigh Choppers, heard them hoon and whistle like a whorl of red kites circling. Kisses are fifty.

My middle grumbles for lunch but Aunty's not moving. Wallflowers scrawl up the wooden fence where the sun hits. Paint blisters. Summer thrums in the alleyway where watchful footsteps make their way to our gate. Tansy.

"Want to get an ice cream?" she says, toeing a stone. She swings on the gate, eyes me to the alley. Holds up a coin. "I'll pay." It shimmers as she threads it through her skinny fingers.

Aunty is sleeping. Her eyes are petal-soft closed. Clouds shift across the sun, and the sky turns the exact colour of a secret. Tansy unravels my pigtails.

I don't know their names.

All summer, coins fall in my tin like rain.

Leanne Simmons (For Leanne's biography see page 243).

Right Choices

The opulence was startling. White marble steps led to a podium where a mahogany desk stretched along the width of the room, and the polished floor reflected two flags: one with scythe and hammer, one with the emblem of the Republic. Red velvet curtains were draped alongside the portraits of Lenin and Husak with the slogan *Labour be honoured* in gold lettering. The sound of documents being handled echoed in the vast space. The clerical silence was interrupted by chanting from the street below.

"Can somebody close the window?" the judge said, waving his gavel at the baroque sash.

The court clerk hurried to comply with the order.

"Continue, Comrade Belinsky,"

"I have nothing more to say." Belinsky's voice resonated in the courtroom. He stood straight with his shoulders pulled back. "You've heard it from those outside and read it in the Manifesto. We demand democratic general elections, release of all political prisoners and freedom of speech. Forty thousand people signed the petition. What are you going to do with *them*?" He pointed at the closed window.

"That's beside the point. You are here to defend yourself against charges of antisocialist instigations. If you have nothing more to say for your defence, I'll call the first witness."

Belinsky frowned and sat down.

Julia straightened her skirt and tucked a strand of hair behind her ear. Her heart was pumping fast. She glanced across the room at Belinsky. He'd lost weight. He didn't look as she remembered. He'd become gaunt and pale, and his shirt hung loose over his shoulders.

The prosecutor, sitting in an armchair next to the judge, sprung from his seat.

"Comrade Dvorska, how did you meet Comrade Belinsky?". He was a short, round man with a greasy moustache. He faced the auditorium, enjoying the sound of his voice like an actor during his first act.

"He is a friend."

"A friend! I see," he crept towards her. "And were you aware that your friend is an agent of imperialism?" His bulging eyes were almost touching Julia's face.

"Yes," she said in a low voice.

"You were!" The round figure turned and walked to the other side of the room, leaving the smell of raw onions behind. "Did you, Miss Dvorska, transcribe one hundred and fifty copies of that antisocialist propaganda?" he continued. "The handwriting is yours, isn't it?"

Julia didn't have to come closer to recognise the transcript of the Manifesto lying on the judge's table. By the time she finished the last copy, she could recite its entire content.

"Objection! This point is not part of the investigation," Belinsky's solicitor shouted.

"I shall rephrase the question," the prosecutor continued. "Were you involved in distributing these samizdats amongst university students?"

"No."

"Was it the defendant who distributed them and gathered signatures for the petition?"

Julia's hands convulsed around the sides of the witness box. She closed her eyes.

"Yes."

"Were you aware that information in the pamphlet instigated oppositional political activity?"

"Yes."

"I have no further questions," the prosecutor said.

Before Julia sat down, she scanned through the witness bench to find her dad.

Julia's father was the director of a wood factory in the town. After three years of proving himself politically mature and ideologically faithful, he was voted in as a member of the Communist Party. On the day he had received his red passport, leather-bound with the Party's logo on it, he came home with a bottle of Sampanske.

"Maruska, I made it! I am in!" he'd said to Julia's mother. "All doors are opened for us now."

When Julia and her brother came back from school, the whole family jumped into the car and drove to National House – the best restaurant in town, where other Party-ists would take their families for special occasions. They spent holidays in High Tatras in one of the Party's recreational centres that summer, and Julia's mother was delighted to shop in Tuzex, using complimentary vouchers Dvorsky had received for his contribution to socialism.

Over a Sunday lunch, he used to talk about his upbringing in Orava - the part of Slovakia where even potatoes struggle to grow. His childhood stories were about hardship, and they often turned into lectures on the importance of making the right choices in life. Julia would listen whilst blowing into a steaming soup, watching liver dumplings sapping the grease from the meat, navigating homemade noodles around the carrots poking through like traffic cones. Dvorsky spoke in a soft accent. Julia had never known him to raise his voice, except for a few years later, when she admitted to seeing Ed Belinsky.

They used to meet in a flat that belonged to Belinsky's friend Rudolf. Rudolf's grandparents lived in the same village as Ed's, a few kilometres outside of the town. The boys spent summers catching frogs, dissecting long worms and doing things boys do during their school holidays. They made a promise to study medicine together after college. Ed was rejected as 'a morally and politically unsuitable candidate', but Rudolf was admitted to university in Prague. His parents moved away, and the city apartment was empty.

The flat was in the basement of the brown, pebble-dashed building from before the war, with oval balconies and Crittall windows. The musty smell lingered inside the thick walls and seeped into every piece of furniture and clothing. The electricity stayed connected to a communal supply and when Ed found an old electric heater in a skip, the flat became their hideaway. Julia spent time lying on the sofa dreaming out their future whilst Ed would write pamphlets for the underground movement meetings. She'd talked about a house in the countryside with an apple orchard and a big kitchen where she would make jams and stacks of pancakes for the little ones and wait for Ed to come home from his doctor's rounds.

"They'll never allow me to go to university," he'd say. "Not until the regime changes."

When summer arrived, they would take a bus to Devin and walk around the castle ruins. The air would tremble from the heat and smell of wild thyme that grew on the rocks. They would rub the tiny purple flowers between their fingers and chase each other around, like lovers do, comparing lengths of daisy chains, laughing. Then they'd eat a cake Julia had brought and watch the border patrol on the other side of the riverbank.

"Would you do it?" she'd asked.

"Yes."

At the narrowest part where the river bent, it was no more than fifty meters. The current was slow, and the water was at its deepest, providing shelter from binoculars and bullets.

"Remember that guy from number thirty-three?" she said, and laid her head on his shoulder, wrapping her arms around him.

"The one who got shot? Loser. I'd be careful," he said.

"And what about me?"

"You'll be fine here. You've got your daddy."

Julia watched her father take the witness stand. The Party's badge pinned onto the lapel of his blue suit. He'd put it on for the occasion. She twitched.

"Comrade Dvorsky." The state prosecutor started the questioning. "What can you tell us about the defendant?" His smile synthetic, and wider than Russian railway tracks.

"I've known Ed Belinsky his entire life," Dvorsky said, "His family live in the same block of flats."

The little man pointed his finger up in the air, turned on his heels and marched to the other side of the podium.

"I see. And would you say that the defendant is of good character?"

"I believe he didn't make the right choices in life," he said.

Julia shivered.

"Can you be more specific, Comrade Dvorsky?" He smiled again.

"Ed Belinsky's father is a political dissident. His son seems to take after him."

"We know about his father. Can you support your claim with regards to his son?" he asked, a trace of irritation in his voice.

"He was influenced by his father from an early age. I had my own doings with that man. He is a dangerous international adventurer!"

Julia remembered Ed's dad. She shared the elevator with him a few times when she was little. He would pretend he didn't know which floor was hers and ask her to point out the right number. "That one, at the top!" she'd said, reaching for number eight on her tippytoes.

He'd pressed the button for her, saying, "A few more bowls of spinach, and you'll be there!" He carried a briefcase like her dad's, but Ed's dad's was full of beer bottles. She could hear them clinking when the lift shuddered and he stepped onto the third floor. He was a historian before they made him work in a recycling plant.

The prosecutor continued with the questioning, but Julia didn't listen. The fat little man was in his element, prancing like a ringmaster around a manège, showcasing his well-rehearsed number. The witnesses and the lawyers, like tamed animals, lured into his circus, performed as required. She stared at the window. Framed like a modernist painting, there was a picture of freedom. It had been a goal to conquer, to reach that sky, since the beginning of time. It had the colour of hope and desperation, the same colour as Ed's eyes.

Julia's parents' flat was on the top floor of the concrete block, built the year Julia was born. The flats were allocated on a first come first served basis to young families, or those willing to swap their houses in the country for city living, to be close to their grandchildren. No money had ever changed hands in property transactions, and the system guaranteed a demographic cocktail of residents. Doctors, crane operators, university professors and factory workers, all shared the same lift and endured snow-clearing duties during winter.

Julia and her brother shared the biggest of the three rooms in the apartment, divided in two by stacks of flat-packed furniture. At bedtime, when the lights went off, the children whispered tales of the school day across the Lego wall. Julia spoke about Ed. That boy from the third floor who never talked much was her classmate. They walked to and from school together, and when the teacher discovered they were neighbours, they sat at the same desk. Ed introduced Julia to chess and Julia showed him how to play table tennis. By the time Ed's voice dropped and Julia bought her first mascara, they'd tried their first cigarette and shared a kiss.

Julia loved school and her aspirations to become a member of the Socialist Youth Union made her dad proud. Ed had a vision. He memorised the Hippocratic Oath and knew the Latin name of any bone in the human body. During weekends, they would go for walks around the city and Ed would be relentless about Louis Pasteur and the importance of his discoveries. When he started private English lessons and impressed Julia by saying, *My name is Ed*, Julia begged her dad to pay for language school for her.

"English? Darling, you don't need to speak English. You can go to any university you want without it," he'd said.

She picked Economics and Foreign Trade. Five thousand students applied for one hundred places on the course. The head of the faculty was a fellow comrade from the Party, and the admission was a matter of filling in an application form.

The two families didn't socialise, apart from the obligatory Easter Monday visits, when men would knock on neighbours' doors in their block, pour water over women in the family and receive an Easter egg for it. A tradition accompanied by copious amounts of plum brandy and ham rolls filled with potato salad. This was the way to maintain neighbourhood relationships. The merriments lasted from early morning to late afternoon. By that time, sixteen heads of families would have each enjoyed fifteen shots. Laughter and screams were heard around the communal area where the residents exchanged their experiences of the day, formed new comradeships, and strengthened established unions, all accompanied by more refreshments. With more shots being toppled, the revellers lost their inhibitions, and their true opinions on politics and life in general emerged. Julia's father was a regular participant in these conversations, and he would return to their flat shouting, "I hate that man! Belinsky! He is nothing more than a subverter! I will show him who is in charge! No one will question my choices! He'll pay for this… he'll cry!"

Julia's mother would help him to bed whilst he'd shout more drunken threats. The following morning, he couldn't remember anything that had happened.

"Julia Dvorska, can you please answer the question?"

"I am sorry, I didn't hear it," she said.

"I asked if you could recount the events that led to Comrade Belinsky's arrest," the prosecutor said.

"Yes, I can."

She had been thinking about that day ever since it was over. Like every Sunday, they'd spent the afternoon in the flat. She hadn't arrived at the agreed time. Ed didn't suspect anything but he did question her lateness.

"The lunch took forever," she said, brushing him off. She sat down to the task. A pile of samizdats she had already transcribed was towering on the desk, with the original pages of the Manifesto pinned to the wall above. Ed was absorbed in lining up the pages for the petition, leaning against velvet cushions on the pea-green sofa.

"What did you have?" he asked.

"What?"

"What did you have? For lunch."

"Oh, the usual. Chicken soup with liver dumplings and schnitzels. I was sent to shop for breadcrumbs. That's why I'm late," she added.

The flat was poorly lit. The only window in the room was obscured by the meaty leaves of a chestnut tree growing in front of it. They kept the main light off, and Julia strained her eyes under a small table lamp placed between Ed and herself. They worked in silence, with no radio on and when they spoke, they kept their voices low. Ed believed that if enough people signed the petition, it could bring down the Communists and establish a democratic Government. He rarely spoke about anything else. He was growing a beard and it suited him. His black curly hair was too long, falling in his eyes, and he puffed it away and tossed his head to one side. He looked up from his work when he felt her stare. He smiled. There was the boy who taught her to play chess.

"Don't cry, baby, what's up?"

"It's nothing. I'm just being silly," Julia said, and wiped her tears with the cuff of her cardigan.

They didn't make love that evening, and when Julia finished the last copy of the Manifesto, Ed stowed the pile into his rucksack, ready for the following day. They walked home holding hands, the warm summer night embracing them in their silence. They passed by the metal recycling plant where Ed's dad worked. Once a professor at the university, he was commissioned to write chronicles of the Communist Party. Seduced by the opportunity to pour out his dislike for the ideology, the book was considered demagogic and flawed. He was dismissed, and Ed's university application rejected.

That night, lying in her bed with her eyes open, the sense of righteousness that usually warmed her stomach was no longer there. A new feeling snaked around, thrusting out the innocence, the value of truth, the purpose of freedom and all those virtues we read about in children's books. It was time to grow up. Time to make a choice.

"Stop tossing around," her brother whispered from behind the makeshift partition wall.

"I can't sleep."

"Why?"

"I think I need to break up with Ed."

"Uh. Why?"

"I don't think he loves me. All he ever talks about is his bloody petition!"

"Oh well, Dad will be glad."

She smiled at the furniture standing between her and Juraj. The structure had long lost its newness and was tattered, with cabinet doors stooping off the loose hinges. But it was there, solid and familiar.

"Good night," Julia said. The events of the day faded into a dozy mist and her last thought before she fell asleep was of her father and his perpetual lecture on choices in life. Choices you make, and choices you must live with.

The Police Station wasn't far. She walked fast, passing by her university and the stadium where members of the Socialist

Youth Organisation, all dressed in their blue uniforms with red handkerchiefs around their necks, practised their routine for Labour Day manifestation. Julia checked behind her left and right shoulder before she entered the building. Her steps sounded too loud on the staircase, like a gavel in the courtroom ordering silence. She stopped halfway to catch her breath and looked down at the revolving doors, the usual conveyor belt of complainers, collaborators and informers, now absent on a Sunday.

A TV in the corner of the reception room was on. Ice hockey. The duty police officer was dipping a bread roll into the plastic pot of cod with mayo, chewing loudly. He glanced at Julia.

"What is it, young lady?" he said with his mouth full, not turning his eyes away from the match. "Did you lose your house key?" he giggled.

"I'd like to report a criminal activity," she said.

"Yeah right," he took another bite from the bread roll, picked up a pen that was attached by a cord to the table and brushed off the crumbs from the logbook. A piece of mayonnaisey pickle was stuck on his grey moustache.

"What's ya name?"

"Julia Dvorska," she said.

"Ah! Old Dvorsky's daughter?" he said, raising his eyebrows.

"Yes. That's right," she replied.

"Uhm. Wait there. I'll get somebody."

Julia sat on the wooden chair by the TV. It was nearly the end of the second third. One nil to Czechoslovakia.

The interrogating officer was a balding man with protruding cheekbones. Julia heard herself talking. Her mouth was dry and the clicking sound of the typewriter pierced her head.

"Well Comrade Dvorska, you've made the right choice," the officer said. "In these trying times, it is all about choices, isn't it?"

They thanked her for fulfilling her citizen duties and conducting herself in the spirit of a member of the Socialist Youth Union.

She ran back home, picking up a bag of breadcrumbs on her way.

Katarina Wilmot

Katarina is a translator by trade who writes songs, poetry and fiction. She draws inspiration from her time in the Slovak mountains where she grew up, and compares it to her life in the south of England, which has been her home for nearly 25 years. She is currently working on a collection of short stories.

Snow Death
(A dark prologue to a beloved fairy tale.)

Josephine was not thrilled at being married off to a widower twenty years older than her father who had a daughter not even ten years her junior. Nevertheless, she agreed to the marriage.

On the wedding day, Josephine donned a rosy gown embroidered with golden flowers. Her groom was clad in an azure mantle exalting his still fiery red mane. And his daughter, acting as ringbearer, wore a white ruffled dress rivaling her snow-pale skin and enhancing the stunning contrast with her blood-red lips and tar-black hair. With their signatures, the couple secured a military defense for the prosperous country of Leona, and economic relief for the poor people of Helmware who had suffered at the hands of famines and plagues for the last seven years.

Josephine's duty towards her homeland was also to birth a baby boy for the King of Helmware, blood ties being the most efficient way to ensure that in the future, Leona could always count on Helmware's military troops to come to its aid.

However, disregarding her expectations, the King did not force himself on her on their wedding night, nor any of the following nights. On one hand, Josephine was relieved, but on the other, dread began to grow in her heart. What if the old king passed away before he impregnated her?

Since the King seemed to be too grief-ridden, to welcome a new woman into his chamber, Josephine decided to pursue the only other possibility she could see to keep Leona safe in the future. She had to make the King's daughter, Snowdrop, fall in love with that land. To win over the girl's heart, Josephine spent as much time as possible with Snowdrop.

They often took a carriage to the grey port of Helmware to marvel at the parade of brightly painted vessels flying Leonas's gold-rimmed flag.

"Each of those merchant ships mimics the colors of its hull and sails after the plumage of one of the many colorful birds that populate Leona's skies," Josephine explained one day.

"Do you really have birds that are blue and red and yellow and pink and, oh so many colors?!" The young girl's eyes darted between Josephine sitting in front of her and the ships visible from the carriage window.

"Yes, we do. Leona is filled with lush vegetation harboring multiple kinds of birds, furry animals, and lizards. Even on our sandy beaches, you can always spot some sea critters scurrying here and there. Wherever you look is green, and blue, and every other color you can imagine."

Snowdrop begged to visit the marvelous realm so different from her own.

Ecstatic with the princess's interest in her homeland, Josephine petitioned the King who regretfully could not foresee any royal visit to the allied realm in the near future. Without losing heart, Josephine wrote home requesting a special cargo of livestock and potted plants to create a greenhouse representing the best of Leona to keep Snowdrop's interest alive until the day a visit would be possible, or a male heir born from the union.

The greenhouse was built in record time as Josephine's parents not only sent plants and animals but also expert gardeners, animal caretakers, and glass blowers. It stood between the castle's walls to allow the royal family to visit it at leisure, and indeed so they did. Josephine, feeling at her best when between the familiar fauna and flora, often invited the King to stroll with her or have picnics together. The thriving vegetation, chirping birds, and lively animals inhabiting the structure brought back the love for life in the King and began to mend his broken heart. Seeing such improvement, Josephine imagined that soon the King could grace her with access to his chambers and therefore an heir, hopefully a male one. Nevertheless, she continued to spend time with Snowdrop.

Doing so, Josephine noticed strange things happening around the girl. Flowers wilted in her proximity, animals recoiled from her, and food rotted on her plate. Josephine found this concerning but, since Snowdrop did not seem to mind at all, she decided not to give it much thought. However, when on the princess's eighth birthday almost every plant and animal in the greenhouse dropped dead, Josephine could no longer ignore the signs and sought advice from her mirror.

The mirror was Josephine's dearest possession. It had belonged to her mother and her mother's mother before. It was a fairy mirror, imbued with knowledge of all things supernatural.

"Tell me, o fair Glass, tell me true! What makes everything wilt and rot in this land?"

"A demon, risen from hell to appease a barren old womb's prayer," the mirror answered.

Josephine was incredulous but she knew the mirror could never lie to its rightful owner. However, she was not one to jump to conclusions. She needed to know more about Snowdrop. And who better to ask if not her father?

One evening, while leisurely strolling through the dried-up gardens of the castle with her husband, Josephine said, "May I ask how it happened that you and your previous queen decided to wait so long before bringing the joy of children's laughter into the castle?"

"It was no choice of ours." The king stopped and turned to look Josephine in the eyes. "My previous wife had been wounded falling from her horse when barely more than a child herself. She healed and was able to regain a normal life, but her womb could have never carried a new life into this world."

"But Snowdrop?"

"Even intercourse was excruciatingly painful for her, and that's why we never attempted it again after our first night as husband and wife. And yet Mary was so eager to have a child of her own. I suggested we raise as ours an orphaned child. She refused. One day her belly began to swell. Nine months later Snowdrop was born. The next spring, blossom season never came. Seeds rotted in the fields before they could germinate, and my wife's health deteriorated. I did not father her. She's the ghost of my late wife's desires."

Genea Piervittori-Vaughn

Spirituality for Sale

From the outside, the place looks like a restaurant. A single-story wooden building with roof trusses covered in long grass; its spiky ends sway with the rising wind, bringing certainty that a tropical storm is on its way. A few stone steps – five or six – rise from underneath meaty green banana leaves onto the veranda, hiding a woman who sits cross-legged on a day bed made from dark stained bamboo. I marvel at the thickness of the wood. Back home, it would grow to the girth of a cocktail straw; this one is as thick as my arm. Flora and fauna are on steroids here. The European *house plants* bloom alongside the jungle path with flowers as big as dinner plates and the coconut trees are the size of wind turbines. Even the mosquitoes look like dangerous animals from a sci-fi series.

I step over a plate made from palm leaves full of yellow flowers sprinkled with grains of uncooked rice. A sweet scent rises from an incense stick stuck into a purple, plum-like fruit. I can't imagine what that thing tastes like. I have been conned by the appearance of food in Asia before; chicken nuggets from dog meat, a rice dish garnished with fried larvae, or a durian – a fruit resembling a Covid emoji sold on the sides of the roads. I bought it from two ladies dressed in traditional white lace costumes with wide, red satin belts around their waists. They waved at me, and I pulled over, thinking they were in danger. I should have known something wasn't right when they giggled as I handed them the money. They couldn't speak much English, just *You like! You like!* They cut it in half and a repulsive odour arose from that devil object, so vile it made my stomach turn. It smelled exactly like vomit on the streets of Manchester on a Saturday night. I left them the money and drove off.

Several rows of sandals and flip–flops are lined up in front of the glass entrance doors. I bend over to undo the laces on my Vans and, balancing on one leg, kick the boots off of my feet. Terrible choice of footwear for the tropics. When I look up, a tall, slender woman stands over me, smiling. She has long blond hair that touches the ground as she bends down with her arms stretched towards me. She is in a loose, floor-length, hessian-coloured dress and is, of course, barefoot.

'Wel-come dear', she says in a soft, fairy-like voice. She accentuates *wel* over *come* whilst *dear* almost disappears into the ether. I put my hands into hers. She squeezes them and locks her pale blue eyes into mine. We stand like that, staring at each other for what seems like too long.

'Thank you.' I blink and smile, but I don't dare to wiggle out of her tight grip. My palms begin to sweat. The intimacy she imposes through that prolonged skin contact is uncomfortable. I count to five and she still holds my hands, staring into my eyes with a smile of the Virgin Mary. I am sure the expression on my face is not like hers, and I worry this realisation has turned my face grotesque. I count to ten and wish the fire alarm would go off. Fifteen. I wonder when this place closes.

'I hope you'll have a beautiful time this evening,' she says, finally.

'Thank you', I reply and copy her Namaste gesture, bowing my head not once, but three times, delighted the standoff is over. Have I been bewitched? Has she uncovered some deep secrets I may be holding?

I follow her into a room where people sit around low tables, cross-legged, on large cushions. Everyone sips a steaming liquid from mini ceramic pots, and I recall overhearing a conversation about a cacao ceremony. For an extra tenner. Pronounced *ka–kao*. The clientele seems predominantly European or Australian, with no natives amongst the cohorts, which I find bizarre, considering cacao is indigenous to this region.

We move to the back of the restaurant, passing the stage with kettle drumming. I glance at a table where an older man wearing an unbuttoned white linen shirt entertains two teenage girls. He is Caucasian but has a tan like someone who has lived in this climate for many years, unlike the girls, who are the fresh pink colour of new graduates at the beginning of their gap year. The man's greying hair is bound into a bun on top of his head. I notice he wears that strange cross with a circle around his neck that is worn by every spiritual person in town. I was told it symbolises a unity between masculine and feminine.

The man and the girls must have finished their hot chocolate, because they are holding hands above the table, eyes closed, their little fingers entwined. Their nostrils tremble as they inhale sharply, and their mouths pout when they exhale. They go *deep*. When one of the girls bursts out laughing, breaking the spiritual circle, her friend throws her a scornful look and apologetically flaps her eyelashes at their male companion.

'There,' says the hostess, pointing to a table, bringing my attention to a group of four women, one of whom stands up and walks towards me.

She is known as Ilumia and, just like her friend, welcomes me with her arms outstretched and a hug that lasts too long.

'My dearest', she says, holding my hand. She introduces me to the group.

'This is my lovely friend, Sarah.' One by one, the ladies announce their names (all have a connotation to nature) and tilt their heads to one side like mechanical dolls. Their eyes are wide open, chins pointing up, lips slightly open, breathing out an ethereal aura. They move with the grace of Tolkien's creatures, but their outward balance makes me feel uncomfortable. I always thought of myself as poised and feminine, but compared to these divine creatures, I am a clumsy, rogue tomboy.

I clear my throat.

'Hi', I say and mimic their smile.

'Ilumia has spoken about you with love and compassion', River says.

Compassion? I ponder her word choice. I only met Ilumia once – last week – buying a coconut at the market. I re-run our conversation in my head, wondering which part of it has given her reason to believe I endure suffering.

'We are all sisters here,' Juno announces.

'Oh, are you?' I scan the group for a family resemblance.

'Not by blood of course,' she adds, noticing my confusion.

'So what brings you to this special town?' Storm interrupts.

'I am a journalist... and a surfer,' I say, wishing I could say something cooler, like a tarot card reader, or a yin yoga teacher; I want to get along with these ladies. 'I want to explore, meet people and ride some waves.' I add.

'Ah! I see… so, you didn't come here to heal?' She looks at me, bewildered.

'Heal what?' I say but immediately regret that, knowing I am about to cause controversy.

Storm turns from me, her eyes fixed on an invisible spot on the floor.

'We all need to heal from something, my dear,' she says when she looks up at me. 'But don't worry. In your own time. When you are ready,' she adds theatrically, reaching to touch my hand.

I pull my hand away. I am offended by her comment. Insinuating I must be troubled, unaware of my conscious inner self, and ignorant to the benefits of spiritual awakening. I stop myself telling her that some of us, after experiencing anguish and pain, have developed a coping mechanism with life, that some have already thrown stuff out of a childhood drawer, and had the strength to sift through it, fold things back again, and firmly shut it. All that without singing *Oh Shiva Shiva* at a Kirtan ceremony.

We sit around a low table, decorated with multicoloured mosaic tiles. The menu, in faux leather binding, is sparse and Westernised. All the dishes are raw. I hesitate between vegan pizza on a coconut base and tacos made of walnuts. Crave a baked fish in a banana leaf.

'This place is quite pricey for Bali, isn't it? I say.

'Oh but it's delicious,' says Storm.

'I am sure it is,' I reply.

'It is not just food, it is medicine. Prepared with love,' she adds, and I wonder how much love must go into grating a carrot to make it five times the price of Nasi Campur from a warrung next door.

When the waitress with brown, almond-shaped eyes comes to take our orders, I ask her to recommend a local beer. She doesn't understand and says she will check with her manager. I feel bad for making an unreasonable demand. She comes back with a purple-tinted bottle that looks like the packaging for a posh ketchup. *Root beer made from rainwater*, I read on the label when I search, in vain, for the alcohol percentage. Oh well.

We order our dishes and talk about the day. River recounts the events at a shamanic course. She talks about it with passion, especially about a Dutch man who studies the Spiritual Perspectives module. He is divorced, recovering from a bitter custody battle with an ex-wife. She says he'll join us in a while to share his experience in person. His story resonates with Storm who has escaped domestic violence and struggled with prescriptive medication abuse all her life. When questioned about my healing experience, I wriggle out of it by asking how long the *sisters* have known each other.

'Oh, we only met the other day at Wom(b)an yoga at The Centre,' Ilumia says.

I am surprised at their willingness to deal their personal trauma cards around a room full of strangers, who are only united by a belief that listening to the sound of an ancient drum in a circle and holding hands will lead you out of your spiritual darkness. I am ashamed to witness their vulnerability. It leaves an unpleasant taste, like having sex on the first date. My initial discomfort and feeling of inadequacy are replaced with pity and worry. I glance towards the table with a man and two teenage girls who are not his daughters. I make an excuse to go outside for a cigarette, mortified at having to admit to such a foul habit amongst people who munch on raw broccoli for a special treat.

The rain arrives with all the drama a tropical storm is known for. At first, the odd drop hits the parched pavement with a thump, in an off-beat rhythm like a jazz trumpet. The tempo accelerates, the waltz becomes a samba, and then the dance breaks into a riot, where the loaded beads shatter on the ground and bounce back into the air, spraying the ankles of passers-by. The water gathers on the hot asphalt filling the potholes and forming a small river that reaches the curb of the pavement. The beeping of scooters ceases and is replaced by the swooshing sound of liquid gushing from the skies.

I remember being caught in a storm on the way home from school with my classmates. We took a detour through the corn fields, eating the raw kernels, which were still soft and sweet. When the rain came, we squatted beneath tall leafy plants, bending them into a shelter. The water ran off our faces, shoulders and knees, making our clothes wet, sticking to our shivering bodies. When the novelty of the survival game wore off, the rescue plan took shape. Being the closest one, my house was picked as a refuge to get warm and have some hot chocolate. My heart sank as the group ran towards my house with anticipation. I was slowing down further and further with each step, for I couldn't think quickly enough about how to prevent exposing my drunk mother to my friends and avoid the social debacle that would inevitably follow.

I sink back into the cushions, close my eyes and listen to the comforting sound of a storm. There is sunshine after rain, rain after sunshine, life is a circle of events good and bad, where the bad has a purpose as a measure of good.

'Have you got a lighter?'

I wake up to a woman dressed in a short tight black dress standing in front of me.

'Yes sure,' I reply, delighted not to be the only one smoking after all.

'Awful weather, isn't it?' she says.

'Refreshing.'

I look curiously at my new companion who, without asking, takes a place next to me on the bamboo sofa. She lights a Red Marlboro and inhales deeply, leaving a lipstick mark on the cigarette. She runs her hand through her short dark hair, straightens the cushions, then finally, when happy with the arrangement, sits back and crosses one leg over the other, leaving her hands on her knees. Her perfectly manicured toenails are the same colour as her lipstick.

'You're new here? You don't strike me as the *type*,' she winks at me and nods towards the Centre, whilst swinging her leg, amused by my apparent misplacement.

'Uhmm… Yeah, I'm missing a *tree of life* tattoo, don't I…'

We both laugh at that joke. She seems interesting and oozes the confidence of an achiever. I bet the linen fairies despise her.

'Where are you from?' she says in a New York accent.

'I live in England now.'

'*Now?* Oh, that sounds interesting,' she says whilst taking a puff.

'Yes, I'm originally from Eastern Europe.' I continue.

The conversation flows around my upbringing in communist Czechoslovakia, and my life in the UK, then turns to more general topics of politics. We discuss the impact of globalisation, life in Europe versus life in Asia, weather changes and snorkelling. I am glad I don't have to listen to mindfulness techniques for opening a third eye chakra.

'Let's order some wine,' she says when I ask her to tell me about herself.

'Wine?'

'Don't tell me you don't drink,' she says and waves at the same waitress who brought me the rainwater brew.

'I don't think they sell alcohol here,' I say.

'Oh come on! If you can become a shaman in three weeks, there is a way to get a bottle of wine. Trust me,' she laughs.

I like her. She says something in Indonesian to the waitress who, contrary to my prediction, brings a bottle of Australian Shiraz. I sip the wine. It tastes delicious. Vivien – that's the woman's name, tells me how she came to the island with her husband ten years ago. He was a property developer, looking for new opportunities. He died in a tragic diving accident in the south of the island. With no family in New York, she decided to stay and continue what he started. I say I admire her courage and willpower to keep going.

'The only way is up,' she says, taking a sip of wine. 'We all have strength inside we need to unlock.'

I say I agree, that in my opinion, the only way to receive help is from within, and that's why I find these spiritual ceremonies bizarre and fake. It forces people to rely on external elements to resolve internal issues. They adopt an image, a persona they believe will empower their ego to cure them, but it only creates distance from their own identity. Doesn't that go against what they preach? They hang on a hope that by taking part in a gong bath séance they will connect with their inner selves. They blame astrological occurrences for failure in their interpersonal communication and rely on taking various plant extracts to find the meaning of life.

'And actually, is it so important to find the meaning of life?' I ask. 'Isn't the answer in simply living it?'

'It's an identity crisis,' Vivien says. 'People have lost the sense of belonging. Communities are virtually non-existent, everyone tries to find their tribe in a society of individuals… this,' she points at the Centre, 'fills the void of absent relationships with partners, parents, children.'

'But is it healthy?'

'Uh… healthy? Western society turned away from their Christian tradition and by doing so, the society lost its moral institution. This is the replacement. Look,' she adds, 'it is certainly better than belonging to a murderous gang. And it pays my bills.' She laughs, and raises her glass.

I realise who I have just clinked with.

'Oh, you didn't realise who I was, did you darling?' Spirituality is in demand. And I have it for sale.'

We drink in silence. She leaves me perplexed. More than ever, I question righteousness, morality and common sense. On one hand, I see attendees of the healing centres indulging in spiritual egocentrism, and becoming insufferable in their patronising mannerisms towards us – the latter-day saints. On the other hand, I see them being exploited by entrepreneurs preying on their vulnerability. Is this a natural progression of our society? Is it a supply and demand mechanism that is feeding this bizarre business? Has capitalism evolved from trading goods into trading psyche?

Vivien is correct in one thing. The concept of the family unit in the Western world has been warped. Men seem to have lost their masculinity for showing their emphatic selves to please women who ultimately find such behaviour unattractive, label men useless, and seek independence by bringing up babies on their own. If the family is the first molecule that builds up the organism of a community and it is corrupt, how can a society grow healthy?

The rain stopped.

'I think I might make a move,' I say and yawn.

'It was nice to meet you,' Vivien says.

I put my helmet on and start the engine. She shouts something after me into the darkness but I don't acknowledge it, change gear, and speed up towards the other side of town.

Katarina Wilmot

Stargazing

"There's no point in having a roof if we're not going to use it," Mom said. "Shooting stars are nature's drive-in."

Dad and I followed her lead, bundled in puffy jackets, wrenching ourselves through my bedroom window onto the sloped roof.

The three of us laid on our backs, shoulder-to-shoulder, staring at the night sky. Mom raised her arm to name the constellations, tracing them with her finger. Her perfume mingled with the cool night air and the petroleum smell of the roof, its rough surface against my scalp. With every glimmer that streaked above us, Mom turned her head toward me and winked—my cue to make a silent wish. I crossed my fingers for extra luck, even though I knew my biggest wish couldn't come true.

Dad made us popcorn and we tossed the kernels into the air, laughing as they landed on our faces, missing our open mouths. They collected on the roof shingles, in Mom's thinning hair spread around her head like a halo. The puffs were like stars, briefly suspended against the night sky before transforming into buttery bites as they fell.

"It's getting late," Dad said, rubbing his hands. "And chilly. Should we call it a night?"

"I'd like to stay," Mom said. The look on her face, in her eyes—Dad couldn't say no.

Dad brought up pillows, scarves, and hats for each of us. He zipped sleeping bags together to make an extra-large blanket. We shared body heat and stories into the night.

When dawn colored the sky, we eased our stiff muscles to life and brushed the remaining popcorn crumbs from our clothes.

The air was thick inside—stifling, warm, with a tinge of sourness. It flipped my stomach, and made me eager to return to the clean, clear air outside.

After Mom's diagnosis, she insisted on throwing a party. *A Celebration of Life* was printed on the invitation, every letter a different, bold color—red, purple, orange, turquoise, fuchsia—with a silver foil confetti background. She insisted on being present if people were going to say nice things about her.

We rented the community center, decorated with balloons and streamers inside, and a canopy with string lights over the patio. There was a photo booth, and a DJ who played music, heavily weighted toward hits from the early aughts, when Mom and Dad were dating. Pink's "Get the Party Started" followed by Bon Jovi's "It's My Life" got the ball rolling. Mom and her best friend Carol sang along with NSYNC's "Bye Bye Bye", and others joined in. Even my friends and I sang along, embarrassed to admit we knew the words.

Family I'd never met were there. People from Mom's college days, coworkers, neighbors and friends, and seemingly all the people Mom and Dad had collected throughout their life came to celebrate. A projector showed pictures of Mom from childhood to the present, rotating on a loop. Those watching exclaimed when they saw themselves:

"I remember that!"

"Oh my gosh, they look just the same!"

"Right after this shot was taken…"

If Mom noticed someone getting teary-eyed, she gave them a long hug and brought them to the dance floor.

"I don't have time for grief—you've gotta dance that shit out!"

Ricky Martin's "She Bangs" poured out of the double doors. People and food were everywhere as the day shifted into the evening. Mom's boss brought his smoker, and several men gathered around it, fussing over chicken legs and sausages as smoke wafted overhead.

"She always loved a clear sky at night," someone said, quickly correcting themselves: "Still does, I mean."

The tables were piled with potluck: pizzas, lasagnas, casseroles, fruit salads, potato salads, chips, and brownies. Nearly every food I'd ever tasted, as well as a few dishes I'd never get close to (like the "salmon soufflé" my aunt Trina brought). Coolers of sodas were everywhere. There was a self-serve freezer of Stellar Ice Cream Sandwiches, which my friends and I enthusiastically enjoyed—the Lemon-Ginger-Blueberry my favorite.

I brushed crumbs from my shirt after eating my fill of pizza and treats, then played a round of corn hole with my friends and some of my cousins, squeaking out a narrow victory. The DJ played a bit of Taylor Swift and Billie Eilish amid all the oldies. I laughed and danced as much as everyone else and wondered if anyone felt as awful about doing so.

Was everyone really having a good time? Or were they just pretending, for my Mom's sake? How could I have joined the Conga line that wound out the community center doors and through the parking lot?

There I was, playing along with everyone. Why was no one tearing out their hair and screaming the obvious? My mother was dying.

I still go up to the roof.

Dad grunts, clambering through the window to join me.

"Up here again?" He asks, catching his breath.

"Uh-huh."

"Do you want to talk?"

"I'm okay," I answer.

"It's okay to not have the words," he says. "I miss her too." His eyes are red and puffy.

He settles beside me with peanut butter and jelly sandwiches, blankets, and a thermos of cocoa for both of us. Languid stars flicker in the night sky.

I sit up on the asphalt shingles, grateful for the picnic. Together, we watch the sky darken, the pouring and slurping of cocoa breaking the silence.

"It's a nice evening for it," he says.

I reach my hand toward the sky and pinch the North Star. I cover up three stars with my remaining fingers, like staking dibs on the cashews in a bowl of mixed nuts. I close my fist, scooping them all into my greedy hand.

"What are you looking for up here?" he asks.

I can't answer him. I can't say that if I could somehow swallow the cosmos, take in all of the stars in the night sky, it might keep her close. I know that's not how it really works, but somehow, that's the only thing that makes sense to me.

I chew my sandwich as a satellite blinks above us.

Dad brushes crumbs off the blanket and puts his arm around me. His flannel shirt smells of Old Spice, and his arm is warm around my shoulder.

"You ready to come inside? I don't want you to catch cold," he says.

"I'd like to stay," I say, and lick some stray peanut butter from my thumb.

We lean against each other, gazing up as the evening wanes. I'm jealous of the moon as it creeps across the sky, its ambient glow gobbling the stars in its path.

Sarah Sharp

Sarah is a lover, and writer, of short fiction. She lives in Vancouver, WA, where she and her partner dutifully serve their cat, Tiger.

Statue

It started in my feet. Crept. Slowly at first.

This disease. It has a Latin name and a rarity that intrigued the doctors. Something to do with collagen and thickening of the skin. Scleroderma. And as it creeps, it hardens. Turns to stone. My toes locked in. Unmoving. Feet like blocks of concrete. Throw me off a bridge and feed me to the fishes.

When it reached my calves, they said I was an unusual case. Unique indeed. They wrote about me in the *Lancet*, took pictures of my, now useless, feet. Foundations. The pedestal, maybe, of a statue. Doctors debated the creeping, relentless, unstoppable. Shook their heads. Tutted. But no cure could be found.

'We're looking', they said. 'And in the meantime, we'll write another academic article so that those who follow us will have something to read.'

The day he left, my husband recommended roller skates. Said I could wheel myself to the supermarket rather than sit and wait for the inevitable. I watched him run down the path to his car, throw a suitcase in the back. Trying to follow. Wishing for the lightness which had once been ignored. I peered at the skin on my knees, as if staring at my legs for hours on end would change the outcome. Maybe I'd see it creep up, tendrils of stone wrapping my thighs. Like ivy on a worn-out tree.

'What will happen to my mind?'

They couldn't say, but wrote notes on lined paper. What will happen to my mind, I wondered again. But I was already losing it in the waiting.

'You're going to have to choose a position', the consultant said. 'One where you're most comfortable. Sitting maybe. We can hoist you then, put you on the commode. Yes, sitting I think.'

As this monster came for my thighs, I sat. My knees at ninety-degree angles. They gave me a wheelchair but no one came to push me, my world shrinking. I tried to manoeuvre it into the corridor but got stuck in the door frame. They found me a room in a rehabilitation centre. Somewhere to live, they said. To live and watch others walk again, live again. While my own life was measured in the passage of crawling granite-like skin. Grey. Uncompromising.

I didn't need a hoist to transport me to the commode. Incontinence beat them to it. Nappies. My body reverting to helpless baby as my mind raced.

'I want to write a diary,' I said. 'Record how I feel about this.'

'We're keeping records.'

'No, your writing about a condition. I need to write about the condition of my mind, my heart and my soul. Oh, God! My heart. I can't let my heart turn to stone. Kill me,' I said.

'We can't do that. There might be a treatment, a cure.'

'Kill me please.'

But they wouldn't. Promised that when the time came, they would make it painless. Took samples. Scraped dead toes and put the shavings in a test tube.

I took out my laptop and began to write. *I am watching myself die.* Over and over again, until I filled a hundred pages and the pattern of the words made a picture of my pain. I screamed but the sound was the quietest shade of loud. I cried but no one dried my tears. In the rooms up and down the corridor, people were rehabilitating. I was receding. My words could not describe the awful pressure of my petrifying.

I knew when it had reached my womb. The sharpness of loss. Tears for children unknown and no more blood flow. In my mind I held funerals for the children I would have had with my husband, if he hadn't run away. A boy and a girl. Blond hair and blue eyes like me. Their names were Noah and Molly. I could feel them as if they were real, love them as if I knew them. That night I cried from the stone in my gut. Primal. Emptying.

The next day, my fingers seized. Body. Arms. Like a drowning animal gasping for breath I tried to push back the tide with the might of my mind. Wished it would turn. Prayed for a miracle cure. Heart still pounding.

Someone once told me that everyone is given the same amount of heart beats and we die when we have used them up. I used up a great many in the next days. The relentless surge of granite-like me. Unstoppable. Prepared myself for whatever came next. Bargained with God.

It reached my heart at midnight, just as the clock struck. Tick tock. The only sound. My own beat silenced. Forever. This is it. I'm going. I'm ready.

But I didn't float skyward or see the white light. I didn't hear the call of Jesus or run naked through a field of wheat. No waiting room emerged and no pearly gates with judgement standing by, a list in his hand. No. I remained, trapped in a body that no longer pumped blood.

They found me the next morning. Didn't check for brain activity. Pulled a sheet over my head and said, 'How sad. Her heart has stopped. She's gone.'

They wrapped me in a black bag. Zipped it up and placed me in a freezer. But the disease hadn't stopped creeping. I lay in the cold I knew was there but couldn't feel, as the stone reached past my shoulders to my neck. Surely now, I thought. Please.

The day of my funeral they lowered me into the ground. My mother said it was what I would have wanted. But I longed to burn, to disintegrate. Ashes into the ether. I was sure I had told her that. I shouted it as they sang Amazing Grace, a hymn I hate.

The worms have found a way into my coffin but cannot break me down into nutrients. The darkness both overwhelms and comforts.

I wait to be excavated by future archaeologists, placed on a pedestal and admired.

Statue.

Sarah Wilson

The Cailleach

Every year we'd burn my grandmother's face.

She'd laugh as she led the chanting, her crinkled eyes reflecting dancing flames.

"Bare birch for a bold, bright flame, lass!" she instructed each spring, while setting a fresh cut log aside to season. As the nights drew in, she carved. Her soft, shrewd mien imitated by the raw grain but now potent and puissant.

"It's a prayer," she murmured as she toiled.

"A prayer for what?" I asked, looking up from my screen. She contemplated me with sad, solemn gray eyes.

"For health, and hope. But mostly for forgiveness." She turned away then, her concentration refocused on the features slowly emerging from the pale, fragrant wood.

Come solstice, we'd place the log at sunset, kindle the fire, and watch as blue smoke wreathed the old red sandstone fireplace. A meandering stream of warmth, mingling with the chilly downdraught just as Yuletide meets Midwinter, before reluctantly making for the sky. *I love her old ways and traditions*, I mused. *All that effort for something so quaint. To even think of having a fire these days—*

"A blaze. An appeal to winter's champion to withdraw," Grandmother interrupted my thoughts.

She embraced me, her heart fluttering as she tried to convey her disquiet.

"Someday the carving will need a steadier hand than mine. Your mother lacked the patience to learn, before she left."

***

Years later I fret over the log.

"The Cailleach is agony, darkness and suffering," she sighs. "And it haunts my dreams.

"It perceives its image burning, and is repelled by the coruscating plea within. The more of yourself you pour into the carving, the further it flees. The power proceeds from your pains."

I humour her counsel while wielding her hammer and gouge.

Later as she sleeps, my iChisel loads her profile and blitzes the hardwood. A blizzard of splinters and shards brings an early winter snowstorm. I draw in the familiar tang of tree sap and admire my handiwork with satisfaction.

"How are the eyes?" she enquires while preparing breakfast. "And the cast of the face?"

"It could be your twin!" I assert with pride.

Knees creak as she eases herself down to inspect, rheumy eyes staring intently at the hewn visage. She glances at me, hushed for once. Conscience-stricken I study the amber and russet gale whipping past the window outside as the forest gives up its clothing for the year.

"You think there's a resemblance?" She looks again, and her hand rises to her cheek. "I had no idea…" She bites her lip, a habit I'd assumed was solely mine.

***

Snow seethes against the icy windows as I set the fire. I ignore winter's last desperate attempt to secure its foothold before the seasons turn, and throw the Yule log onto the nascent glow.

"It kens," Grandmother observes uneasily as she wraps her

183

gansey tighter. Unsettled, she peers through the dendrites growing up the rime-frosted glass, but the night is pitch-black.

I peek out as a brief fracture in the clouds allows a feeble shaft of moonlight through, and gasp in shock at the still figure illuminated on the path.

"Someone's out there!" I blurt, reaching for the door as a sudden keen of lament cuts the night air.

"The Cailleach!" Grandmother whispers. "See to the log!"

The fire snaps and pops as its flames lick the bricks of the hearth, but the log hasn't caught. The blackened countenance appears to gloat at me with malign glee. Bile burns my throat at the sight of such an alien expression on so familiar a face.

I swallow it back.

"It could be someone gone astray, or needing help?" I offer, reaching for any explanation that might fit. Unable to escape the malevolent sentiment emanating from the unearthly pilgrim outside, I feel myself breaking into a cold clammy sweat.

"It is that!" returns my Grandmother, as a hysterical shriek rattles the panes.

Her gaze sweeps the sooty grate with concern. "The features are faithful, but lack the power to drive her away. She is unshackled!" A frigid gale of glacial wind tears down the chimney and snuffs the fire, leaving us in sudden darkness.

Hinges creak as the door cracks ajar. Ropes of cold air writhe across the floor, entwining my legs, numbing and paralysing, pulling me to the ground. I open my mouth to scream but gelid air is forced down my throat, stifling any sound I might make.

The door bursts open.

The silhouette in the doorway emulates my grandmother in brittle misery. Surrounded by pale azure flame, the skin is sallow. The eyes, a cold piercing blue. It opens its mouth and its voice is an avalanche of despair.

Blood pounds in my ears, and my vision blurs. I have never tasted peril so close.

I cannot get away.

A warm hand rests on my shoulder. I twist my head, fearing another horror. The old lady who has cared for me all my life fixes my hair and plants a kiss on my brow.

She cups my face in her hands, and commands, "Look at me."

I ignore her, unable to tear my eyes from the abomination on the porch.

"Look at me!" she insists.

I shift my gaze.

"The Cailleach haunts each winter with shadow and death. It is the way. Burning her likeness drives her away.

"Or she takes what she needs to end her torment.

"A successor."

She glances at the doorway, eyes glistening, this time crinkled with regret. Smiling a sad, tearful farewell, she beseeches me.

"Remember.

"Remember my face next time. And let your spirit and strength flow."

My Grandmother hugs me one last time, and without hesitation turns and stands to face the monstrosity. I witness her walk to the doorway, and pause briefly before stepping into the conflagration.

Above the torrent of pain and suffering from the tortured soul she embraces, her final words leave me more numb than any winter wind ever could.

"Hello Mother, I've missed you."

Jeff Parke

The Deal

Just need that weasel out of the picture and the promotion will be in the bag. A seat at the table with the big boys.

It's just before 8 o'clock. Miles is sitting at the bar in The Alchemist, his favourite watering hole, already halfway through his third Old Fashioned. He is oblivious to the hum of city chatter around him, getting louder as the Friday night buzz takes hold. He is brooding, thinking about Bruno Rotte, the new hotshot. Nothing but trouble since arriving from Munich six months ago, and now in line for the job Miles had been working towards for years.

"So, with him gone, there'd be nothing in your way?"

Miles jumps, spilling his drink. It pools like liquid copper on the bar. Had he spoken out loud? He stares at the man sitting on the stool next to him. Surely he hadn't been there a moment before. He is thin and even sitting down it is obvious that he's tall. He is wearing a long patchwork leather coat — clearly old, but the red and yellow patches are not at all faded with age. Over uncombed hair the colour of straw, he wears a large red hat which casts a shadow on his face but does not obscure striking blue eyes.

What on earth is he doing in here? thinks Miles. Surely he'd be more at home round the campfire drinking hemp juice. He smirks, looking round out of habit for someone to appreciate his wit.

"Sorry, fella, I must have been thinking out loud."

'Fella' hangs between them, a misjudgement. The stranger stretches out a hand. His long fingers are bony and pale. Miles feels rough callouses on the thin forefinger as he reluctantly shakes hands.

"Piers Pfeiffer," the man says. "I can help you, Miles."

"Help? With what? How do you know my—"

"Bruno Rotte. I can help."

"Listen mate, I don't know—"

Piers silences him with the slightest move of his hand.

"I can help you get what you want. Competition out of the way and the job of your dreams." He smiles. "For a certain sum."

Miles glances round to see if there is anyone near who might overhear them. There is no one. Even the bartender has vanished. It has grown dark, the air still. The bar is silent. He can hear distant laughter outside on Leadenhall, an occasional car passing. All muffled by the softly falling rain.

He takes a slow swig of his drink, loosens his tie.

"How much?" he asks, matter of fact.

"A thousand pounds."

"A thousand pounds!" Miles tosses a bulging wallet onto the bar. "I've got more than that in there. You sell yourself cheap, mate."

"I only need what I need" Piers says, and he smiles.

Miles waves his almost empty glass at Piers, ice clinking against the crystal.

"And that, my boy, is why you'll never earn the big bucks."

Miles swallows the rest of the drink, picks up his wallet, and claps Piers on the back with a laugh.

"A thousand pounds! Why not?"

Still chuckling, he puts on his coat, pulls his cashmere scarf tight and heads for the door. The bar is noisy once again, the lights bright. Before stepping out into the street he turns to give a goodbye salute to the strange man, but there is no sign of him.

***

On Monday morning an email comes round to let the team know that Bruno Rotte had fallen onto the tracks at Liverpool Street on his way home on Friday night. Sadly, he was killed. There will be drinks later for anyone wanting to pay their respects.

You just didn't know what was going on with people did you? Chickenshit obviously couldn't hack it. Nothing in my way now.

Miles doesn't go to the memorial drinks. He stays late in the office, getting up to speed with the project Rotte had been heading up. Happy to step into the breach he tells his boss, for the sake of the team. It's what Bruno would have wanted.

It's after midnight when the taxi pulls up outside his building. Miles hands the driver two fifty-pound notes.

"A little something for you, pal," he says. "I've had a big win today."

He jumps out and dashes towards the building, head down against the sheeting rain. He is so focused on getting inside that he doesn't notice the figure who has stepped from the shadows into the rectangle of light spilling out from the glass doors

"Jesus!" snaps Miles, "Watch where you're going".

"Good evening, my friend." says the man.

"You can't beg here," snaps Miles, not looking up.

"I'm here for payment, Miles."

Miles stops.

"I'm sorry, what?"

For the first time he looks at the man, registers the long patchwork coat, the red hat, the bright blue eyes.

"How did you—"

"We had an agreement. A thousand pounds." The man's voice is soft, matter of fact.

"Agreement? What?"

"Competition out of the way. A seat at the table with the big boys."

"What? I hardly remember speaking to you. Drunken chit-chat in a bar. I don't think we have anything else to say to each other, do you?"

He pushes past and swipes himself into the building. As the doors slide open, he turns back and jabs a finger at Piers.

"Don't come here again. Don't ever speak to me again. Understand?"

Piers doesn't reply. He stands and stares, then slowly turns and disappears into the darkness

***

Days pass. Miles gets the promotion, a seat in the box at Chelsea, a new Porsche. Months pass. A six-figure bonus and an insatiable new fiancée. He is on top of the world. Invincible.

***

Midsummer's Day. Miles is striding through the lobby at work when a man and a woman approach. They are out of place with their scuffed shoes and polyester suits.

"Miles Hamlyn? You are under arrest for the murder of Bruno Rotte. You do not have to say anything but…"

Miles doesn't hear the rest, his attention caught by the figure leaning against the wall over by the lifts. How did he get in here? No one else notices the tall, thin man — they are all transfixed by the drama of Miles' arrest. Piers stands tall, his red and yellow coat reflected in the jet-black marble floor. He watches for a few minutes then gives a little smile and turns, his coat billowing out behind him as he goes.

***

A photograph sent from an anonymous mobile phone showed the exact moment Miles had pushed Bruno under the train. There was no doubt it was him – the Savile Row tailoring, the distinctive red scarf. CCTV showed him entering the station moments earlier and standing on the platform behind Bruno. No-one remembered seeing him at the bar, and the taxi he claimed took him home that night was never traced.

And, after all, why would anyone else want Bruno dead?

Jodie Kennedy

The Ghost of McVey House

This is not a ghost story.

It's a story about a boy, looking out.

There's a house on a hill. A house where, if you look long enough, you will see a figure standing in the window of what you think is the main room downstairs. If you look long enough, you'll see the way he lingers in the dark. And if you look long enough, you'll see the longing in his eyes.

He might wave at you. He might nod his head in subtle acknowledgment. If you're lucky, he'll give you a smile that will light up the darkness he seems to be trapped in.

He doesn't move from the window.

You won't approach. Instinctively, you know there's something that won't let you take a further step toward the house. Those hairs on the back of your neck stand to attention if you think about moving closer. You can't put your finger on exactly what it is. You'll walk away. You're haunted by the look in the boy's eyes when you're tucked safely in bed at night. You'll find yourself wondering about him hours and days later.

The McVey House.

Abandoned almost a century before, the house has fallen into disrepair. The McVey daughter died young, and her parents – heartbroken – left McVey House. You remember that people say the McVey daughter used to haunt the halls, singing sad laments that travelled to the town through the wind. But it wasn't a little girl that you saw at the window.

Then, you think you might have seen the boy before. Near the quarry. It's abandoned just like the McVey House. There are stories of a boy who drowned there. It's much more recent than the McVey story, and people who knew the boy claim to have seen him standing at the drop where he had jumped that fateful night. They say they've seen him walking through the town, but you don't think ghosts can travel from place to place as they please. They're rooted where they died, aren't they? You start thinking again about the boy with the sad eyes, who waits in the window.

This is not a ghost story.

July 17th, 1987

The stereo was blaring the music from the tape that Jess Emerson had hastily stuffed into it. His choice was met with cheers and whooping sounds. He stood, throwing one hand up in a way that meant his choice was the best, before reaching for a can of beer. His friends chanted his name, overpowering the music. He laughed when he stumbled as he crushed the empty can with his hands, his girlfriend gripping his shirt and hastily kissing the underside of his jaw. A friend slapped him hard on the back, and another shoved another beer into his hand. Only his second for the night. The music continued to bellow, cutting through the silence that surrounded them at the late hour.

The quarry had always been their place to hang out. As kids, Jess and his friends would ride their bikes up and throw stones away from the cliff edge, trying to see who could launch them the furthest out into the open air. None of them had dared to look over the edge when they were in their pre-teens, but as they grew older, the bravado took over: they stood, sat and dangled their legs over the edge. The water was deeper than any of them liked, but Jess always brushed it off. He was the unofficial head of the group, despite being the youngest. He was the first to stand on the edge of the drop, to sit there and dangle his legs. He was first to be called in the latest dare.

"Emerson! Are we finally gonna jump off the edge, or what?"

Jess felt his girlfriend's hand still holding onto his shirt, fingers curled loosely in it. He downed a mouthful of beer before he heard his name being chanted again. That was all it took for him to give in. His hand shot up and pointed into the night, earning raucous cheers. Another kiss was pressed against his jaw, followed by a few more until he was lost in the moment of kissing his girlfriend. He was tugged back into his surroundings by a harsh yank on the back of his jacket. He pulled away with a grin, finishing the last drop of his second beer and crushing the can in his hand once again before taking off his jacket—a gift from his parents on his twenty-first birthday, now carelessly thrown next to the stereo on the bonnet of a friend's car. His shoes were next, one dumped after the other. He tripped, gripping the shoulder of a friend.

"You going first, Jess?"

"Duh," Jess replied, rolling his eyes. The mix of music, chatter, and laughter was exactly what he enjoyed being surrounded with. The atmosphere was so *alive*. His friends were pushing each other as they removed their jackets to follow Jess's lead. A trail of shoes lead up to the edge of the cliff.

Jess glanced to his left, then to his right. One of his friends grinned. Another squeezed his shoulder. His girlfriend tugged at his shirt and told him to be careful.

"I'm always careful," he reassured her.

"You're the clumsiest person we know, Jess." His friend squeezed his shoulder once more. Jess rolled his eyes, brushing off his hand. He turned to face where the car was parked. Jess knew the last track would end soon. He touched his hair as if in front of a mirror, almost readying himself for a performance.

"C'mon," he grinned, taking one final look at his friends.

Jess leapt into the darkness without a second thought.

The water was freezing.

They had been near the water more times than he could count, shoving each other around and dunking each other under the water, but never close to the deepest part. The temperature of the water shocked him. It seeped into his bones and kept him still. He dived so deep, he was shrouded in darkness. The water was murky at best during the day. At night, there was little chance of visibility.

He struggled and fought his way upwards. With the blackness blocking his vision and causing him to panic, he did not see a jagged edge of a rock before him. He collided headfirst. The sharp edge tore into his skin, splitting open the curve of his cheek. His mouth opened in a silent scream of pain, and it was then that he inhaled – and inhaled.

Jess couldn't remember being dragged out of the water. He couldn't remember his friends shouting his name as they dragged him to shore with them after jumping in themselves. He couldn't remember the screams from on top of the cliff. He could only remember how cold the water was.

Jess watched from the shore. It didn't make any sense to him, at first. He didn't understand. He was confused as he looked at himself while his friends frantically pumped at his chest. Hands over his heart, someone breathing into his mouth every few seconds. *What were they doing?* Jess shouted at them, but no sound came out of his mouth. Water spilled out instead, flooding him through. His clothes were soaked, but the biting cold when he jumped was gone. His friends were all soaked too, shivering and shouting desperately. One was still pumping his chest. Another had his hand pressed under Jess's neck, feeling his pulse. His girlfriend repeated Jess's name over and over in mounting desperation.

Yet he still hadn't woken up.

His attention shifted down *his own body* lying on the ground surrounded by his friends. His skin was a shade of pale as the dead's in the horror movies they'd seen. The only movement coming from his body was the involuntary motion of his chest as it was forcefully pumped to revive his breathing. His eyes were closed. He opened his mouth to try to shout again and get his friends' attention, but there was still no sound. With the realisation starting to set in, he grew hysterical. No tears rolled down his face. Even the gravel crunching under his feet when he stomped around produced no sound. His plea to be brought back was an empty silence.

The four of them – five, if Jess counted himself twice – were illuminated by the lights of the car as it skidded to a stop. The screams started all over again. Jess shouted at them until it felt as though his throat would fall apart. A sound rolled deep from within him, almost like a shriek. But nobody heard it. They pulled the body into the car with them. Jess jumped in alongside them. They left the quarry.

7th August, 1987

It had been three weeks since he was pronounced dead. Drowned, they said. Too much water in his lungs. They were lucky to have pulled his body out of the quarry at all, his friends were told, given how dark, murky, and big the quarry water was.

Three weeks.

While his body had been buried a few days ago – closed casket – he was still around, except nobody could see him. He was now part of all those crazy stories about ghosts that he never believed. He tried moving things around. He tried shouting and screaming at his parents to get their attention. Nothing he did worked. His mother sat around the house, crying. His father slammed the door shut on Jess's bedroom on the night they were told of his death and hadn't been in it since. His friends walked right through him. People kept stopping by to give their apologies, or to leave flowers. The fridge was overflowing with food that people kept bringing by for his parents. They all did the same thing: they offered a smile full of sadness while his mother teared up again, and his father shrugged his shoulders even though his brokenness was reflected on his face.

Jess was still around, but nobody could see him.

Present Day

It's a question he asks himself even now. Why is he still here? Why had fate kept him for herself, forced him to an existence between life and death? He had tried the ways he thought would let him part from this world. Tried to amend mistakes. Tried to settle his family. Tried to do the things he assumed would earn him penance, a place further beyond. None of it had worked. Jess had then had to make peace with dying. It was the only thing he had left. A stupid accident, he decided. It could have happened to any of them. It was just unfortunate that it happened to him. Much like Elide McVey, who looked as lonely in her portraits as Jess felt. Unfortunate luck for both of them to die so young; to haunt a place that would only ever know her story when she was nothing more than a rumour and Jess was a cautionary story of why no one should leap from the cliff tops of the quarry.

His friends have all moved on with their lives. Still in contact with each other, they sometimes go on vacations together. They have families. They have children. They have homes they love and lives they enjoy. Jess is barely a memory to each of them. There's an odd picture of him here and there in albums they have, a passing comment to their children about how he's the kid that drowned in the quarry. None of them ever tell their children that they were there that night, trying to bring him back to life.

He wishes he could drop one of the small pebbles beside him down into the endless abyss beneath. That his hands could close around one and allow him the small pleasure of feeling something beneath his fingertips again, however fleeting the sensation would be. Instead, he rises without a sound, not even a murmur against the wind. The quarry has been closed down many years ago. He wandered until he found himself in Elide McVey's home. It's not his and never will be. It's the McVey House; not Jess Emerson's.

The moth-eaten curtains hang limp at the windows. The glass is filthy as it always has been. Even the furniture had been destroyed from years of neglect. Jess could not even remove the peeling wallpaper.

"Why do you leave?"

Elide McVey, Jess discovered, is more than a rumour. She revealed herself when Jess had been at his lowest. Fine thick hair that Jess could never touch. Wide doe-like eyes in a mix of brown hues that held all of Elide's secrets. Those eyes that watch him as he strains to look through the murky glass, his memories searching for familiarity between the world outside and inside behind the window stained by the grime of neglect.

A person stands at the gate and looks at the house. They are staring directly at him. Sometimes, he wonders if people can see him at all. They certainly try their best not to notice, if they do see him. Those who are living can only comprehend so much, he decides. That was why he didn't raise his hand to wave at the person at the gate.

"Because this isn't my place," Jess answers Elide.

And that boy that waits in the window – you might forget about him. You'll go about your life without thinking about him again, perhaps. But Jess? He won't forget. He hasn't forgotten a single living face that's looked at him. Not through him. He'll still be walking the corridors of the McVey House, the quarry, the streets of the town, long after you pass to where he can never get to.

This is not a ghost story.

Shanice Khan

The Life of Artemisia Gentileschi
(as told through her art) – An Essay

Naples 1606: David with the Head of Goliath (Caravaggio)[3].

The severed head is dripping blood from its ragged neck where the sword has sliced and hacked. Its eyes stare sightlessly into the void, the mouth gapes. David, his right hand still holding the sword, lifts Goliath's head up, grasping the matted hair. But David is not savouring his moment of victory; his expression is full of sorrow.

Caravaggio painted this subject as both a confession and a plea for mercy. He wanted Cardinal Borghese to repeal the sentence against him and let him return to Rome. In 1606, he got into a drunken argument. It may have been over a woman, or a tennis match; at his trial he could not remember. There was a duel, and a young man died; Caravaggio was found guilty and escaped with a price on his head.

In a macabre twist, this is a double portrait; a juvenile Caravaggio is holding the head of the older one. He has painted the younger self with an expression of deep regret. As Simon

---

[3]https://en.wikipedia.org/wiki/David_with_the_Head_of_Goliath_%28Caravaggio,_Rome%29#/media/File:David_with_the_Head_of_Goliath-Caravaggio_(1610).jpg

Schama puts it, "Perhaps by offering his head in a painting, he can save himself in real life." [4]

The subject is lit by a diagonal shaft of light against a dark background. Caravaggio was famous for inventing this technique, *chiaroscuro*. It creates a startling focus on the subject at the centre, surrounding the scene with sinister darkness. His friend Orazio Gentileschi had begun to paint in the same style, and Orazio's daughter Artemisia was also experimenting. *Tenebroso*, some call it, in the dark manner.

Rome 1610: Susannah and the Elders (Artemisia Gentileschi)[5]

A solitary young woman, interrupted while bathing in her garden, is being harassed by two intruders. She recoils in horror from the advances of the leering, predatory men. Pale-skinned and naked, with only a towel to protect her modesty, she is twisting violently to the right, away from her assailants, with an expression of horror. Her arms are lifted, hands raised in a gesture of both defiance and defence. The story of Susannah and the Elders is from the Apocrypha[6]; a Hebrew wife is bathing in her garden when she is spied upon by two lecherous Elders. They blackmail her: if she does not consent to having sex with them, they will say that they found her with a young man.

The Elders are portrayed in contemporary Italian dress. They could be prosperous Roman merchants. The senior of the two, with his greying hair and whiskery face, is leaning over the back of Susannah's seat, invading her space. His younger companion has an arm around his shoulder and is whispering into his ear,

---

4 Simon Schama's Power of Art, (2006) BBC DVD, 1min. 41 s.

5 https://joyofmuseums.com/artists-index/artemisia-gentileschi/
susanna-and-the-elders/

6 "The History of Susannah" in The Apocrypha (1894) page 302-306, London: Oxford University Press

his free hand toying with Susannah's hair. The older man puts a finger to his lips suggestively; they are huddled together, conspiring.

In the Bible story, Susannah rejects their advances. The Elders are as good as their word: she is tried for adultery and sentenced to be stoned to death. Enter the prophet Daniel, who points out that the Elders too should be questioned. Fortunately for Susannah, their statements do not tally, and she is set free.

Artemisia was not the first to tell this story; Lorenzo Lotto painted it in 1517, as did her father Orazio, and it became a popular subject in the Baroque period. But Artemisia gives the subject something unique: she tells the story from the woman's point of view. She makes Susannah the central figure, and her body language unequivocal. Her Susannah is determined, though ultimately doomed and dominated by these predatory men. Orazio's version[7] makes the fleshy Susannah passive, almost complicit. This is the first painting by Artemisia that can be reliably dated and may represent the end of her apprenticeship in her father's studio, a "masterpiece" in that sense. Her father was proud of her talent and wrote to the Grand Duchess of Tuscany that she had become "so skilled that I can venture to say that today she has no peer."[8]

Artemisia was just seventeen when she painted "Susannah and the Elders" for the first time. The subject, a young woman being pestered by older men, is significant. As a female artist in a man's world, it seems to reflect her own experience. Her vulnerability. Less than a year after this was painted, she was raped by a fellow artist. The case went to court.

---

[7] https://upload.wikimedia.org/wikipedia/commons/d/d8/Orazio_Gentileschi_-_Susana_surpreendida.jpg

[8] https://www.newyorker.com/magazine/2020/10/05/a-fuller-picture-of-artemisia-gentileschi

Rome, 1611 (real life).

They take hold of her hands, her artist's hands, and prepare to break them.

So silent at their work, the torturers. Practised, efficient, methodical.

Strings are wrapped around her fingers, twining like some unholy cat's cradle. They pull them tight. The pain begins.

They are waiting for her to speak, but she says nothing. Tighter still.

How far will they go? Will they break the bones? Will they leave her like this, until her fingers blacken and die? They say nothing, concentrating on their grim endeavour.

Artemisia is an artist. She makes her living at the studio of Orazio Gentileschi, the famous painter who is also her father. He has taught her well, and her talent has come to match his. The commissions roll in. One day everyone will know her name.

That is, so long as they do not cripple her. Could she learn to hold the brushes if her fingers were reduced to stumps? She would surely try. The urge to paint is a fire within her; compelling, unquenchable.

The court expects her to change her testimony. The judge has ordered this torture to persuade her to withdraw the charges. Perhaps they think that pain will break this woman. They are mistaken.

They have invited her attacker to watch. Agostino Tassi. He stands there, as the cords are tightened further.

"Now what do you say?"

"I have told the truth and I always will, because it is true," she says.

Tassi. This thief who came to her father's house to lie and to steal. They say he has stolen paintings, but from her, he stole something beyond price. Her virginity.

And afterwards, so that he could fuck her whenever he wanted, he spoke of marriage. What could she do? She was a maid of seventeen. No man had touched her before. Even her father was won over by his words. Tricked, deceived, hoodwinked. Tassi already had a wife, though no-one seemed to know where she was.

He raped her, though he swore she had consented. So why did he hold a handkerchief over her mouth? Why did he collude with Tuzia, her companion, to leave them alone together? Tuzia walked away and left him to it.

The cords are biting deep. "Look. This is the ring that you give me, and these are your promises."

The judge reads out the written testimony; *I was a virgin, and Tassi raped me.*

Does she still claim this is what happened?

She holds up her bleeding hands for all to see:

È vero! È vero! È vero!

It is true. It is true. It is true.[9]

After the trial, Artemisia was married off to Pierantonio Stiattesi. The couple settled in Florence, at the home of Pierantonio's father on the Via del Campaccio, where Artemisia set up a studio in her own right. She already had family ties to Tuscany: her father Orazio was originally from Pisa, and she adopted the Tuscan family name of "Lomi". Her first child, Giovanni Battista, was born in September 1613. Sadly, he died before his first birthday. Two more children, Agnola and Lisabella, also died in their first year. Her fourth child Cristofano died age five. Only her daughter Prudentia, born in 1618, survived into adulthood.

---

9   https://www.nationalgallery.org.uk/exhibitions/past/artemisia/artemisia-in-her-own-words

Despite being almost constantly pregnant during these years, Artemisia continued to paint and achieve great success. Cosimo de Medici, Grand Duke of Tuscany, was among her patrons. In 1616, she became the first woman to be welcomed into the Florentine Academy of the Arts of Drawing. Among the Academy's members was astronomer Galileo, who became a friend.

As a married woman, Artemisia could now step out independently in the world. She forged a career as a successful, highly regarded artist among the powerful, the wealthy and the intellectual elite of Florence.

In 1618, Artemisia began an affair with a wealthy patron, Francesco Maria Maringhi. Despite her professional success, she and her husband were haunted by debt and in 1620 Artemisia left Florence to set up a studio in Rome. She maintained her relationship with Maringhi, complaining at times that she did not see him often enough. By 1623, her marriage was officially over, leaving her to bring up her daughter alone.

Rome 1620: *Judith Beheading Holofernes* (Artemisia Gentileschi)[10]

The windpipe has been severed but the head is still attached. Judith is sawing at the neck with her sword. Drunk though he is, Holofernes is strong, and it takes both women to hold him down on the bed. His right hand is raised against the maid, but his strength is failing, the arm is bent. The maid is hanging on with unshaken resolve, pressing him down with all her weight. Blood spurts, drenching the bedclothes. Judith is leaning back, to keep it off her face and her clothes; only a few tiny red drops

---

[10]   https://upload.wikimedia.org/wikipedia/commons/4/4e/Artemisia_Gentileschi_-_Judith_Beheading_Holofernes_-_WGA8563.jpg

speckle her dress. She has rolled up her sleeves, workmanlike. Not so much an execution, more a butchering.

Perhaps Artemisia has seen somebody killing a pig. Perhaps she has helped to kill a few pigs herself. According to chef Anthony Bourdain, there is a trick to it. You slip into its pen, concealing the knife. Somebody must hold it down while you rip through the trachea and hack at the blood vessels. The pig screams and struggles, fighting back. It takes strength, determination, teamwork.

The painting is based on a story from the Apocrypha. Judith, a respectable Jewish widow, uses guile to defeat Holofernes, the Assyrian warlord who is threatening to destroy her village. She goes to his tent and persuades him to be alone with her. Then she gets him drunk, *overflown with wine*[11]. Calling upon her maid to help her, Judith beheads him with his own sword.

Artemisia's Judith needs all her strength to restrain Holofernes; she has one knee up on the bed, bracing herself. With her left hand, she grasps his hair and wrenches the head back, exposing the throat, pulling the flesh away from the cutting edge to free it for the next stroke. The sword is in her right hand as she slices vertically through the neck. The Israelites are avenged.

Artemisia has embraced Caravaggio's trademark techniques and made them her own, as she learned to do in her father's studio: rich colours, chiaroscuro, a dramatic subject. She paints the background a sinister black, spotlighting the drama of the action: dazzling white sheets, the flesh tones of three pairs of arms, a grid of diagonals. The dark, velvety red of the bedcover tangled around Holofernes' lower torso and legs matching the dark blood-spatter. Judith herself is in heroic burnished gold.

---

[11] Apocrypha, *Book of Judith*, p146. London: Oxford University Press (1894).

The foreshortening of Holofernes body creates a three-dimensional effect: the head is towards us, seeming to emerge from the canvas, about to tumble alarmingly at our feet.

Caravaggio himself painted this subject in 1602[12] but his young, elegant Judith holds the sword as if it were too heavy for her. It is severing Holofernes' throat, but there is no conviction behind the stroke. Caravaggio's maid, an old crone holding a bag ready to receive the head, looks detached, wary.

By contrast, Artemisia's protagonist and her maid are wrestling Holofernes down by brute force, fully engaged in this bloody slaughter. These women, painted by a woman, embody competence, determination and power.

The realistic blood-spatter was informed by the work of her friend Galileo, who wrote about the parabolic motion of projectiles[13]. This is the second time she has painted this subject. The first version, painted in 1612, lacks the gory detail of the blood spurting from the neck. It is tempting to conclude that (a) she enjoyed painting this subject and (b) she reprised the work specifically as a compliment to her friend.

Rome 1620: Jael and Sisera (Artemisia Gentileschi)14

Darkness. Two figures are picked out in a shaft of light.

The young man is lying on the ground, sweetly asleep, curled in a cosy foetal position at the knees of a young woman. His white stockings are rolled down, exposing naked thighs. His head is resting on his forearms, nestled in the golden folds of

---

[12] https://en.wikipedia.org/wiki/
Judith_Beheading_Holofernes_%28Caravaggio%29#/media/File:Judith_Beheading_Holofernes_-_Caravaggio.jpg
[13] https://artlark.org/2022/02/15/art-and-science-galilean-influences-in-artemisias-judith-beheading-holofernes/
[14] https://en.wikipedia.org/wiki/Jael_and_Sisera_(Artemisia_Gentileschi)#/media/File:Giaele_e_Sisara.JPG

the woman's brocade skirt. His carelessly abandoned sword lies impotently nearby.

The woman's sleeves are rolled up and she is calmly concentrating.

With her left hand, she is holding a sharp spike against his head.

Her right hand, grasping a hammer, is lifted high. She is about to bring it down and drive the spike into his brain.

This story is from the Old Testament, Judges 5: 26. The Kenite woman Jael, kills the defeated Canaanite general Sisera, by driving a nail through his skull: *She put her hand to the nail, and her right hand to the workmen's hammer; and with the hammer she smote Sisera.*

Artemisia suffered sexual harassment, rape, a lazy husband, and a negligent lover. In the 1970's and 1980's, feminist writers such as Germaine Greer interpreted the ferocity of this painting and the previous one (Judith Beheading Holofernes) both from 1620, as an expression of rage against men in general[15]. Artemisia certainly seemed to relish depicting a heroic female protagonist despatching a male adversary; her style is gruesomely realistic. In both, the man is incapacitated, by drink or sleep, and the woman is in control, seizing the advantage. The sword and the spike have phallic connotations, and they are both taken from men: Judith employs Holofernes' sword, while Jael uses a workman's hammer to drive home the spike.

In 1630, Artemisia moved to Naples where she established herself once more. Here, she started work on paintings for churches and Spanish patrons; her first works intended for a public space. The Birth of Saint John the Baptist was commissioned by the Viceroy of Naples as part of a six-part

---

work depicting the saint's life story, executed by a variety of artists. It captures the moment when Zacharias, literally dumbfounded when his ageing wife is declared to be pregnant, is writing *His name is John*. In the Bible story (Luke 1:13) this act miraculously restores his powers of speech.

1635 Naples: *The Birth of John the Baptist* (Artemisia Gentileschi)[16]

Four women are bathing a newborn baby. Much of the room is dark with the babe itself at the centre of the lit area. Chiaroscuro. The Bible may have made Zacharias the hero of the story, but Artemisia puts the baby and the women at the centre of the action, literally relegating the old man to the shadows.

In the left foreground a well-dressed woman, presumably Elizabeth, is seated. The silks of her dress and headdress glow sumptuously. She is looking in wonder at the infant, who seems to be returning her gaze. To her left, a midwife in more simple clothes is holding the baby over the bowl of water, expertly cradling head and legs. The tender realism of this scene reflects Artemisia's own experience of motherhood. Her surviving daughter, now 17, was working as an artist alongside her.

Standing behind the midwife, the high point of the composition, a maid is holding a bowl of fresh water. She too has her eyes fixed on the central figure of the child. Lastly, Artemisia has depicted the fourth female figure on her knees with a hand in the bowl of bath water, looking up at Elizabeth as if saying something to her. It is an energetic pose, caught as if in a fleeting second. To me, this looks like Artemisia herself. The painting radiates joy and the companionship of practical women.

---

[16] https://www.museodelprado.es/en/the-collection/art-work/the-birth-of-saint-john-the-baptist/65572d18-d9a1-42b8-bddd-f931c4b88da6

Artemisia had painted for a Grand Duke in Florence and a Viceroy in Naples. Now she was coming to London to paint for a king. Her father Orazio had been court painter to Charles I since 1626. In 1638, he began work on a huge canvas for the ceiling of the Queen's House in Greenwich, an allegory of Peace and the Arts, with Peace surrounded by twelve personifications, all female figures. Orazio, 74, was by now a sick old man; Artemisia was summoned to assist him. Orazio's rival, Rubens, had finished the ceiling of the Banqueting House in Whitehall just two years earlier, which must have lent a piquancy to the commission. Orazio died shortly after it was completed.

We do not know which of the female figures in Greenwich can be attributed to Artemisia, but while in London she also completed a self-portrait for the king.

1638 London: Self-Portrait as the Allegory of Painting (Artemisia Gentileschi)[17]

The background is dark brown, a prepared canvas awaiting the image. Artemisia is lit brightly from top left by a window or skylight, the pale flesh tones glowing: her trademark technique. She has put on a brown apron, rolled her sleeves up, tied back her hair, workmanlike, as Judith and Jael did. She is leaning forward, brush in hand.

The subject is at a difficult angle as if we are looking down on her from top left, perhaps through the skylight. It is a masterful piece of perspective. It does not look like a self-portrait done in a mirror, in the way that Rembrandt self-portraits look squarely out at the observer. The artist is not looking at us, she is concentrating on her work.

So many of Artemisia's heroines seem to resemble her. The

---

17   https://www.rct.uk/collection/405551/self-portrait-as-the-allegory-of-painting-la-pittura

bright-eyed, bird-like face. The ample bosom and muscled forearm with its rolled-up sleeve.

What panache, what confidence, to depict herself as 'Painting' itself.

When the commission was complete, she returned to Naples where she continued to paint until her death in 1656. The English Civil War, and the death of King Charles would come to her as news from a distant land.

London 1649 (real life).

The ceiling of the Banqueting Hall[18] is exquisite. If Charles looks up now, he will see a vortex of angels and swirling drapery, drawing the soul of his father up to heaven, where a cherub waits with a heavenly crown. Rubens' royal masterpiece.

But Charles is being escorted directly through this sumptuous room and out onto the scaffold beyond. He is to be executed.

The block is low; he must prostrate himself before the assembled mob. The wooden floor is cold through his two shirts, damp.

The executioner lifts his axe; ten pounds of steel, a thirteen-inch cutting edge, honed with care.

The axe falls.

Skin, muscle, bone, sliced through.

A collective groan. Muffled cheers.

The executioner retrieves the severed head before it rolls away, and holds it up for everyone to see. A slippery lump of meat, surprisingly heavy. Spectators elbow their way through the crowd to dip their handkerchiefs in the royal blood as it runs off the scaffold and drips onto the cobbles.

---

[18] https://www.hrp.org.uk/banqueting-house/whats-on/rubens-ceiling/#gs.k8734s

Conclusion

Artemisia was written out of history after her death, ignored. Some of her work was attributed to Orazio. She was "rediscovered" in the early twentieth century by Roberto Longhi, a scholar of Caravaggio's work.

In recent years she has been depicted as a feminist icon: the rape survivor who became a great artist. She certainly had many obstacles to overcome; her mother's death when she was just twelve, sexual harassment and rape at seventeen, pregnancy, childbirth, and the deaths of four of her five children. But to focus exclusively on this diminishes her as an artist and deflects attention from what matters.

She was a stellar talent, trained by Orazio, and influenced by Caravaggio. She rolled up her sleeves and worked hard to perfect her craft, leaving an extensive and varied body of work. It is this, her art, that will continue to tell her story and to speak her truth.

Sue Nicholson

The Magpie's Baby

It wasn't the first time Amy had seen the Magpies, but it was the first time she had really noticed them. She'd been waiting by the window for Jenny, who was late again, and saw them sitting on the lawn over the road. She started saying that rhyme in her head, 'One for sorrow, two for joy, three for a girl…' And she had a girl hadn't she. Little baby Eliza: seven pounds, two ounces and six days old. So, at first, she had been pleased to see the three magpies, a sign from Mother Nature. How did they know about her and her baby?

But then a fourth strode out from behind a patch of daffs. 'Four for a boy…' She didn't have a boy. Not a boy, like Jamie had wanted. They'd had a baby girl.

***

She was sure that they had agreed on 10.30, Jenny in her high-pitched sing-song voice, head tilted, as if her hearing only worked that side. Kind smile, but sharp eyes. Her tiny, bony hands grasping Amy's engorged breast as she tried to show her how to get Eliza to latch on properly. Amy, too stunned by the enforced intimacy to be shocked, felt too large, soft and lumpy next to the swift efficient midwife.

Finally, the shabby fiesta pulled into the drive and Jenny jumped out, grabbing her scarf and her bag as she slammed the car door behind her. Amy felt a rush of irritation.

"How's Mummy doing?" Jenny smiled brightly, sweeping into the front room. "Oh, it looks super tidy in here, someone's been up with the Hoover this morning." Jenny's dark hair pulled back into a ponytail, swishing efficiently behind her bobbing head.

She chirped on and on, setting up her scales. Amy wasn't listening. The magpies' angry chatter was all she could hear as they were spooked into flight. Interrupted, Jenny shuddered at the birds cawing into the sky.

"Hello Mr Magpie!"

Amy must have looked quizzical.

Jenny, caught mid salute, blushed. "Sorry, my grandma used to say you must greet a magpie for luck."

"I thought that was if there was only one. There were four; four for a boy, even though we've got a girl."

"One for sorrow, two for joy, three for a birth and four for a death…" Jenny said, then paused. Flushing furiously, she laughed, as she began packing up her scales.

"Baby has lost a little weight, but that's expected in the first week, so nothing to worry about. We'll weigh her again at day 10 and I'm sure she will have regained her birth weight and a bit more; now shall we have another look at how the latching on is going? Is that nipple still sore?"

***

Amy hadn't expected Jamie to be standing behind her. Cleaning the top of the cooker, radio playing and the kitchen window open above the sink, her hands encased in the rubber gloves, a blur in foamy suds. She wasn't sure when the hob had last been cleaned properly.

"Amy?"

He had made her jump; in that moment of surprise her temper rose. She turned, quickly picking up the kettle, biting back her anger.

"Do you want tea?"

"What I really want is to talk." Jamie took a step towards her.

"Why? What about?" Back towards him she filled the kettle.

"You. I'm worried about you, how you are, how you're coping…you seem…"

"I'm fine. Honestly, I'm fine. Or I would be, if I could get on top of this cleaning. I don't know how I let it get so bad!" Amy turning, picked up the Brillo pad again.

"It's not bad, really."

Amy resumes her scrubbing, tucking a stray wisp of hair behind her ear with her damp glove.

"Please leave it and talk to me?"

"About what?" She regretted her tone nearly as soon as it was out of her mouth. "Sorry, I'm just a bit tired," she said.

"Of course, you are, you must be. Thats what I'm worried about. You've just had a baby, you're exhausted, but rather than resting you just seem to be obsessing over how clean the bloody oven is—"

"I just want things to be tidy, I need to stay on top of things, especially now."

"Then let me help you, please. You don't have to do all this on your own." He gestured at the sparkling kitchen vaguely.

"I will, promise. If I get more tired, I'll let you know; but honestly, now I'm not lugging all that weight around I feel fine. Honestly better than I have in ages"

"Lugging all that weight! That's our daughter you're talking about," he chuckled, his eyes crinkling at the corners.

"You're the one who looks tired, I'll make you a cuppa." Reaching into the cupboard for mugs she glances through the open window, the magpies are back on the lawn, stretching shiny feathers in the spring sunshine.

"Thanks. What time is the midwife coming today?"

"I don't think she is, not today. She had a full list and I didn't think we needed her today"." She can't look at him as she tells this lie.

"Oh, I wanted to see how much weight she's put on!"

As if on cue the monitor stirs into life, whimpering rapidly turning into desperate cries.

"Can you get her please? I'll make the tea."

Jamie jumps down from the kitchen stool, making his way towards the stairs. Through the window she sees the magpies, one, two three, four… four for a boy.

***

Gazing out of the bedroom window the sky, a leaden pre-dawn grey. Amy looks at the baby in her arms. Mid feed she has nodded off, her cheeks full, top lip pert with the wind she needs to release. Amy needs to wind her, she knows this. Knows that she daren't risk lying her in the cot. But, just for a moment she gazes into her new daughter's rosy face. She waits. Surely this feeling that they all talked about would come. The moment that she will feel the overwhelming rush of maternal love. She waits.

Objectively she knows that she is a pretty baby; aren't all babies pretty? Her fine dark hair, snub nose and silken lashes resting on a cheek flushed with sleep, but still. Amy searches her heart for the feelings that she knows must be within. Maybe it's because she looks so like Jamie. His dark hair and perfect ears? Is it possible that the baby that Amy carried reluctantly for 9-months, that she stopped drinking, ate healthily and did pre-natal relaxation classes for, bears no resemblance to Amy at all?

A lone tear drifts down her cheek as she remembers the other baby. A miniature doll of her, he had seemed, as they laid him in her arms. Her nose and mouth, an unruly mop of hair the colour of burnt sugar. Tiny hands, the smallest finger bent at the tip, just like hers and her Mums. Amy had cradled the silent doll baby for what felt like only moments before the kindly nurse had suggested they take him away. Alone in the delivery room she had folded the memory and her feelings into her maternity bag, with her blood-stained nightie and unused nursing bra.

Amy's breath catches, searching for some part of her in these tiny features. A noise through the open window draws her attention. In the half-light she sees wings flapping and the dark outline of three, no four birds rising from the roofline. Amy shudders. Had the window been left open all night? Thinking that she must remember to close the window before she leaves the room, she glances back down at the now deeply sleeping infant. Adjusting her position so that she can move the baby into the cot, she catches Eliza in profile. Maybe it's the glow from the soft lamp, or the lack of sleep, but somehow the baby skin that was so rosy pink, now looks a translucent parchment pale. A desperate chill of fear runs through her. Is Eliza ill? Turning the baby's head slightly, Amy feels a sudden wave of revulsion. Eliza's skin at her hairline is tinged a sickly yellow.

***

The sight of the shabby fiesta on the drive signals the arrival of Jenny. Tiny, smiley, chatty Jenny enters the front door in a shaft of late afternoon sunlight. Head-tilted smiling manner, which usually irritated Amy so much, was welcomed today.

"Oh! Its ever so dark in here! Shall we just open these curtains and let some sunshine in? Seems a shame on such a lovely day."

"It's the baby—" Amy began, talking to the back of Jenny's head as she fussed over the curtains.

"There now, that's better! What about Baby? What seems to be the matter?"

"Look at her…"

Both women bent over the Moses basket, resting on the sofa. Eliza was sleeping soundly, oblivious to their attention.

"She looks peaceful enough. When did she last feed?"

"Two hours ago, it's not that really—"

"And how is she taking to the formula feeds?" Jenny cut across Amy as she opened her bag, found Amy's notes and fished about absentmindedly for the pen that was in the top pocket of her uniform.

"Fine, better, I think. She seems to prefer it to feeding with me."

"Nonsense! Babies all love the breast! But at this age it will be easy to move her over onto formula, if you are really sure that is what you want to do? You were doing so well on the breast though. I swear if I didn't know, I'd say you'd done it before."

"No, never," Amy cut in too quickly, a sharp squeeze in her tummy. "I mean, yes it's definitely what I want. It's just that her skin, with it changing colour, I thought that it might be my milk, that if I stopped feeding that she might… I don't know, change back…" Amy trails off, unable to finish her sentence. Jenny eyes her sharply.

"Let's have a look at Baby, shall we?" Jenny lifts the sleeping infant from her basket, cooing at her gently as she undoes the sleepsuit fastenings, until she has exposed Elizas little arms and legs.

"What were you worried about with her skin? Nice and healthy. No sore or dry patches I can see. Is her bottom sore? I can give you some cream if you think that she has a nappy rash?"

"No, no, it's not that. I just thought, her skin, it looked yellower somehow…"

"Touch of birth jaundice, nothing to worry about. Nice walk in the fresh air will soon clear that. It's a lovely day. Might do you both good to get out in the sunshine for a bit!" Jenny smiles up at Amy in a way that Amy is sure that she is supposed to find reassuring.

"Let's get her weighed, shall we?"

After Jenny has gone, Amy tries to feel reassured. She has googled jaundice in babies; all the articles assure her that Eliza will grow out of it. Somehow, looking at the pictures online she can't find any that look like Elizas skin. The jaundiced babies look yellowish, as if there is a filter on the photo. Eliza doesn't look like that. Elizas' skin looks more transparent somehow, as if it was becoming see-through. Shutting down the laptop, Amy decides that she will defrost the freezer before Jamie gets home. She can't remember when it was last done properly.

Tonight Amy dreams about Eliza for the first time. Until then all her dreams have been about the baby before. She often wakes feeling guilty somehow, as if she has cheated on Eliza in her sleep. Gazing into her daughters' face as she has her early feed, Amy wonders if Eliza knows that her mother dreams of another baby. Can she tell that she isn't the first? That Amy's arms have held another? The tiny secret doll boy that she never told anyone about. Sometimes when feeding her, Amy had the feeling that Eliza knew that Amy's arms ached for the first baby. Did Eliza know that the milk she drank wasn't made for her?

That another had been before? The realisation of this had actually made Amy jump in alarm. Eliza, snoozy suckling had jolted awake, an insistent cry emanating through the upstairs rooms.

But tonight, was different.

Tonight Amy dreamt about Eliza. In the dream Eliza lay cooing in her basket. The basket, which appeared to be in a garden with tall trees, which grew dark and cool as evening gathered in. As Amy walked down a winding path towards the baby, she was aware of flapping above her. It wasn't evening at all, but the day was darkening because the sky was filled with birds. The birds were zigzagging; their shrieks filling the sky, as their movements began to coordinate until a slowly orchestrated pattern of flight emerged. The birds were flying in a wide looping circle, some on the outside, some on the inside, the centre of which seemed to be directly above the basket. Amy felt her limbs stiffen in panic, urging herself onwards she began to propel herself towards the now silent basket. The path wound behind a group of trees, and in that moment, Amy lost sight of the basket on the grass. As she rounded the screen of branches, she saw, sitting on the flimsy pastel Moses basket, four magpies. Their enormous, clawed feet gripping the sides of the wicker basket, which bowed and warped under their weight. Although the birds above still moved in a cacophony of wing beats, the Moses basket remained deathly still. The bird at the head of the crib, bending over, head on one side, fixed its shiny sharp eye on the inside of the crib. In the dream Amy stood frozen to the spot, unable to move forward or to cry out.

***

Amy started awake. It takes her a moment to orient herself, eyes focussing on the edge of the coffee table, the sideways profile of her mug of now cold tea. She blinks twice, shifting her arm to rub her numb hand, pins and needles bristling through her fingers. How had she fallen asleep? What time was it? What had woken her? Her mind races through these questions as the baby monitor crackles into life.

Through the monitor, Amy hears the cackling call of a bird. A voice she has heard before, for a moment she can't place it. Sitting up, Amy stares at the monitor, as if the maker of the sound were actually going to appear through the plastic vent. Again, the angry chatter crackles into being, this time with a gasp Amy's brain knows the author of the sound, can picture its blue-black and white feathers, beady eyes watching her, ready for the reckoning that Amy now knows, has always known was inevitable.

One for sorrow.

Leaping from the sofa, Amy races to the foot of the stairs. She cannot lose another baby. She must not let the magpie take her. Amy stifles a scream as her mind plays the film of the magpie's claws clutched around Elizas pale flesh.

Two for joy

Running down the worn carpet path of the landing, Amy sways at the sight of the closed nursery door. Heart racing, she steadies herself, one shaking palm flat against the pale wall. The cackling now louder than before.

Three for a girl.

Amy's hand touches the cold door handle, her eyes blurred with the tears that have been waiting all this time, now set free. Heart pounding, Amy pushes open the door. As it slides away from her, she hears the beating of wings, the sound of birds taking flight.

Four for a boy.

The cot is empty. the room is empty. Even as Amy turns wildly around the realisation dawns. The room, clean and tidy. Cot sheets made up. The monitor, plugged in, sitting neatly on the windowsill. The bedroom window open to the warm spring day. Gripping the side of the cot, knuckles white Amy looks out and along to the end of the cul-du-sac. She can just see Jamie, strolling along with the pram, smiling at a neighbour. His sweater off and tied round his waist. The baby safely tucked inside the cocoon. Beyond the father and daughter, silently watching from a garage roof, sits the magpie. Wings folded; head cocked. It's beady eye watching all. For a moment Amy thinks it looks directly at her. It's eye contact sending another shudder down her spine. Her breath catches, arms instinctively wrapping around her frame. The magpie stretches its jewelled wings and with a flick of its long tail feathers flaps slowly away, turning lazy circles in the bright blue sky.

One for sorrow.

***

Amy is perched stiffly on the edge of her Mother-in-law's overstuffed chintzy sofa. Amy's dark dress is too tight, pulling across her breasts and tummy. She hadn't wanted to wear it but knowing that a dress would be expected she was low on choices, settling for this one because at least it fitted, mostly.

Jamie had branded the look 'a bit gloomy for a party', which Amy felt summed up how she felt. She was still unsure why they were having a party, or a "get-together" as Diane liked to call it. A cup of lukewarm tea cooling in its saucer in her lap, unwanted sherry abandoned on the hexagonal side table, Amy's attention drifted in and out of the conversations that surrounded her. A group of flowery women cooed and gushed over the baby that Diane proudly proffered round. Almost as if she herself had delivered Eliza, Diane accepted the praise modestly, head bowed. Another woman, overstuffed into a chintzy dress that made her look like a walking part of the lounge suite, was trying to take Eliza from Diane's arms. Amy saw her mother-in-law's hands grasp her granddaughter's blanket tightly, fingers curling claw like around the sleeping form. Her painted nails, scarlet against the pale crochet of the blanket. In her mother-in-law's arms lies the treasure the women are fighting over. Her eyes open, staring solemnly from her pale face.

Turning to look for Jamie, her heart thumping in her mouth, Amy realised that he was drinking beer in the kitchen with his dad and other lost men. There had been lots of back slapping when they had arrived. "Wetting the baby's head," being mentioned more than once. Bored of this now, the men's talk had turned to sport. Amy had briefly become alarmed at mention of "The Magpies"; she knew they were a team, funny that they should choose that name.

Her head started to pound. Amy, standing suddenly, made an excuse to leave the front room. Skirting the hall, she managed to make it to the back door without being waylaid by any more good wishes. Stepping out into the cool shade of the garage, Amy placed a shaky hand on the brickwork to steady herself. Consciously trying to slow her breathing, she focused on the plants in the neat garden. Spring was just getting into its stride and everywhere were tiny green shoots. The hedges looked fuzzy as new leaves appeared. All of Mother Nature burst into new life. Blinded by the bright blue of the spring sky, Amy's attention is drawn by birdsong coming from a neighbouring roof. A proud blackbird sits singing from the eaves. Amy can see its tiny chest moving with each note.

An ominous flapping makes Amy jump. Turning her head, she is eye to eye with the solitary magpie. He bobs his head, a polite greeting. His eyes never move from Amy's face. Mesmerised, Amy reciprocates the movement. She feels that the magpie is expectant.

"One for sorrow,

two for joy,

three for a girl,

four for a boy,

five for silver,

six for gold,

seven for a secret, never to be told."

"Umm, good morning Mr, Magpie, how's the family?" Amy pauses, her words, barely more than a whisper, sound loud to her ears. "I'm sorry about the baby. The other baby I mean… I'm so sorry for him. I couldn't do it then, I wasn't ready… I didn't look after myself, I know I couldn't have looked after him. I was so young… and he was so early, so tiny…" A sob escapes her throat, but this time she doesn't try to stifle it, she allows it and the fresh tears that are now unleashed.

"But this time I am ready. I can look after this baby, I want to, but I need to know that you will let me, that you won't take her too?" Amy wipes her face with the back of her hand, snot and tears smearing on her dark dress.

"Please let me have her, this… Let me be happy in this house, with this life."

"I never forgot him, never… I carried him with me, I'll always carry him with me, but she isn't him, is she? She's new…" Amy's voice trails off as she hears her own words, echoing hollowly in the small garden. Sinking onto the damp grass, Amy feels the weight of something shift inside her. She is silent, tears finally slip easily down her face. Amy looks up and for a brief moment locks eyes with the bird.

She holds her breath. The moment stretches and warps. Amy can see herself, damp and tearful, sat on her in-laws' lawn. Hands by her side, finally resting. For the first time she can see her pale, exhaustion-ravaged face. Amy's vision pans out and she can see all the gardens in the row, the rooftops, treetops, and expanding horizon, until she is only a solitary black and white blur amid the fresh green gardens and the warm red roof tiles. Awoken by the flapping of wings, Amy's eyes focus as the beautiful bird circles away into the sky of a bright, hopeful, spring day.

Sarah Croker

Sarah grew up in rural England, migrating North to eventually settle in the Yorkshire Wolds. She takes inspiration from the lives of 'ordinary' women and the natural world. Her research takes her all over the UK to towns, buildings and countryside to uncover the everyday yet extraordinary details of life.

The White Lady

Bare branches tap on warped glass as the wind whistles through the window's hairline cracks. Tonight, twilight lingers: a haunting shade of blue, and a soft ring encircles the moon. She is often seen on nights like these, when moonlight bathes the old chestnut tree, a hazy figure, forlorn and grey. Four hundred years have passed since the rumours began. A broken heart is her most noted cause of death, but rope has scarred a beam upstairs.

Headlights bring Mary's attention to a ball of mist by the roadside. She pulls her cardigan tight across her chest as a chill runs down her spine, unrelated to a breeze that seeps inside. At first, she blames the weather, but it hasn't rained, and the sky is clear. The mist dulls and brightens like it's breathing slowly, then drifts towards the chestnut tree. Under a low-hanging branch, there is a barren spot where even weeds won't grow. There it stops and lingers before sinking into the soil.

There are hundreds of tales attached to Brampton Hall's history; every room has its own ghost story. On a cold autumn night, not long after Mary started working, the owner, Mr Matthews, told her about the White Lady. And though she isn't the most dominant spirit, the story pierced Mary's heart and left a lingering impression.

It was love at first sight for the soldier and the laird's daughter; a serendipitous meeting around the summer solstice. But the laird didn't approve of his daughter's Protestant acquaintance. They'd meet in secret, cloaked by nightfall and the greenery of the forest, consequences be damned, come hell or high water. But by the harvest, her cycle had failed to bring blood, and they knew her family would never approve of their union.

On a bed of golden leaves, he got down on one knee and promised her something more priceless than land or money. He held out two rings, both gold, with their initials engraved, and asked her to elope once everyone was asleep. She glowed with hope as they embraced each other, unaware the trees that concealed them also hid an onlooker.

Some speculate her brother followed out of curiosity, others presume he knew their secret and was incensed and bitter. But when it comes to why he told their father, most agree he was trying to protect his little sister. As stars began to poke through a darkening sky, the laird and his faithful son crept into the garden. The laird stalked the property, hiding in the shadows of the outbuildings and evergreens. The brother took up watch in the torch-less stables, confident he wouldn't be seen. The night was silent and slow, so he settled onto a hay bale and made himself comfortable. His eyes grew heavy, and his body relaxed as he waited for his sister to show.

A maid witnessed him return early in the morning, eyes weary and clothes heavily soiled. He waved off her suggestion of breakfast and went to his room without saying a word. The atmosphere in the house was thick and dreary. The dogs wouldn't settle, their ears twitched and their demeanour was uneasy. During the night, the maid had woken to a woman's guttural cry. And from that day forward, the daughter never left her room. They brought her meals to eat, which she refused. It seemed the soldier had abandoned both his post and her. By the next full moon, her body lay six feet under.

Call it intuition or coincidence, but as she watches the mist, Mary comes to know why the White Lady won't rest. She rushes through the great hall and into the kitchen, grabs a set of keys off the dresser, and slips her feet into someone else's slippers. The back door creaks as it opens, and she steps into a wall of frigid air. A garden light clicks on, alerted by her movement, and illuminates the path to the old stables: a derelict structure where the family stashes unwanted possessions. Dew seeps through the slippers as she races to the door. There are dozens of keys, but the one to use is clear: thick rusted iron that matches the keyhole.

The stables smell like mildew and sawdust, and the garden light barely pierces the darkness. At the back of the room, the dark appears to move, but she tells herself it's her mind playing tricks. Mary props open the door with a forgotten flowerpot and begins to feel along the wall. The spade should be where she left it in spring, from when she planted roses and marigolds. Once her hand finds the wooden handle, she exits the stables swiftly, dragging it behind her.

The walk to the tree feels long and treacherous. The chill on her skin is no longer something she registers. Her eyes are wide, and her hearing heightened. With each step, her heartbeat increases, and her breathing quickens. The barren spot is easy to see in the sparse winter grass. Conkers speckle the ground, their shells cracked and decaying. The cold weather hasn't yet hardened the earth; the spade sinks in without effort.

Dirt piles up at her feet as her fingers begin to stiffen and freeze. By the time the mound reaches the height of her thigh, her palms feel bruised and her shoulders ache. She considers the hole, still small and shallow, and starts to think she made a mistake. Frustrated, she stabs the centre of the hole with the spade, where it hits something hard and ricochets. She scrapes away the mud, revealing something long, thin, and pale. She hopes she's uncovered a tree root or buried branch, but no matter how hard she tries, it won't snap or scratch. With a lump in her throat, she scrapes down its length, shifting dirt and small stones, until she uncovers the delicate bones of a hand.

Feeling unsteady, Mary gets down onto her knees as she stares at the remains, wondering if she's discovered a crime or piece of history. At such close range, she can see the bones more clearly. There is a smooth band above the knuckle of the ring finger. She uses her hands to dig until that section of bone is free, then slips off the ring and hides it in the pocket of her jeans. She replaces the bone fragment, leaves the spade in the dirt, and runs back to the hall to wake the other residents.

In the light of day, a team excavates the site. The skeleton is roughly six foot and believed to be male. They pick out the bones, section by section, and carefully store them so they can be further examined. The sergeant in charge confirms it was likely a murder but tells Mr Matthews not to worry; it's been four hundred years since the culprit hid the body.

The following days are a chaotic blur, and visons of that haunting night won't leave Mary alone. Unable to sleep, she sits at the kitchen table with a cup of tea, when Mr Matthews enters wearing a curious expression.

"There is a version of the White Lady's story that is quite sinister," he exclaims.

Mary looks at him expectantly, a silent plea to continue.

"As the brother began to fall asleep in the hay, a guttural scream echoed through the estate. He rushed out into the yard then stopped suddenly, swaying on his feet. A full moon sat high above the chestnut tree, illuminating the scene beneath. His father stood over a slumped figure, sword in hand; his sister was on her knees screaming at him to stop."

Mary gets a flashback of the chestnut tree lit up by the moon, then receives a vision of an ageing man stood over a beautiful, bleeding soldier. Dorothea's heartache washes through her. She holds out her hand and strokes her thumb along the gold ring, now free from dirt and glistening. In her mind, she speaks to the White Lady and prays that she now rests peacefully. With her thumb and middle finger, she slips off the ring and turns it to the light. Carved on the inside are the initials D and R.

Amy J Sayner

The World Tree

Reader discretion advised
(Contains themes of Suicide, self-harm, body horror)

I was 8 years old the first time I considered sacrificing myself. I climbed into a cove that would soon be cut off by the tide. I would soon drown, I thought. I took off my shoes and let the waves lick my toes, re-enacting a scene from Sylvia Plath. I don't know who had let me read, The Bell Jar. The sea secreted the sand from beneath my feet. I considered walking into the sea to speed up the process.

I don't remember walking away. I don't remember deciding not to die and climbing back over the rocks that separated me from safety. Maybe I didn't have the right God to sacrifice to. My childhood suicide would have been meaningless. Pointless. What good would it have done anybody? All I had at that point was the silent God of my parent's church. He had not asked me to sacrifice myself as he had asked Abraham to sacrifice Isaac. At that time, I believed in that God as firmly as I believed in the sun and the wind. And I wished to understand all three.

I picked at my faith like a scab. I wanted to know more, and all I found was pain and blood. That didn't make sense to me. This was not the meaning I thought I wanted. I read religious history with fervour and researched the wives of Mohammed and the practices of popes. I studied the spread of Hinduism,

Buddhism, and the resurgence of Paganism. It drew me in like the sea.

I loved sources of the mystical. I craved the logic and truth I found hidden behind the magic and the divine, explanations of why our land looked the way it did. I loved the image of Benandonner tearing apart the Giant's Causeway, Mélusine hiding her tail from her husband, and Polyphemus blinded by the mysterious "no one". I have found the truths in these tales and grown in them. Truths are comforting. I have collected facts jealously and will cling to them when I am drowning.

I did not grow up in a household based on facts. So much of what was told to me in my childhood was a lie. "I am fine." And, "I love you." No wonder I clung to the truth of the tides and death in the cove. I cannot tell you more about my childhood. I am still protective of that twisted nest. I feel guilty when I spill my family secrets, as if I am attacking my mother by sharing the things she did and said—this woman who wielded food as a weapon. There are things you do not need to know.

I unearthed sources of religions and superstitions. Pinned their locations to maps on walls. I loved climbing mountains named in folk tales and visiting the sources of healing springs. I have discovered the truth about trolls and ogres. They exist. Not in the fairy-tale way of creatures crashing through the countryside. There are spirits in some rocks who demand payment for travel over their land. Those who will not pay will suffer, even if they do not know the cause. I have learned to listen to them. Conversations with them may take hours. Or days. A rock does not experience time as a human does. You must be patient. You must sit. You must have an open heart and mind and allow them to say what they will.

When I found Mimir's well, I sat for three nights and three days while he spoke to me. I was dizzy from the lack of sleep and water, but I paid the price he asked of me. I do not know all that he saw when I opened my heart to him, but he must have seen my want for truth. I was to be granted the same choice as Odin. I took it. It was not violent. I pulled my eyelid up between thumb and forefinger, and with my other thumb and muscles I did not know I possessed, I pushed out my eye. What a rush! The landscape spinning away while staying still! I could see through both points of view for a few seconds before I took my knife and finished the work. I scooped up the jellied ball and laid it gently in the well. I was expecting it to float - I don't know why - but Mimir spirited it away to the depths. I was permitted to drink from the well.

I was overcome. It was like a full orchestra suddenly burst into being. I was aware of the language of the trees, plants, and rocks. Mimir laughed at my joy. And to think, he only gave Odin runes! I danced and wheeled about in my new-found world, giddy until sleep took me, and I fell asleep at Mimir's lap, comforted by his favour.

My family did not take kindly to my decision. People who saw me were horrified. They called the police and doctors and accused me of mutilating myself. With my newfound knowledge, I could find the words and gestures to dissuade these interlopers from further action.

I mention my family reluctantly. I do still see them. I still love them. I am almost as ashamed of this as of admitting our history together. People cannot seem to hold the two states in their heads. People cannot believe that my mother has told me to be grateful to a partner because I am difficult to love and that I still love her and want her in my life. I eat the food she gives me. I cook her food. She talks about my body and teaches me to go hungry and to be proud of the fact. I was well trained for those three unfed days with Mimir. My mother hated my eye socket.

She cried. She said she had given me that eye; I should have been grateful.

I started to realise all that I had sacrificed and almost sacrificed. I had sacrificed my comfort on the altar of beauty. I had used my teeth to sacrifice my nail beds to my anxiety. I had sacrificed my time and energy for money. I had sacrificed my skin on hot surfaces and watched. I had sacrificed my heart to people who would never treasure it. It was time to make a sacrifice to myself.

This is what Odin truly went through: casting away all that was and all that had been to a future, better self. I would cast away this body and this sprained mind of mine for a self that was happy and whole and had never heard the bedroom door open in the night.

I returned to Mimir. He was not surprised to see me. I don't know if he would even understand what was meant by surprise. I greeted him and sat in his presence. Calming myself and tying the knots. I am almost ready now. If I am right, my weight will be supported by every point in my body. Every part will feel the pain. Every part will be given in sacrifice to myself. I am full of anticipation. Like I am about to marry a wonderful stranger. I have not eaten in a week. I cannot wait to meet the self who comes down from the tree. I wonder how she will cut the bonds I tie.

Florence Hood

Florence lives in Oslo, Norway and specialises in learning (and forgetting) languages, fibre arts, and owning too many teapots. Since her first play was staged in Moscow, Russia in 2016, she has used her writing to protest the decriminalisation of domestic violence, explore other worlds, and build community. She loves creating intimate and uncomfortable pieces that stick in reader's throats.

Train Ticket

I was startled by the clunk of a cabin suitcase hurled overhead, followed by an aged, chocolate-brown leather bomber jacket slammed on top, with half of one sleeve left dangling. I eyed the handle of my holdall to check if it was caught under the suitcase, and was relieved that it wasn't. My deliberately heavy sigh ruffled the pages of the book I was reading.

The morning came in disarray. I didn't wake up to my alarm, and when I did, I only had half an hour to prepare to catch the tube to the rail station. The first sign of daylight had not shown itself yet between the gap in the curtains. In my rush, I stubbed my toe on the edge of my bed. I braved the icy water for a quick splash on my face. Under the bleary light, I haphazardly drew the lines and strokes that sketched a decent face. On my way out, I realised I forgot my train ticket. I went back to retrieve it, struggled to extricate my key from the keyhole, and remembered just as I missed the first available tube that I had the ticket saved in my email. Lugging my holdall in the train, I noticed that other passengers stared at me — perplexed — and quickly looked away when our eyes met. I checked my ticket: I was in the right train, the right coach and the right seat. Perhaps they could tell I was not in the right place.

"May I sit here?" the person who flung the suitcase asked. My peripheral view could see a blurry finger pointing at the seat.

I couldn't tell whether he was pointing at the aisle seat next to me or at the aisle seat in the opposite row.

"Suit yourself," I flatly replied without lifting my eyes off the book I brought for the six-hour train journey.

"I take that as a yes."

"You're welcome," I said sharply.

"For what?"

"I thought I heard you say thank you."

"Oh, sorry. I meant to say thank you. I'm Matt, by the way," extending his hand.

I shifted my eyes from my book to his face for the first time. A train slowly moving on the tracks caught the morning sun's rays which reflected on his blue-grey eyes. The glint evoked an image of a bright morning in a placid lake towards the end of summer, while his smile had the excitement of the season's beginning. His sea-blue jumper set off his sun-bronzed face framed by unkempt, short, wavy dark brown hair flecked with silver-grey. He looked like someone who was in the tropical sunshine for the most part of the year, on his way to a winter hiatus. A beautiful view seemingly without a veneer.

For a brief moment, my cinematic imagination urged me to abandon the thorny vein my morning took. But my will was pinned down by a lingering disenchantment.

I didn't shake his hand.

"Since we're gonna be sitting together for the longest time, I hope it's not gonna be a bumpy ride, Matt."

"Where you off to?" he asked, without looking at me while he briskly patted his thighs to remove some invisible fluff.

"Why do you ask?" I questioned back. I felt the heat rising from beneath the pores of my skin.

"Since we're gonna be sitting together for the longest time, I thought I'd be a bit friendlier to my seatmate." He flashed a grin.

"That's genuinely nice of you, but I'm reading, so if you don't mind, I'd really love to be left alone. By the way, you don't have to repeat after me. And you don't have to sit next to me."

Matt turned to an elderly man in the opposite aisle seat, showed his ticket, asked if the seat next to mine was his and if he could keep it. The man peered down from his reading glasses, nodded and waived his rights with a wave of his hand.

"Ok, I'm really sorry. I'll leave you alone. For now."

"For now?" I abruptly turned to him, my brow creased.

"Yeah, for now," he assured, wearing an amused smile.

The train started moving.

"Why are you annoying?" I asked without looking at him. I had been stuck on the same sentence in the same paragraph that I had read a few times without comprehending.

"Am I?"

"Yes, you are," I insisted.

"My friends say I'm quite cheeky, but I'm only ever really cheeky around people I think I can be cheeky with, or who look cheeky themselves."

"So, you're saying I'm cheeky?" I closed the book and turned towards him.

"I don't know, maybe, or you look like someone who doesn't care much about appearances or what people think of them. I don't know, I'm just saying based on what I see."

"OK, you're not only annoying, but you're also implying that I'm a mess and I'm sloppy," I said, as I quickly ran my fingers through my hair and tucked both sides to the back of my ears.

"Oh no, no, I don't mean anything like that. I thought it's just your fashion statement, or whatever it's called."

"What fashion statement?"

Matt pointed at my eyebrows.

I rummaged in my bag for a mirror. My eyebrows were perfectly shaped and contoured. In dark red.

"Oh, my god!" I gasped in horror and embarrassment. My laughter felt as if it bolted out of solitary confinement and basked in the rediscovery of an old pleasure. I chortled until I could hardly breathe. Matt echoed my laughter until we had dewy eyes. I caught my breath and sighed. My laughter came to a halt; I was then uncomfortably aware that the joy I'd been suppressing had unabashedly shown itself to the surface. I excused myself.

I stared at the train's lavatory mirror. The harshness of the last five years had been worn by my untended face. The creases and folds were as deep as my grief. Silver-grey tufts of hair that lined my forehead had grown into strands as lifeless and dull as my daily aspiration to get by. Until my dark-red shaded brows this morning, the only other presence of colour in my life came from the flowers I'd been laying on my husband's grave. Stepping away from the mirror, I smiled faintly at the reflection of the person I had become.

I glanced at him when I returned to my seat; the amused smile had not worn off.

"I'm Maya." I offered my hand. "Lovely to meet you, Matt."

MZ Akil

Treading On Eggshells

Tina crunched up the driveway with ten minutes to spare. It had been a toss-up – face the bus queue and clamber of passengers or risk a random taxi driver's probing conversation. In the end, she had plumped for the latter. When the silver Octavia pulled up outside her flat – far too early – she'd got in the back, pressed AirPods into her ears and taken out her phone. At least he'd got the hint.

A signpost to the clinic entrance sent her to the left of the main building – a double-fronted Victorian villa – where a waist-high wooden gate greeted her. Someone had pinned a laminated notice on it: 'Closed for Lunch – 1.00 – 2.00. Wait Here For The Gate To Be Opened.' She looked around. It was bright but chilly for April, with a slow breeze that made the layers of evergreens in the clinic's gardens tremble. Not too long to wait. Clumps of hydrangea, bristled by winter, lined the ground's perimeter. Are they mopheads or lacecaps? Mum would have known. And she would have pruned them by now.

A short, greying lady wearing a burgundy tabard made of wipe-clean material emerged from an outbuilding set behind a wall of laurels. Her hips swayed with every step and the mop clanked against the bucket she carried.

"Someone's busy," she said.

Tina unhooked an AirPod.

"Me?"

"No. Her."

The lady nodded towards a tired patch of earth a few feet away. The reddish-brown plumage of a female blackbird hopped amongst straggles of aubretia that spilt onto the shingle. The bird pecked at the ground, turning dried leaves over in its beak and discarding them as if it were looking for something in particular. She reminded Tina of the last couple who had viewed the house, the one who had eventually bought it. How they poked around, opened cupboard doors and commented about storage to the smarmy estate agent who had looked down at his iPad rather than make eye contact with Tina. She had more or less emptied the place by then. The white goods in the kitchen were included in the sale, although Tina had heard the woman make noise about ripping the whole lot out. But they were impressed with the dimensions of the rooms. The height of the ceilings. Just Dad's old armchair to get rid of and do something about the greyish outlines on the walls where family photos had hung for so long. Every time she looked at them, they had brought Tina a fresh sadness.

"She's building a nest. Might get five eggs in a clutch. It's got to be sturdy."

"Predators," said Tina. She unhooked the other AirPod and popped them both into their case. "Crows and magpies are the worst. For nestling birds."

"Scavengers," said the lady and continued to the front door of the main building, the mop clanking against the bucket. She tapped in a code, disappeared into the lobby and the door clunked closed.

Tina leaned against the wall and pressed the back of her head into the brickwork. She took a deep breath in through her nose, closed her eyes as she held it for a second then blew it out through the perfect 'o' of her lips. Tuned into the rhythm of the birdsong. This was one of Janice, Tina's therapist's favourite strategies. Focus on something you can see or hear. Wisdom imparted bi-weekly over Zoom. You've got this.

A stirring of stones opened Tina's eyes. An elderly man hobbled towards her, a newspaper snuggled under his arm. He wore corduroy trousers the colour of cedar and well-worn tan moccasins whose leather looked soft. Tina made fists with her fingers and fought the familiar urge to touch them. His casual zip-through jacket was open at the top revealing a tight half Windsor knot. She remembered what she was wearing and wondered if she should have dressed smartly. Not that she could have – most of her clothes were in boxes in the hallway. She was still settling into the flat.

"Having your toenails cut, are you?" he asked.

"Oh, er, yes. Maybe. I think I have a problem with them." Tina slotted her left fingers into the gaps between her right and rubbed at the little fiery patches of eczema.

"Me too. Problem I have is I can't reach 'em anymore!" He chuckled.

Tina took her cue and smiled. Should have kept her AirPods in.

"It's the nails on my big toes. I've tried to manage them but I think they're ingrown."

She pictured her big toes inside her trainers. Nubby, ground-down nails where she'd gone at them with the metal file and cuticle pusher until they looked like a couple of old farmers' thumbs. The man sucked in his breath sharply and shook his head.

"Nasty".

"I think someone needs to take a look at them. Have done for a while."

"Well, they're very good here. All trainees."

Panic, like the shadow of a small bird, fluttered across Tina's face.

"Supervised. All supervised, of course."

"Oh, good," said Tina, her out-breath jagged. "You've been before then?"

"I haven't, no. My first time. The wife has. Comes here regular. Well, she did. She, uh. Passed. Quite recently. George, by the way. Better not shake your hand."

"I'm sorry. Tina. Always good to have a recommendation."

A blotch of eczema had started to bleed so Tina stuffed her hands into the pockets of her joggers. She'd always been a picker.

"Nervous?"

"Yes, I suppose so. Kind of. Silly really. Always a bit nerve-wracking going into something new. Something unknown." Tina said 'unknown' in a childish, silly voice, as if saying it that way would somehow make this unknown less scary. Her cheeks reddened with regret.

"But you do want your nails seeing to," he said, with a new tone of gravity. "And you need someone to look at that um, nasty business." He nodded towards her feet. "Right painful if you don't get that seen to. You don't want infection."

"I know. You're right. Just the thought of it more than anything…a stranger at my feet. My bare feet. Holding…sharp things—"

"Well, they're very good here. My wife recommends them."

Silence fell between them and George unfolded the newspaper with a deftness Tina recognised. Something fatherly about him. The way he tucked it under his arm.

It had started with the wallpaper. Anaglypta wallpaper that hung in the stairwell of her childhood home. Tina loved the feel of it. Pressing the little bubbles in. She had systematically picked away at it. Ripped a little bit, piece by tiny piece, every day, step by step, an inch above the skirting. That's where it started. She thought of her toenails, how she'd hacked away at them until they bled, trying to dig them out. Her parents had tried to understand. But now they were gone and someone would pull what was left of the wallpaper down.

"I lost my parents," said Tina. "And I guess I'm out of practice. At going out. You know, after all the lockdowns. Seems like a lifetime ago." The sun grew brighter and she felt warmth emanate from the wall. She unzipped her hoody. "I got used to staying in."

"Got all your jabs, have you?"

"Yep."

"You'll be alright then," said George, looking up at the sky as if he were hoping to see something new. A few other patients gathered near the gate.

"Hope so. I mean, I was nervous about it. All the stuff on social media. I was in two minds. Didn't know what to do and didn't have anyone to ask. In the end, I thought it was the best."

"Way I see it," said George, his voice, gentler now. Softer. "You just have to keep going. Take each day as it—"

"Masks on please!" barked the receptionist.

She was exactly as Tina had imagined. Officious and sharp-featured, she blustered down the path, unlatched the gate, then turned and marched back into the clinic. Tina had thought her schoolmarmish when she'd made the appointment over the telephone. The way she explained to Tina that as a private practice, they were at liberty to continue with the mask-wearing policy in the clinic as the majority of their patients were elderly. Vulnerable. As if attempting to put Tina off. How she had stressed the importance of no nail varnish and emphasised that a twenty-five pounds no-show fee would be charged for missed appointments or failure to provide twenty-four hours' notice of cancellation. "In all cases", she admonished, which made Tina wonder what in her voice suggested she would object to wearing a mask, or insist on wearing colour on her nails or be lax about keeping appointments.

"Shall we go in?" asked George.

Tina's top teeth found her bottom lip and bit. She could turn around and head back down the gravel driveway. Call a cab. Get back to the flat.

"After you." George gestured towards the gate.

Tina scrunched her toes inside her trainers. Or maybe she could get this over and done with. Give her toes a fighting chance to heal. She could even take a chance on catching the right bus home. Make a start unpacking boxes.

As they walked up the path towards the clinic, the blackbird emerged from the scrub, a tangle of mossy twigs bunched in its beak. It hopped, took off, and disappeared into the blue.

Leanne Simmons

Leanne is from Berkshire, England where she lives with her husband, three sons and two cats. She enjoys walks in the woods, pottering on her allotment and writing short fiction. Her work has been published in Writing Magazine and various online journals. She is working on her first novel.

Vixen and the Brother Bears

The winters were long and harsh in this forgotten part of the world.

In the deepest forest, where midday and midnight shone the same, Vixen lived alone as such animals must. Spring to spring she measured her existence in snowfalls and twilights, the dark months pulling the woodland deeper in on itself. She had lived many winters, each one different, each one harder. Feared by the other forest animals and hunted by Man whose dwellings on the forest edge she was sometimes forced to visit, her lonely existence had become fearful as age slowed her hunting and dulled her instincts.

One year the winter had been especially cruel. Vixen had been forced to stray far from her usual lair. She had become lean and nasty, her body eating itself from the inside to survive. Catching the scent of something on the frozen air, she had tracked for many lonely miles. Driven by an instinct that was not only her hunger, Vixen cautiously entered a clearing in a strange part of the wood. Hidden in amongst the ancient trees she came across a small dwelling. Wary of Man (an ancient fear passed down through feral genes) she watchfully flattened her lean frame behind a fallen log. The cottage was tall and strange. Her own home hidden deep underground was dark and earthy, the floor smooth from generations of footprints with the survivors spread far and wide through the vast frozen forest.

Occasionally in the warmer months she would catch sight of a young fox, prowling in the dusk and wonder.

Driven by her hunger, Vixen sniffed at the opening window. The aroma was sweet and warm, unmistakably food, but mixed with something else, something both familiar and strange. Could it be something male?

Crossing the threshold, she transformed into a beautiful young woman.

She barely registered the large, bright room because her new skin bristled at the sensation of the fire's warmth on newly naked skin. Her hunger overriding her screaming instincts to flee, she ravenously gulped bowls of food. As she sprang to the window she changed back into her fox form. Her four legs were fuelled by her warm belly and she fled into the deepest woods, away from any returning inhabitants.

The Brother Bears also lived in the woods. They had lived for many years together.

Hidden. Alone. They too feared Man and his discovery of them. The smallest bear sniffed cautiously. Something familiar and strange was in the air around the cottage. As the two larger Brother Bears started to argue over their missing food, Little Bear found three beautiful long russet hairs next to his empty bowl. Human hairs. He held them, gossamer thin to the light, but did not tell the others.

Back in her lair, Vixen was haunted by the memory of the woodland home. The snow continued to fall, the days became shorter and darker. She found her hunting had drawn her back to the mysterious cottage. No matter which direction she headed, her foraging circled her back to the clearing. Meanwhile the smallest bear sniffed the hair gently, marvelling at its exotic fragrance. Strange, yet stirring an ancient memory deep within. Something familiar and comforting from his time as a weening cub. How lonely Little Bear felt, trapped in his isolated home. Although he knew that he was a bear and was feared and hated by Man, his heart ached to see the creature with the beautiful auburn hair.

Winter tightened its grip on the forest. The fallen leaves so brittle in the sharp frost that they shattered under Vixen's tread as she tried to move swiftly through the silent forest. Her short breath stinging with icy air, Vixen dreamt of the warmth of the fire in the cottage grate spreading across her pale soft skin as she stretched her long limbs in its amber glow. Curling her bushy tail around her thinning frame she listens to the wind whispering its ancient secrets from deep within her lair. Then suddenly the wind dropped. The silence was absolute. Vixen was out, bounding through the forest, drawn by an invisible thread back to the clearing.

The Brother Bears were also drawn out of their warm home in the search for more wood. The Little Bear sniffed the frozen air, but its silent stillness held onto all secrets. Vixen slunk between trees and logs, her instinctive fear overridden by the pull of something stronger that she didn't understand. Entering the cottage, Vixen was once again transformed into a beautiful young woman. She hungrily approached the fire burning in the grate, marvelling as the flesh on her limbs rippled, downy hairs standing up against the pinking flesh in the fire's amber glow. She stretched on the earthen floor, flexing her cold cramped muscles. An icy blast from the doorway announced the bears' return. Tearing back through the cottage Vixen jumped up onto a chair and stumbled clumsily against the bears' furniture. As the wood splintered, one of the bears lunged forward. Springing to the window, Vixen was once again transformed, and the bear roared in frustration, a tuft of auburn tail left in his claws. As the two largest bears gave chase through the forest, roaring in frustration at the rapidly retreating Vixen, Little Bear held the tuft of black tipped fur. He marvelled at its exotic softness, the way its colour changed in the firelight.

As the shortest day approached and the forest entered its deepest, most magical days, Vixen was visited by strange dreams. She was a beautiful woman once more, stretched out upon a bed in the cottage. Soon the afternoon sun dipped low into the frozen sky and the colours began to bleed from the day. The sky hung heavy with snow, the forest holding its breath awaiting its fall. Every animal sensed that magic. The earth swayed on its axis, the day and night balanced awaiting the surrender of the other. Vixen, driven as much by her haunting dreams as by her frozen bones, crossed the cottage threshold again, landing on her two naked feet. The cottage opened up silently before her, inviting the luxury of her curiosity. Vixen looked beyond the warm fire and the empty bowls of food.

Vixen found the bedroom and saw the three beds outlined by the soft glow of the snowy sky. As the night began to take its victory from the day, she chose the smallest bed and sank into its cosy warmth. Her beautiful auburn hair fanned out behind her on the pillow and she let the darkness enclose her, gratefully falling into a dreamless sleep.

Upon their return, The Brother Bears were shocked to find the cottage disturbed. While the older brothers searched the clearing, the little bear sniffed the air leading him to the beautiful woman asleep in the bed. He gazed at the sleeping form, her hair soft and shining. He knew that when his brothers saw the beautiful woman they would have to eat her, for the bears were starving too. Although she smelt different - earthy and primal - she was unmistakenly Man, and therefore the enemy of the Bears. If only she weren't a woman. If only she were another animal, then the brothers would be able to spare her.

Bursting into the bedroom the Brother Bears startled the sleeping woman. She leapt naked from the bed, baring her teeth, instinct sharp. She ran clumsily on two legs, her golden tail flying behind her as she sprang from the bedroom window. The largest bear swiped at the pale flesh and Vixen cried out as five deep wounds tore through her flank. The brothers saw a sleek vixen disappearing silently into the trees behind the clearing and into the snowy night. As the skies finally give up their icy burden, the dark trail of blood matching her swift paw prints marked her path. Soon the forest was transformed by its soft quilt of snow. Only the Vixen's trail of fresh blood left any trace of colour in the darkening forest.

Alone in her den Vixen licked her wounds. At this time of the year she was so lean she knew her wound could be fatal. Outside the snowstorm wreaked havoc on Mother Nature. For many days and nights the snow fell, sometimes obscuring the sun and sky altogether so that it felt like an angry long night. The Vixen curled around herself and slept, dreaming of her other self, buried in the warmth of the Brother Bears' bed.

The Brother Bears were also trapped within their nocturnal hibernation. Little Bear dreamt that he followed a path of tiny red flowers to the Vixen's door. When he saw her she was not a woman but the Bear who had birthed him, alive again. As he reached out for her he saw once again the fatal wounds Man made. As he looked into her soft face it began to change into a sharper smaller muzzle, the ears pointed and tufted with black-tipped, auburn fur.

Eventually days begin to lengthen again as the earth turns once more. The snow melts and the forest comes to life, tiny green shoots offering up their hope. Vixen moves cautiously through the undergrowth. Her wounds have left her with a slower leg, a limp that makes her vulnerable. She is now heavy with what she knows will be her last litter of cubs. She knows she must see these weened before her time is finished. She stays close to her den, knowing she must keep herself and the unborn safe.

The Brothers Bear have also been punished by the ravages of winter. The oldest Brother has not woken from his hibernation. His carcass will provide much needed food for the remaining brothers, but Little Bear feels the weight of his own inevitable fate. He will eventually eat his remaining brother unless Man gets them first. He will be alone to live out his time hidden in the forest, until age or starvation takes him too. The last Bear in the forest.

One summer evening Little Bear sniffs something on the dusky air. It stirs a memory within him and looking out of the cottage window he catches a glimpse of red between the dark trees. A young Vixen tentatively lifts her nose into the air, the new scent stirring some inherited memory. As he watches, the young Vixen silently skirts the clearing. As she disappears into the undergrowth's embrace the Little Bear sees a flash of white, five streaks of white fur on her auburn flank. He catches a glimpse of the stubby end of her beautiful auburn tail, it's pointed tip missing.

Sarah Croker

Acknowledgements

I am deeply indebted to all my fellow graduates for joining in with this project and taking the time to write their submissions.

Especial thanks to Leanne and MZ, for helping me in the editing of the works and of course, to Dr. Barbara Henderson for her fantastic foreword.

Thanks also to all our tutors on the MA in Creative Writing, to the administrative staffs at Hull for the help and assistance they gave throughout our time studying, and to the Alumni organisation for helping us to stay part of the University of Hull's community after our graduation.

Finally, as I am sure all the contributors to this anthology will wish to echo, a massive thanks to our families, who helped and assisted us as we spent long hours preparing assignments and pouring over books, trying to craft sentences that would make our work worthy of the conferment of a Masters. And in my particular case, for supplying endless cups of coffee and not feeling the need to answer as I debated if a semi-colon or a comma was the way to go.

Ian Hooper
Editor and Compiler
Australia, 2024